FACE OFF (RIVALS)

SCOTIA STORMS

CATHRYN FOX

COPYRIGHT

Face Off
Copyright 2023 by Cathryn Fox
Published by Cathryn Fox

Discover other titles by Cathryn Fox at www.cathrynfox.com. Please sign up for Cathryn's Newsletter for freebies, ebooks, news and contests: https://app.mailerlite.com/webforms/landing/c1f8n1

ISBN ebook : 978-1-998943-15-9
ISBN Print: 978-1-998943-13-5

ABIGAIL

The bell over the door jingles as the last customer of the night exits the premises, and the forced smile I've been wearing all night falls from my face. I glance at my phone and exhale an exaggerated breath, happy it's finally closing time.

Honestly, after this morning's hour commute to college, attending classes all day, and an hour's commute home, only to run Boondocks—our family-owned restaurant/gift shop—until closing, I am officially exhausted. You'd think after burning the candle at both ends for the last year, I'd be used to it. But no, I'm not.

I stifle a yawn, desperate for sleep. Unfortunately, I can't fall into bed and get a good solid eight hours like I need. Midterms will be here before I know it, and if I want to keep my scholarship at Scotia Academy, I need to pull an all-nighter.

The good news is that it's the end of September, which means tourist season in Nova Scotia is slowing, and I won't have to spend as many late hours in the shop. Good for me, but not good for business.

Fortunately, lobster season begins at the end of November, and selling to local grocers will carry us through to May, to when the tourist season starts all over again. Just thinking about the never-ending cycle makes me tired and dizzy.

But now, with Granddad's decline in his mental health, Mom and Dad need the help, and with the powerful Dunn family trying to destroy our retail fishing business and take our much-coveted oceanfront land, which has been in our family for generations, they don't trust anyone outside our small immediate family. Mom and Dad think everyone in the community is a spy working for the Dunn's multimillion dollar fishing conglomerate with its huge commercial fishing fleet and manufacturing and distribution facility. The company hires most people in this town, so my folks probably aren't wrong, which, of course, is why we're all run off our feet simply trying to keep afloat.

I close out the cash register and remove the fish fillets from the display showcase, putting them in the large fridge in the kitchen out back. I check the burners on the stove and turn off the fryers. We don't do big, fancy meals here at Boon-docks. We're known for our fish and chips and lobster rolls, and they're served in take-out containers customers eat at the picnic tables outside, overlooking the Atlantic Ocean.

Once the place is secure, I gather up my backpack, toss my phone inside, and lock up behind myself. Outside, the cooler night air falls over me, and I take a moment to breathe it in. With any luck, the sea salted breeze will fuel me with a second wind and I won't fall asleep over my books.

A pinging sound rings out at the end of our dock, and I narrow my eyes to see if the local kids are messing around with the buoys again. The light at the end of the dock is burnt out, preventing me from seeing further than two feet in front of my face. Is someone sitting in one of the Adirondack chairs? I make a mental note to bring them in for the season come morning.

I stare for a moment, and when silence reaches my ears, I glance across the water, to where light falls over the golf course. It really is a picturesque community here in Lunenburg, and while I wish I could live in the city, closer to campus or even in a sorority, like my best friend Ocean does, it's out of the question.

Is moving to Miami after college to do a master's degree in marine biology out of the question too?

I groan, not wanting to think about that, but knowing soon I'll have to give it more consideration. There are summer grants and scholarships I can apply for—need to apply for in the next few weeks—but how can I leave my family during the busy summer tourist season?

I hike my backpack up higher on one shoulder and walk along the dark waterfront path leading to the well-lit narrow road, where tourists can catch horse drawn carriage rides and learn the history of our famous fishing village. Our house is just up over the hill, and it's a safe enough community, so I usually take the path instead of walking the long way around the winding streets.

As I'm about to cross the quiet road, a car slows, and my stomach tightens as loud male voices reach my ears. I straighten my shoulders and do a fast glance around. The town is pretty much shut down at this time of night.

Dammit, I'm alone out here. The window on the sports car rolls down and I cautiously peer inside.

"Is that you, fish bait?"

Oh God, no. Is this really happening? Fight or flight instincts kick in, and I back up an inch. Running is out of the question, since there are four college hockey players in that car and my chances of escape are slim to none. Nope, I'm going to have to play it cool here, like I'm not intimidated by them, like the names they call me don't hurt at all.

"What do you want?" I ask, and the front, driver's side door opens. What are these guys doing in Lunenburg this time of night?

"I thought I smelled something fishy," one of the guys quips as he slips from the back seat.

As I stand there facing three of them, my heart thunders. Okay, this isn't good. Not good at all. I do another fast glance around, calculating an escape route if they try to come closer.

"If you're here to buy seafood, we're closed. Come back tomorrow." I start walking, but one of the guys moves in front of me, blocking my path. Real fear gathers in my stomach, and I try to keep my breathing normal.

"What if we want something fishy now?" one of the assholes snaps, and my throat squeezes tight. I grip the straps on my backpack harder. Do I have anything in there I can use to protect myself if they come at me?

"What do you have in there?" the tallest of the three outside the vehicle asks as he towers over me.

"My books. Now if you'll excuse me, I need to go home to study." I make a move to push past the guy blocking my way, but it's like trying to stop an eighteen-wheeler with my pinkie.

"Hey Abigail." I turn at the sound of the fourth man, as he exits the front seat and I know I'm in real trouble when my gaze lands on Sebastian Turner—Scotia Storms' left winger. Sebastian is a local, and I've known him since kindergarten. He's trouble with a capital T, and has always gotten away with things because his father is a powerful provincial politician. For some reason, he's always hated me. Well, maybe not always, but definitely since I reluctantly went to a party with Ocean in high school.

There was a guy she liked, and she begged me to go with her. Sebastian was drunk and hit on me—rumor has it he wants to sleep his way through the alphabet with every girl in our class. I naturally turned him down. Apparently, that pissed him off enough to tell everyone I wanted to fuck him, but he couldn't go through with it because I smelled like fish.

"What do you want, Sebastian?" I start breathing faster. I'm in serious freaking trouble here. I slide my backpack from my shoulders, hoping to get to my phone so I can press the emergency button, but the guy blocking me grabs the bag from my hands before I can get to my phone. He tosses it to his friend as Sebastian stalks closer. He sniffs the air as the other guys kick my backpack around and laugh.

"Still want to fuck me?" he asks, his breath reeking of alcohol.

"Sebastian," I begin. How am I going to talk my way out of this when he's not even in his right mind? "It wasn't like that."

"I can't fuck a girl who smells like fish," he slurs, anger and hate in his voice. What did I ever do to this guy, other than defend myself from his drunken advances? He lifts his head and gazes at the wharf, like he too heard a noise. A cruel smile parts his lips. "Maybe I'll have to dunk you in the ocean before I put my dick in you."

A gasp I have no control over catches in my throat, and seems to please him. Think, Abigail. Think. He takes a step closer, and I move back the same amount of distance. It's clear he thinks I ruined his reputation and is out for revenge, when the truth is he was the one trying to ruin mine—simply because I said no to him. Apparently, no one has ever said no to Sebastian Turner before. I back up, knowing my only choice here is to run.

With the three other guys distracted, tossing my backpack around and laughing like idiots, I steal a fast glance over my shoulder to see how far I have to run. Sebastian seems a bit unstable on his feet, so maybe I can make it back into the shop, unlock the door and lock it again before they can catch me.

They have my backpack, but right now, getting myself to safety is the priority. I take a step back, and turn to run, but when I do, I hit something so hard and solid, it steals the breath from my lungs. Big hands grip my shoulders as I bend forward and gasp, clamoring for air.

When I can finally breathe again, I push myself up to my full height and when I set eyes on none other than Liam Dunn—Scotia Storms' toughest defenseman, and a guy I despise—I instantly realize my night has gone from bad to worse. My legs go weak, and my heart thunders in my ears as the world closes in around me.

"Abigail," he says quietly, and so damn gently, I figure I'm hearing him wrong. He's probably yelling and the pounding in my ears is softening the noise, making it sound tender, when it really isn't. He glances over my shoulder to take in his hockey buddies. It's five against one here, and I'm out of ideas. Okay, maybe not entirely. I could kick Liam between the legs and maybe still make it back to Boondocks. "Are you okay?" he asks.

I freeze, and blink and as much as I'm trying to put on a brave front, I can't stop shaking.

Liam's eyes narrow in on me as I squeak out the word, "No."

"What's going on here?" he asks, his voice deep and hard as he aims his question Sebastian's way. It takes me by surprise, but what surprises me even more is the way he's positioned me behind him, his hand grasping mine. Not in a hurtful way, but in a worried, supportive way.

No way would Liam Dunn be trying to help me here, right? His family hates mine. We're like the Capulets and Montagues in real life. Not that Liam and I are Romeo and Juliet. We are far from star-crossed lovers. Quite the opposite. We hate each other. Why then is he protecting me? I quickly glance at the sky to see if it's falling.

"We were just having some fun with fish bait," Sebastian says with a laugh, and every muscle in Liam's body stiffens.

"Don't call her that," he bites out, and his thick muscles bunch as he inches closer to Sebastian, every movement in his body calculated and threatening.

"Hey, we were just having some fun." I note the way Sebastian stiffens as Liam towers over him.

Liam squares his shoulders, somehow making himself look even taller. "Abigail didn't look like she was having fun at all."

The other guys all stop kicking my bag around.

"What, are you fucking the fish bait or something?" one of them asks.

"No," Liam snaps so forcefully, so defensively as a hard quiver goes through him—like that's the most disgusting thing he's ever heard—he might as well have just sucker punched me. I have no idea why I'm suddenly hurt. I hate the guy and his family, and wouldn't have anything to do with him if he was the last man on earth and we were responsible for repopulation. "And I said, don't call her that."

They all stand still, sizing one another up, until Liam steps forward and picks up my backpack. "This is yours?" I nod and he hands it to me before turning back to Sebastian. "What are you guys doing out here, anyway? A long way off campus, aren't you?"

"Just out for a joyride, and I thought I'd show the guys my stomping grounds," he replies. I glance at Liam, and he doesn't much look like he believes that either. He was there the night of the party, and knew what went down. I assumed he believed Sebastian, like so many others. Was I wrong?

Liam tugs his phone from his pocket and checks the time. "Coach won't be too happy about this. We have practice first thing tomorrow."

"Yeah, we're leaving," the tall guy responds, and gets back into the car. It's clear he doesn't want any trouble from Liam or the coach. The other three grumble under their breaths as they follow.

"Don't come near Abigail's dock again," Liam warns. The car revs and the tires squeal as they take off, and the second they round the corner, I bend forward, fighting back tears as I take deep, gulping breaths.

"Are you okay?" Liam asks after a long moment.

"Adrenaline dump," I explain my chest so tight it hurts all the way to my throat. "I'll be okay in a second." I take a few more breaths and stand. My heart picks up pace again as I take in the dark eyes watching me carefully. "Thank you."

"Do you want me to call the authorities?"

"No," I answer quickly. God, that will just cause more trouble for me.

He gives a small nod and gestures with a flick of his chin to his car parked near one of the restaurants across the street. "Let me take you home."

I'm about to nod, when I remember how defensive he turned when asked if he was sleeping with me. Am I that repulsive to him? I don't know, but it does remind me we hate each other and I should never get in a car with him. Only problem is, I'm not sure my legs will actually carry me home. Somehow, I'll have to find a way to make them work. I straighten my shoulders to present strength and confidence, despite the roiling storm inside me. "I can walk."

He lightly touches my arm and I pull it back. "Let me help you, Abi."

"It's Abigail." No way is this man allowed to give me a nickname.

"Fine, let me help you, Abigail." He holds his hand out. "I'm not going to hurt you."

A car horn blares in the distance and my entire body stiffens. Maybe I should go with Liam. We might hate each other, but he did help me tonight. "I..."

"Better the enemy you know," he murmurs, taking the words right out of my mouth. I nod and silence surrounds us as he leads me to his car.

I'm about to get in when something niggles in the back of my brain. "Wait, was that you out on our dock?"

2

LIAM

My heart jumps into my throat as she glares at me, suspicion all over her face. Shit, she's not going to be happy that I was hanging out on her family's dock, and she's probably going to think I was trying to sabotage the place or something equally horrific. I might be a Dunn, from Dunn Industries, but I'm not like my father. I don't hate the Hart family or want anything other than friendship from Abigail.

Christ, I have no idea why my father hates them quite so much. Sure, their land is prime, and we can't expand in Lunenburg without it, but come on, is that any reason to hate them? We have a multi-million-dollar business. How much more do we need? My father swears he's hasn't been behind the trashing of their dock in the past, or responsible for ransacking their lobster storage facility and traps.

I want to believe that—I have to believe that. I'm part of the Dunn family, and have to believe we're not the type of people who'd resort to crime simply because we can't get what we want. Dad is a man who always gets what he wants, and not securing the Hart's land has eaten him alive for years.

As far as I'm concerned, we have all we need and family is the most important thing in the world to me, which is why I believe were above victimizing a small family business. Honestly, I'd do anything for my family, as long as it fit within my morals and beliefs.

"You have the best sunsets," I respond as she impatiently waits for an answer to her question. Christ, I've snuck down to her dock more times than she ever knew. Okay, maybe I don't just do it to see the sunsets—considering it set hours ago. Maybe I do it to get a glimpse of Abigail. I only surfaced tonight, only showed my face because a bunch of assholes from the hockey team were harassing her. No way was I going to stay in the shadows—even if admitting I was trespassing went against my own best interests and might result in Abigail hating me more. Hey, no one ever accused me of being the sharpest knife in the drawer.

But seriously, bad shit could have happened tonight, and I wasn't going to sit back and let anyone touch one hair on Abigail's head. Sebastian is a douche bag. I've known him forever. I think when push came to shove, he wouldn't have touched Abigail. I hope. I just couldn't take the chance, and after my warning, I don't think he'll bother her again. I'll kick the living shit out of him if he does, and he knows that.

Abigail glances past my shoulders, distrust all over her face. "That's why you were on my dock? The sunset?"

"Have you not noticed the sunsets, Abi...gail?" Right, I can't shorten her name.

"No, Liam. I'm usually inside working when the sun goes down," she shoots back, her words as sharp as a fishing hook.

I nearly wince as they pierce me, but I need to keep things light. She has to be pretty traumatized by what just happened.

"Yeah, well if you ever get a chance, you should join me on the dock."

"I'd prefer for you not to be on our dock."

"I wasn't hurting anything," I point out softly, and as my stomach tightens, I notice a bit of the fight drain out of her. I stare at her as light from the dashboard spills from the car. Jesus, she looks exhausted and I'm sure she is. Between school, work and the long commute, I bet she doesn't have a moment to herself. "Let's get you home, okay?" She hesitates for the briefest of seconds, then glances over her shoulder, no doubt gauging the distance to home. "I'll have you there in two minutes."

Shoulders sagging, she nods and climbs in, and I slide in beside her. After a moment, she breaks the quiet. "Why are you here and not in the city?"

"I needed a break," I tell her as she eyes me suspiciously. "All the noise at Storm House can get to me at times." It's not a lie. My first year at Storm House, I tolerated the parties. Now I don't quite have it in me. My father wants me in the dorm, though. He thinks it's good for the team for us to be together and since he's footing my bills, I do what he says. I honestly miss the solitude on the boats. I enjoyed getting up before the sun, the comradery with the other fishermen, and a good hard day's work on the water.

My parents, however, think such menial work is beneath a Dunn. They wanted more for me and I guess it's a good thing I excelled at hockey. It's the only thing I'm good at. If they'd put the pressure on me to be a scholar, they'd have been sadly disappointed. I struggle in school, a lot. No tutors were ever able to help me in my younger years and now, because I'm on the hockey team, many of the professors give me a pass, which makes me feel that much stupider. I don't need my academic intellect—or lack thereof—rubbed in my face like that. All brawn and no brain is what many wrongly say about the hockey players. In my case, they'd be right.

"You'll have to head in early for practice," she says, dragging my thoughts back.

I shrug, and pull onto the street. "I don't mind. The drive is peaceful." I glance at her as she stares out the window. "You never really sat and watched a sunset from your dock?"

"When I was younger, sure." She exhales, and examines a hole in her backpack. "It's just that I spend so much time on the water, I'd rather look at something else before I go to bed." I eye her, not sure I believe that. "Besides, I prefer sunrises. There's something magical in them, and it helps me put things in perspective."

"Such as?"

She shrugs. "I don't know. I guess it allows me to see the bigger picture and reflect on my place in the cosmos." I angle my head as I listen. "I guess what I'm trying to say is it makes my problems seem miniscule."

"Funny, sunsets do that for me," is all I say, even though I'd like to ask what problems she's talking about. I pull into her driveway, and the house is pitch dark. One porch light illuminates the front door and the cracked stone walkway. She gathers her bag and hugs it to her chest.

"I guess we're different like that."

I nod. Yeah, I get it. We might have grown up in the same small town, but our differences are night and day, like sunsets and sunrises. Does that mean we can't be friends, though? I guess it does, considering she stopped talking to me in elementary school, when their storage facility was ransacked and tension intensified between our families. My dad's hate for her family started long before they accused his company of sabotage.

I glance at her ripped backpack. "I hope your books are okay."

"Thanks."

Her door opens and the dashboard light showcases her blue eyes, which look big and stark against her thin, heart-shaped face. My heart skips a beat. My God, she's so pretty. "Those guys won't bother you again, Abigail," I tell her trying to keep my voice even. "You have my word on that."

Dark lashes fall over tired eyes. "I never...you know...with Sebastian..."

"I know," I agree quickly. "Anyone who believed his lies are nothing but idiots, and not worthy of an explanation."

"I must have damaged his frail male ego when I refused to let him put his tongue down my throat," she says, her body relaxing. "He handled rejection like a three-year-old. I don't think he's ever heard the word no before."

I can't help but laugh, and a small smile turns up the corners of her mouth. Jesus, I'm certain this is the first time I've seen her smile, or even joke—at least since elementary school. And that smile...Fuck, I thought she was pretty before, but wow, she's actually drop-dead gorgeous.

"Men and their fragile male egos. I apologize for all of us." She stares at me for a moment, probably wanting to call me out on my own ego, but instead closes her mouth and steps from the car.

"Thanks for the lift."

"See you around." Seconds before she shuts the door, I say, "Maybe you'd like to give a sunset a try sometime."

A humorless laugh crawls out of her throat. "Sure, right after you give a sunrise a go."

The door closes, and I sit there grinning. I guess she doesn't know how much I love early mornings. While that might not have been an invitation—heck, I'm pretty sure there was an insult in there somewhere—I think I'm going to take her up on it. I also think—and this could be my fragile male ego talking—that we might have actually formed a tiny truce tonight.

I stay in the car until she opens her front door, and just when I'm about to back out, she turns back to look at me. I grin, taking that as a good sign. She gives a little wave and disappears inside. A light turns on in one of the rooms, and I watch her figure walk past. While I'd like to stay, I'm not a creeper—much—so I back out and drive along the shore until I reach our place.

I pull my car into my spot in the four-car garage and kill the ignition. I check the time. It's late, and I need sleep, but I also had an adrenaline rush tonight. Sebastian is lucky I didn't tear him a new one right on the spot. My rage was not what Abigail needed at that moment, so I did my best to keep my cool. Maybe a good old fashioned body checking is in order for practice tomorrow, just to drive the point home that Abigail is off limits.

I step into the house and find Dad in his favorite lounge chair, a baseball game blaring from the TV as our black lab, Charlie, sleeps at his feet. It's late, and Mom and my younger sister Ember, who plans to go to Scotia Academy next year, are already in bed.

Dad offers me a smile. "You're out late, son."

"Just driving a friend home."

"Oh," he says, arching a brow. I don't have too many, or any, friends left in Lunenburg. I'm a bit of a loner and spent all my time with my best friend, Josh, until he went to play college baseball for Michigan State. "Anyone I know?"

I hate to lie—nothing good can come from that—and while I expect backlash I truthfully say, "Abigail." His gaze jerks to mine so quickly I'm sure he's given himself whiplash. Anger flashes in his eyes and hits like a puck to the mouth.

"Abigail Hart?"

"Yes."

"I told you to stay away from that family."

I perch on the edge of the sofa, and note the warning in his eyes. "What did they ever do to you, anyway?"

"They're not good people. Stay away from them," he warns, fire blazing in his dark eyes.

"I was just giving her a ride."

Something comes over his face, his anger shifting, morphing into something I don't like. Is he scheming up something that could end up with the Hart property in his hands? If he is, I hope it doesn't involve me.

"If you insist on driving her around, find out what you can about them. See if you can get a look at their books. See if there are any violations at Boondocks that could get them shut down."

My heart leaps into my throat. "I'm not snooping, Dad."

He shrugs but the serious look on his face is a reminder that I'm where I am today because of him and I owe him for that. "You either stay away from her, or get me what I ask for."

My lungs are tight, and breathing is difficult as he turns back to the TV, letting me know the conversation is over and that he's not fucking around here. Which means I need to keep my distance from Abi because I'm not about to get dirt on her family. Jesus, what a horrible position to put me in.

Honestly, I love my family more than anything and have always respected their wishes and went out of my way to make them proud. I don't enjoy conflict and outside of the family, I stand up for myself when provoked. I've never stood up to my father. He's always been a hero to me, a man who is bigger than life. A man who has worked hard for his family and provided all we could need and then some. I'd never want to lose his respect. Never want to disappoint him. But this... what the hell?

I take in his profile as he pays me no attention. A part of me wants to ask what he'll do if I don't stay away from her, and if I don't get information. The other part of me already knows the answer. If any employee steps out of line, they're out, and I fear it could be the same with his family. I can't even imagine being cut out of my own family.

I glance at my phone. "I'd better get to bed. Early morning tomorrow."

"Driving back to campus, you mean?" It's a legit question, but we both know there is hidden meaning. In my younger years, before I had the pressure of college, hockey, and the NHL, I would jump onto one of the fishing boat first thing in the morning before my parents were even out of bed. Sometimes I got away with it, but other times, I wasn't so lucky. But I was willing to get into a little bit of trouble just to spend the day at sea. I never stood up to Dad, telling him I wanted to be on the fishing boat, demanding he let me. I'd always listen with respect. The sea however, always had a hold on me. I couldn't seem to stay away.

"Yes, early morning practice."

"Proud of you, son," he says and I'm truly happy he is. He's not an easy man to please. Just as the hundreds of people who work for him, I always try to do my best. He's an important man in my life.

"Night," I say and push off the edge of the sofa.

"I'm looking forward to catching one of your games soon." I glance over my shoulder and nod. It's nice that he, along with Mom and my sister, come to my home games when they can. Their support means the world to me. I just wish that support was in everything I do. After his warning to stay away from Abigail, it feels like a punch to the gut, because the truth is, I really don't want to stay away. What does that matter, though? Abigail hates me. It's not like we're suddenly going to be besties after tonight. When it comes right down to it, Dad doesn't have to worry about me staying away. My plan to watch a sunrise with her was a stupid one.

Upstairs, I make a fast trip to the bathroom to wash up, and then head to my bedroom. I turn the lights off and flop down onto my bed. I close my eyes, but I'm unable to get the events of the night out of my brain. Is Abigail at home, staring at her ceiling too?

Or is she thinking about the laugh we shared? That laugh filled me with a lightness that I haven't felt in a long time. Jesus, I sound like a goddamn greeting card. I resist the urge to shoot a text to Josh. It's late and he's probably asleep. He knows how I feel about Abi, though—the girl who studies marine biology at college and wants to make the sea sustainable. Maybe that's why my dad hates her. He doesn't want anything or anyone to interfere with his fishing. I like that she's trying to balance the ecosystem, and find ways to reverse the existing damage.

I roll to my side, and try to quiet my mind, and after a fitful sleep filled with dreams of Abi—correction, Abigail—I wake, and press my palms to my tired eyes. The sun isn't up yet, and my family is still asleep. I need to scarf down some breakfast and hit the road if I want to make practice on time.

Forgoing a shower—I'll get one after practice—I tug on last night's clothes, and because I'm extra anxious to leave—some deeper need I can't quite identify—I skip breakfast, which is unusual for me, and jump into my car. I drive along the shore and find the quaint town of Lunenburg quiet this time of morning. Without conscious thought, I take my foot off the gas and my car slows in front of Boondocks. That's when it becomes glaringly obvious as to why I was so anxious to leave the house without breakfast.

Not smart, Liam. Not fucking smart.

Again, no one has ever accused me of being smart. I stop my car, and even though my actions might result in a knee to the groin—the knee I'm pretty sure was on the verge of happening last night—I walk along the wharf. I don't try to be quiet. I don't want to frighten Abigail.

As the long rays of light climb over the golf course and spill over the ocean, Abigail turns, shock widening her big blue eyes. My steps slow as she opens her mouth, but no words form.

I shove my hands in my pockets, glance at her gorgeous face as the morning sun forms an angelic halo around her small frame, and say, "Good morning."

3

ABIGAIL

What the ever-loving hell is going on?

I stare at the big figure moving toward me, sure I'm hallucinating. But no, I recognize the voice and as he gets closer, and his handsome face—a face I hate—comes into view, I once again realize Liam Dunn is taking up space on my property, not to mention in my head.

Okay fine, I'll admit it. After the drive home last night, I kept replaying the incident over and over in my head, and not the parts where I was afraid. No, the part where he put me behind his big body in a show of protection. Now the guy somehow lives rent free in my brain, dammit.

I put one hand on my hip, noting he's in the same jeans and hoodie from last night, and shoot out, "I thought you were a sunset kind of guy."

He shrugs, and glances over my shoulder as he closes the distance. "I thought I'd take you up on your offer."

My mind races back to my comment last night. I think I was just pointing out we're different people who like different things. "I'm not really sure it was an offer."

Then again, maybe it was. Maybe I was feeling a moment of sentiment after he helped me. I don't know. But did I really think he'd show up for a sunrise? No, not even a little bit. He likes me about as much as I like him. Big fat zero.

"My mistake."

"Guess so." I hug myself as a cool breeze washes over me, and make a move to go around him, and he steps to the side to allow me. "Enjoy," I tell him widening the distance between us.

"You're not staying?" Is that disappointment I hear in his voice. Seriously, what the hell is going on in my life? I turn to see him over my shoulder, and he's watching me, not the rising sun. My body tightens, and I narrow my gaze, unease working its way through my veins. What is he really doing here? We don't speak, ever, and now within a twelve-hour period I've seen him twice.

"I come here for the solitude." My God, could I be any bitchier? I guess I'm just used to my family sparring with his, and it's rubbed off on me. The truth is, he hasn't done anything hurtful to me, and last night he did come to my rescue, and honest to God the hurt look on his face right now is doing the strangest things to my heart. I'm not a mean person by nature, and I don't go out of my way trying to upset people. But Liam is a Dunn. And the Dunn family are enemies of the Hart family. Like I've always been told, the apple doesn't fall far from the tree.

"I can be quiet," he whispers and as I continue to glare at him, his shoulders sag in defeat. He exhales and gives a tight nod. "Or I can just leave." He starts toward me and I grab his arm to stop him. His muscles flex beneath my fingers, and strange little pulses of electricity zips through me as the wharf wobbles and his hand closes over mine to keep us balanced.

I glance at the big hand smothering mine, and I must look horrified because he draws it back quickly. "Sorry, I just... the wharf..."

"Come on." I move around him and drop down on the edge of the wharf. I slide my hands under my thighs for warmth and let my legs dangle over the edge. It's not like I'm in a hurry to get to class this morning. I started my car earlier, only to discover a horrendous noise. The garage doesn't open for a few more hours, so I'm going to at least miss my morning classes.

He stays quiet as he walks—tiptoes—toward me and it must take effort, considering the size of his body as well as the size of his boots. His efforts bring a smile to my face and when he drops down next to me and sees my smile, he angles his head, his eyes full of questions, but he remains quiet.

I shake my head and then gesture to the sun as it rises higher in the sky, and we both sit there in silence, enjoying the peace before the world awakens around us. I steal a fast glance at him and take in the hard angles of his face as he stares out over the ocean. There's a peacefulness about him this morning, not one I usually feel radiating off him. Not that I watch him often. But last year, I'd gone to a couple games with Ocean, and sometimes I see him in the halls—not that he sees me. I always go the other way, of course, never getting close to the intensity that always clings to him.

His energy is nice this morning, relaxing. A different vibe for him. I guess he must have a lot of pressure on his shoulders, as one of the star defensemen on the team. He turns to me, catches me staring and arches a brow in question.

I shake my head again, and whisper, "Nothing."

With the sun higher in the sky, he quietly asks, "Are we allowed to talk now?"

I laugh at his seriousness as something inside me softens. Since I was completely horrible earlier, I say, "Yes, and I promise to be quiet during your sunsets." Wait, did I just agree to watch a sunset with him? Do I have sun stroke from the sun rise?

A big smile crosses his face. "I don't mind talking during a sunset. I kind of like the idea of talking." He shrugs. "I usually watch them alone." As I take in his dark eyes, I sense a loneliness there. "I'd be happy for the company."

Any company, or just me? What the hell? Why does that even matter?

"How is Josh?" I ask. Maybe he's missing his best friend.

"Good," he responds, and shifts a bit, his leg brushing mine. Warm sensations rocket through me, and push back the cool inside my body.

Alrighty then. I push on my hands, lift myself up and brush my palms together. "I should get going."

He jumps up effortlessly and glances around. "I guess I'll see you on campus."

"Not today. I don't think I can make it. Something is rattling under my car. I'm waiting for the garage to open to get it looked at. Hopefully they can fix whatever it is this morning."

He frowns, his hair rustling in the breeze. "Want me to take a look?"

"What do you know about cars?"

He looks down, like I've touched a sore spot, and puts his hands into the front pocket of his hoodie. "I know a thing or two. I've worked on mine over the years. I'm pretty good with my hands."

That takes me by surprise. I can't picture him wielding any tool. Don't they have staff for that? Okay, maybe that's not fair and I'm just stereotyping. All the horrible things my parents have said about his family have gotten in my head. Maybe Liam really is different.

When I don't respond, he glances at me. "Yeah, I get it. I'm a dumb jock," he adds, his voice tight.

My heart jumps into my throat. "Liam, I wasn't..." Was I, though? Was I suggesting he was a dumb jock, which I don't think he is, or was I simply suggesting the rich live a very different—pampered—lifestyle. I'm not sure, but I know I couldn't hate myself any more than I do at this moment. I'm not a judgmental person. I just...he's a Dunn. My whole life I was taught not to trust them. Ugh.

"It's okay," he responds, deflated. "I am what I am."

I swallow against a tight throat. He thinks he's dumb? We were in a lot of classes together in our younger years and he's far from dumb. He might not excel in certain subjects—we all have different strengths—but he's not dumb. "Liam," I try again but he cuts me off.

"I can look at your car if you want. Like I said, I know a thing or two."

I glance at my phone. I can't even imagine what my parents would say if they saw Liam in our driveway, underneath my car. "No that's okay. I'll take it to the garage." He nods, but his face is tight, like my words punctured him. "You need to get to practice," I add quickly.

"Shit, yeah. Why don't you drive with me? We can drop your car off. They have that key drop off slot. We can leave a note, or..." He pulls his phone from his pocket. "We can call and leave a message. That way you won't miss classes. I can drive you back tonight."

Why the hell is this guy being so nice to me? I'm not sure. I only know the idea does sound appealing. "You don't mind?"

"Why would I mind? We're going the same way."

I glance over my shoulder, and as if reading my thoughts, he says, "I can meet you at the garage, or I could just wait down the road a bit and follow you to make sure you don't break down."

I was wrong. I could hate myself more. The man is offering to help me, and offering solutions so my parents don't see him. I'm ashamed of myself right now.

"If you don't mind driving me to my place, then you can follow me from there."

"Okay." He nudges me. "I'll park a bit down the road, though, just in case."

I put my hand on his bicep, and his muscles bunch beneath his hoodie. "I really appreciate this. I hate to miss classes." To be honest, I'm shocked I'm accepting help. It's not in my nature. Trying to justify it, I say, "There are these summer grants available, and I might apply..." I let my words fall off. Why am I telling him that?

He doesn't ask for any further explanation, instead he says, "Not a problem."

My hand falls from his arm. "I owe you one."

"No, you don't." He playfully nudges me as we walk. "You only owe me a sunset."

Have Liam and I just formed a truce?

I chuckle at that and glance at the pink streaked sky. "I think it's going to be a nice day."

"Pink at night, sailor's delight," he begins, and I jump in and join him in reciting, "Pink in the morning, sailors take warning."

We laugh at that as we make our way to his car. He hits the fob to unlock it and jokes, "Can't be too careful around these parts."

"I would have laughed at that until last night."

He goes dead serious as he looks at me over the roof. "That won't happen again."

I nod, even though I'm not sure I believe him. He's a big guy, threatening and a leader on the hockey team, but I pierced Sebastian's ego. Although I'm not sure he'd risk an alteration and get kicked off the team.

I slide into the passenger seat, once again finding myself next to Liam and not hating it. I listen to the radio as he drives the short distance to my place, and I try to fight down the nervousness invading my stomach as he slows and stops before we reach my place.

"I'll just be a second. I have to grab my backpack and keys." He nods and puts his hand on the dashboard, his finger tapping away to the beat on the radio and for the briefest—strangest—second I stare at his nice hands and envision them on my body. I shake my head to clear it. What the hell is going on with me? When I banged into Liam last night, I must have given myself a concussion.

I hurry from the car, and Mom and Dad are inside, busy as they get ready for another long day.

"How did last night go?" Mom asks as she fills a cup of coffee and hands it to granddad who's sitting at the table looking at me like he doesn't remember who I am. My heart clenches.

"Good, not too busy." I walk over and put my hand on Granddad's shoulder and for a second his eyes brighten, only to dull again.

"I didn't hear you come in."

"Late customer," I say. Not entirely a lie. I did have someone come in just before closing. I snatch up my keys and backpack as Dad walks into the kitchen, his hair damp from a shower.

"You'll be back before dinner?" he asks. "I have to check the traps before dark, and your mother has to take your grandfather to a doctor's appointment."

Shoot. I totally forgot about that. How can I say yes, when I don't know what time Liam will be heading home? "Right, sure," I agree, the wind leaving my sails. I'm not going to make it to classes after all. I'll have to stay and wait for my car. I hike my bag over my shoulders. I really hate that those assholes ripped holes in it. I saved a long time to get a campus backpack.

"What happened to your bag?" Mom asks as she pokes a finger through the hole.

"Nothing. Just dropped it." No sense in telling her the truth. I don't need them to worry more than they already do. With the shop, fishing and Granddad, they have a lot on their plate. Which means, there's no sense in telling them about my car either. It's not like they can do anything about it. They share one vehicle and they're unable to lend it to me for the day. My problems are my own—which is what I should have told Liam after I mentioned my car.

I walk outside, and open the passenger side door. Liam takes one look at me and narrows his brow. "Are you okay?"

I work to shield my disappointment, a little surprised that he can read me so well. "Yeah, listen. You go on ahead without me. I'll just take my car to the station and wait."

His body stiffens. "You've been gone two minutes, Abigail. What happened in those two minutes?"

Okay, fair enough. "My folks need me back early. They have things to do. I don't expect you to leave the city early because of me." Honestly, I don't expect much of anyone, and I'm not feeling sorry for myself when I say that. I'm used to solving my own problems, and taking care of myself. My parents are busy, I realized that when I was very young, and I never wanted to be a burden.

"Why not?" he asks, without hesitation.

I stare at him for a second. This man would go out of his way for me? Why would he do that? "Because I'm not your responsibility, Liam. I really appreciate the offer. I'm good. I don't need any help. Thank you, though." My stomach is tight, and as exhaustion overwhelms me—which must be why I'm feeling a little broken and sad—I jokingly add, "Hey, we'll always have the sunset." I don't really think I'll be joining him. We've seen enough of each other this century.

I close the door, and he remains on the street as I climb into my vehicle. I back up and cringe and something underneath clangs loudly. I pull onto the street, and glance in the rearview mirror. Liam follows behind me in his capable vehicle as I drive the short distance to the garage. I expect him to speed past and take the exit to the highway. Instead, he follows me into the parking lot, parks beside me, and hops from his car.

I step from mine as he circles the front, a fierce kind of determination etched on his handsome face. Is he clenching his jaw? What is he angry about?

"What are you doing?" I ask as I tentatively slide from the driver's seat.

He steps closer, his big body hovering over me. Not in a threatening way, but a protective way, very similar to last night. "Driving you to school." He has a sheet of paper in his hands, and a pen. "Here, leave them a note with your keys." He points. "You can shove it through the slot there, and I'll phone the garage. I have a buddy who works here, and he'll put a rush on your muffler."

"My muffler?"

"I told you I knew a thing or two about cars. If they have the part, they can get it fixed today. Tomorrow at the latest."

I shake my head as this comes at me fast. "Liam, I told you. I'm good. I don't need your help, or for you to make arrangements."

Catching me by surprise, he slides my backpack off my body, shoulders it, and points out, "You didn't even give me a chance."

4

LIAM

I take in her big eyes as they stare at me with something that looks like concern, and not hate, like I usually see when I glance at her. Wait, maybe it's more like bravado. Does Abigail Hart not like asking for help, or accepting it, either?

For as long as I can remember, heck, before she could even see over the counter at Boondocks, she was running menial tasks in the store and helping her parents out. Come to think of it, the tasks weren't that menial. She was measuring seafood, wrapping it and ringing it in. That's an awful lot of responsibility for a young girl. One would think the parents would be responsible for their child, not the other way around.

A tinge of anger grips my stomach at that realization. Abigail has been doing for others for quite some time now. Why did I never see that before? Oh, probably because she always ignored me, and I was pretty self-centered, thinking I had all the problems in the world because my folks didn't want me on the fishing boats.

Really, is becoming a famous NHL player a hardship? Hell no. You know what a hardship is? Not having a way to classes when you're attending college on a scholarship, and what were these grants she was telling me about, or rather almost telling me about? Is she embarrassed that she's there on college funding? Hell, she should be proud that she had the grades. If I had to rely on academics, I wouldn't be in college at all. I'd be on the boat.

Where you're actually happy, Liam.

I shut that thought down as she continues to stare at me, shifting from one foot to the other. Her eyes dart from me to the key slot and I can almost hear her searching for another excuse to turn me down.

I get it. Abigail holds a lot of responsibility on her shoulders and just once, I'd like to lighten her load. I'm not sure if it's her wobbly stance, the granite look hardening her face from her forehead down —like the world can't hurt her if she's made of stone—or the fact that I know she's desperate to get to class, that brings out the protector in me. I only know I want to give her a hand, even if it's just a once in a lifetime ride to campus.

"I have to be back to Lunenburg early too."

"Why?" she asks.

I don't want to lie to her, so I explain, "I do have to be back early, because I'm giving you a ride and you have to be back early." She opens her mouth to protest, and I take one of her hands into mine. "Abi..." I shake my head. "Abigail," I begin again. "I don't mind, really. I'd actually like the company for the drive." I smile. "Just like I'd like the company for the sunset. Practice is early this morning and I'll be exhausted when classes end anyway."

She exhales, and glances around the empty parking lot. "You can call me Abi. You seem to have a hard time with Abigail."

I point to my head. "Not too bright like that."

She frowns. "That's not true, Liam." When I don't respond, she continues with, "You don't want to go to the library after classes, or hang out with your buddies at Storm House?"

I have friends, or rather acquaintances, on the team. I was never a guy to have a lot of friends, just one good one, Josh, and he's in Michigan. I'm a bit of a loner, and not sure I've bonded all that well with any of the guys on the hockey team, which is one of the reasons I rarely stay at Storm House. Getting away from the party scene is another. Usually, the guys get tired of the all-out partying by their third year. I'm only in my second and already over it.

"No. I actually prefer my own bed at home." A beat of silence and then, "It's just a ride, Abi."

Her stance softens, and as her shoulders fall, I realize I've won this small battle and she's going to take me up on my offer. "Girlfriend, or boyfriend, won't they be upset if you're leaving early?" she asks.

I grin at her. "If you want to know if I have someone special in my life, all you have to do is ask."

Her jaw drops open. "I was not—"

"I'm kidding," I say quickly, before she changes her mind. Maybe it's too early in our truce to be joking with her. She is rather serious all the time. "Write your note, and I'll be waiting for you in the car." I walk around to the passenger side of my vehicle, and open the door. I don't look at her, but can feel her eyes drilling into me as I drop her bag onto the back seat next to mine, pull my phone from my pocket and slide into the driver's seat. I finally glance at her. "You better get at it, or we're going to be late."

That prompts her into action. She walks up to the glass door, presses the paper against it and scribbles her information. After dropping the keys and note into the slot, she circles my car and gets in. I note how tiny she looks in the big seat. I sort of tower over her, and so do the guys on my team. What a bunch of fucking bullies. How could they get off on intimidating a small woman like Abi, or any woman for that matter?

"You know, you're kind of bossy."

"Just don't want you to be late for practice, my friend."

She goes quiet, not commenting on the 'friend' remark, and once again I feel her eyes on me as I back out of the lot and head down the winding back road.

"What station do you like?" I ask and nod toward the dashboard. "You can change it if you want."

She glances in the back, like she's checking on her backpack. "This one is fine."

"Classic rock, hmm."

"What?" She shoots back, accusation in her tone.

"Nothing. I guess I was just thinking that might be something we have in common."

I pull into our local coffee shop, and head to the drive-thru. "I forgot to eat. Do you want something?" I grin, thinking of my teammate Dane, who has an addiction to breakfast sandwiches, which would hit the sport right about now.

"No, I'm good."

I glance at the big poster board. "I'm starving." I order two big coffees with cream and sugar on the side since I don't know how she likes hers, and get an extra breakfast sandwich. After I pay, she shakes her head.

"Are you going to eat all that?"

"They had a special on. It was cheaper to get three." I pull one sandwich from the bag and hold it out. "Help a guy not make a pig of himself." She arches a brow and I continue with, "If I eat all this, I'll likely lose half of it on the rink."

"Then why did you order it all?" she shoots back.

"Did you miss the part where I said they had a special?"

"You're a strange man, Liam," she laughs and takes the sandwich. "I can't remember the last time I had one of these." She unwraps it and takes a bite, and it's followed up with a small moan.

"Sounds like you like them."

"Yeah, but do you know how bad these are for your heart? Are you even allowed to eat these when in training? Wouldn't they make you sluggish?"

I press my fingers to my lips. "Shh, I won't tell if you don't." She grins, and I kind of like having secrets with Abi. "That coffee is yours. I wasn't sure how you liked it."

She doesn't argue. "Thanks. Just a bit of milk actually." I drive slowly and avoid potholes as she takes the lid off and pours in a milk. "How about you? Can I fix your coffee for you?"

"I like it black." I bite back a grin. Look at us, conversing like everyday adults who don't hate each other. I avoid saying that and risking this fragile truce. I flick on my signal, and take the ramp to the highway. I pick up my phone from the console and hand it to her. "You should put your contact info in here."

"Why?"

"In case I can't find you after classes."

"Oh, right." I steal a glance at her as she runs her fingers over my phone and it's kind of odd how much I like her touching my things. "For the record, I don't. Do you?"

"Don't what?"

"I don't have a girlfriend, or a boyfriend." She shrugs, coming off like it doesn't much matter to her and it probably doesn't. I just wanted to put that out there. "Do you?" I ask again.

"No," she says. "Not anymore."

"There was someone special?"

"It was a while ago." She takes a sip of coffee and goes quiet, contemplative. "First year, college." Ah, I know exactly who she's talking about, not that I kept tabs on her...much. "Until Sebastian tried to ruin my reputation by calling me names in front of him." She glances away, but not before I catch the humiliation on her face. I grip the steering wheel tighter.

"Sebastian is an asshole. I'm kind of glad I beat the crap out of him in elementary school now."

Her gaze jerks back to mine. "You did?"

I laugh at her expression. "Don't you remember me getting expelled from school for a week?"

She glances down, her eyes narrowed in thought. "Ohmigod, Liam. I forgot all about that. I can't remember what happened."

"He was picking on Willow White. Tugging on her hair until he made her cry." I bite into my sandwich, and follow it with a big sip of coffee.

She arches a brow. "And you punched him in the face?" I nod. "My God, I'm surprised he was expelled. His father always got him out of trouble."

"Yeah, I know."

"Do you run to every girl's rescue?" she asks.

"When I'm around, sure."

That brings a smile to her face, and it fucks up my insides. "Well, I don't want you fighting anyone on my account, or doing anything that could mess up your hockey career. I can handle my own battles."

"Noted."

Her smile falls. "You know what I hate about that," she says, and stares out the window. Before I can ask, she continues, "Girls are brought up to think hair pulling is a sign of affection. It's not. It's abuse. Why are we told that?"

I stare at her, a bit confused, until I realize her mind has gone back to the playground incident. "I don't know. I only pull a girl's hair when she…" Her gaze flies to mine. Shit, what the fuck was I about to say.

"When what?" she asks. Are her cheeks turning pink?

I cringe. "You know."

"No, I don't…" I glance at her, and that's when I see the light-bulb go off in her brain. Her eyes widen. "Oh, right." She gulps and toys with the lid on her coffee before taking a big swallow.

"Sorry, I don't know why that slipped out." I flick on my signal and pass the truck in front of us. "I shouldn't have said that. Can you please forget I ever mentioned it?"

"Forget you mentioned what?" she asks, a small grin on her face, an indication it's already forgotten about.

I laugh. "Right." I stare at the road, wanting to know more about her. "So marine biology, huh?"

"Yeah, why does that seem to surprise you?"

"It doesn't. You're worried about the ecosystem and overfishing. I like that."

"I'm sure your family wouldn't." My chest tightens at the comment. She's right, they wouldn't. "I'm sorry, Liam. I shouldn't have said that. That wasn't fair to you. Can you please forget I ever mentioned it?"

"Forget you mentioned what?" I ask and as we both laugh it lightens the tension in the car. "You're applying for summer grants. Which college?"

She exhales and pushes back into her seat. "It's a pipe dream."

"Why?"

"I have the grades, and Miami has the best marine biology program in North America but I just can't see it happening for me."

"I can."

"Well, thank you for the vote of confidence." She glances out the window, and I sense she doesn't want to talk about it.

"I guess we have something else in common."

"Oh, yeah?" she asks without turning my way. "What?"

"I was drafted. I'll be playing for Miami."

She makes a small noise, like a hmph. "I'm never going to get away from you am I, Dunn?" Her words cut but when she turns to me, she has a playful grin on her face.

"You want to get away from me?"

"I'm kidding. It's just we haven't always been on the best of terms."

"You know, we can let our parents' fight stay our parents' fight."

She stares straight ahead, not agreeing or disagreeing, and we both remain quiet, lost in our thoughts for the remainder of the drive. I'm glad I at least put the idea in her head that we could be friends, despite the fact that our parents would lose their minds if they so much as saw us speaking to each other.

As we approach campus, I ask, "Where should I drop you?"

"The Ocean's institute, if it's not out of your way."

"It's not." I maneuver the streets and pull up in front of the big stone building which is located at the other end of campus, far from the rink and the main lecture hall where I take my business classes. "Where should I meet you this afternoon?"

"Right here is good. If it's not a problem. If it is—"

"It's not a problem, Abi." Doesn't anyone ever go out of their way for her? She nods and stares straight ahead. She looks like she's trying to puzzle something out. "What's up?"

"I just..." she shakes her head and reaches for the door handle. "It's nothing."

I touch her hand to draw her attention and she doesn't pull it back. "No, you can tell me."

"Do girls really like having their hair pulled, when they're... you know?"

5

ABIGAIL

As I stand outside the Ocean's building, I can't help but wonder what the hell is wrong with me? Why would I ask such a stupid question? I didn't mean to, it just popped out of my mouth all on its own. Probably because I couldn't stop thinking about it as soon as he mentioned it. I was supposed to forget about it, instead I let it fester in my brain until I became obsessed with the idea.

I'm not all that experienced. I've had a relationship, and sex with Brennan Langley—who I was talking about earlier—first year of college, but it was straight up vanilla and messy with no hair pulling. Would I like that? Without conscious thought, I lift my hands and tug on my hair, imagining it was Liam's hands doing the deed. I drop my arms quickly, when I spot Liam's car come around the corner.

God, I hope he didn't see me, or think I want that. I don't. At least, I don't think I do. How freaking embarrassing would it be if he thought I did, and we had to drive back to Lunenburg together with that knowledge taking up space between us.

I give an awkward wave as he drives down the street and once again wonder what is wrong with me. I ran into my best friend Ocean earlier. It's funny, her name is Ocean and she's an architecture student and I study the ocean. I guess her parents chose her name because they have a house overlooking the ocean. Clever and original. That almost makes me snort. Ocean and I have been friends since middle school and she's a sorority girl here at Scotia Academy. After I told her about my car, she offered to share her bed so I didn't have to travel back and forth. That's when I told her about Liam helping me, and I swear to God, I thought she was going to swallow her tongue.

Liam pulls up beside me, and, trying for casual and normal, like I ride with him every day, I open the door and climb in, setting my torn backpack at my feet.

"Hey," I begin as I buckle in. "Thanks again for the ride."

"Not a problem." He checks something in his rearview mirror and runs his hands through his hair. The move releases a pleasant fruity fragrance and I assume it's his shampoo. I breathe it into my lungs. I'm not sure I ever noticed how nice he smells and he changed his clothes since this morning.

He's about to pull into traffic, but stops to reach into the backseat. "Oh, I got this for you."

He hands me a backpack, identical to the one at my feet, except it's missing the holes. "What's this?" I ask, even though I already know.

"I feel responsible for the dickheads on my team. I wanted to make it up to you."

I stare at him, shocked, appalled and maybe even a little upset by the gesture. "Liam, you didn't have to do this."

Honestly, I wish he hadn't. I don't want to be indebted to him. "I can buy my own bag."

His body stiffens and he goes quiet for a fast second, and I guess he's realizing how this must make me feel. "I just...I thought..." He shakes his head. "You're right, it was stupid. I'm stupid."

Dammit, this was actually a nice gesture and I'm making him feel bad for it, plus he's not stupid. "I didn't say it was stupid and you're not stupid. I can...buy my own bag. I didn't have time today." It's a lie. I did have time and I can't buy my own. I splurged on this one and I rarely splurge on anything. I bought it my first year. A little treat for myself for getting a full scholarship.

He reaches for it. "I can take it back."

I pull it from his reach, my stomach cramping at my bad behavior. "No, it's very thoughtful of you and you've already ripped the price tag off. Thank you. Also, you're not responsible for your asshole teammates' actions."

"Asshole teammates, huh?" he asks with a grin. "Why don't you tell me what you really think?"

I snort and examine the bag. It's actually a newer, updated version with more pockets. I kind of love it. "We don't have a long enough drive home for that, my friend." I open my backpack and start transferring stuff over to the new one. He's sitting there grinning. I think he liked that I called him my friend. "Thank you, Liam."

"You can pay me back if you want."

"I'd like that."

"It doesn't have to be in cash. We could do a trade or something."

My hand goes still as I reach into my bag for my notebook, and I cast him a fast glance. If he doesn't want payment in cash, what does he want? He stares straight ahead, nothing about him suggesting the trade could be sexual in nature.

Sexual?

My God, why would he want sex from me? I'm not like the girls who hang out after his hockey games wearing very no clothes and getting piggyback rides to the pub. I'm definitely not his type so why on earth would my brain go straight to sex as payment?

Oh, maybe because you're the one thinking about sex, Abi.

Good God, one little comment about hair pulling has my traitorous mind going down a path it has no right going. Never in a million years am I going to have sex, of any sort, with Liam Dunn.

Confident that he's not talking about getting naked with me, I ask, "What do you have in mind?"

"Maybe you could help me out with some classes." He almost looks sheepish, ashamed, as he admits his shortcomings. "I'm falling behind in calculus, and it could affect my game. You're pretty good at it, so I thought maybe you could tutor me."

"How do you know I'm good at it?"

He snorts. "You're good at everything, Abi."

"I'm not good at hockey."

"You want me to teach you some hockey moves?"

"Would you require a trade for that too?"

He grins at me, and it's so adorable, my heart does a weird little twirl. "Not everything has to be a trade."

Is this what Liam is up to? Hanging out on my dock because he needs me to help him with something? I realize people will always see me as a poor fisherman's daughter. I pretend to be okay with the name calling, and while I consider myself strong, there's a small part of me that hurts when others are cruel. The times they're not cruel are times when they want something from us, like a deal in the market, or...tutoring.

I finish moving things over to my new bag and Liam stretches out his arm. "I can help you with calculus," I tell him. I shift, about to toss the old bag into the back when his hand slides between my thighs. Whoa. His throat makes a noise as he quickly pulls his hand back.

"Sorry, I was just reaching...your bag...I was going to..."

"It's okay, I got it." I toss the bag into the back seat and try—unsuccessfully—to ignore the burning imprint of his hand between my thighs and the way heat is travelling upward, to settle in parts of my body—one in particular—that has been neglected for quite some time now. What was that I just said about never in a million years?

"Yeah, okay, uh. We should get going then. We need to get you back for your shift."

"Right."

I stare straight ahead as awkwardness overtakes us. Is it awkwardness or is it sexual tension? I don't know. I could be misreading this because my body is completely betraying me. How could one touch of my nemesis—between my thighs—turn me into a woman obsessed about sex?

Is he your nemesis now though, Abi? Didn't you two come to an understanding?

It's true we did, but that doesn't suddenly mean he wants me or I want him. I don't. It's just my stupid body, all five foot five inches of it, is suddenly getting a mind of its own.

We drive in silence and I continue to examine my new bag. Every few minutes, I catch Liam glancing at me. "Did you hear back from the garage?" he eventually asks.

"Yeah, muffler. You called it."

"Did they give you a quote?"

"Yeah, it's not going to be that bad."

"Glad to hear it." He taps his big thumb on the steering wheel and it's a bit mesmerizing. "How long will you have to work at Boondocks tonight?"

"Until closing. Around eight. Seven if it's quiet." I take a deep breath, and consider the assignment I need to finish. "Let's hope for seven."

"Do you want some help?" I snort out a laugh, and he quietly adds, "I was being serious."

"Oh, sorry." I steal a glance at him. Honestly, I never knew Liam was so sensitive. "I guess I was just picturing my father's heart attack if he saw you."

This time he snorts out a laugh. "I guess you're right and I don't want to harm your father."

What he doesn't add is...*like my father wants*. His father has been wanting to destroy us for a long time now. He owns half of Lunenburg, and employs even more. Why our little piece of oceanfront land and shop on the water irks him so much is a mystery.

Liam pulls off the highway and begins down the long winding road leading home. "I can help you with calculus tomorrow, if you want. That's not too late, is it?"

"No, and I'd really appreciate that."

"Meet at the library?" He frowns, and nods but it's tight. "You don't like the library?"

"It's fine. Sometimes I just have a hard time concentrating when other people are around, and we'll probably need to be quiet at the library."

"I have access to a lab in the ocean science building. I have my own key and there's a chalk board. Might come in handy if I have to write out equations."

His face lights up. "That's a great idea."

"The lab is in the basement of the building. It's a bit dark, and—"

"No one will see us together," he says, a grin on his face. "We don't want anyone thinking the world is ending."

I laugh at that. "Did your parents warn you to stay away from me, Liam? Like mine said to stay away from you?" I'm a rule follower, and I don't sneak around, but oddly enough, there's something very exciting about all this.

He nods, and scrubs the soft bristles on his cheek. "Yeah."

"Is it true you steal the dreams of small children when they sleep?"

"Only if they don't have candy for me."

That makes me laugh, and he chuckles along with me as he pulls into the gas station. He parks, and I reach for my door. "Thanks for the lift and the backpack. I really like it." He unbuckles and is about to climb out. "It's okay. I can take it from here."

"I just want to make sure it's done. Did they say they had the part when they called?"

"They said it was the muffler and asked me if I wanted them to fix it."

"Okay, let's check it out then."

I arch a brow and point a finger back and forth between the two of us. "You and me...together. I thought we didn't want people to think the sky was falling."

"It's fine, and I just want to make sure they're not going to gouge you. You know how it can go sometimes. A beautiful woman walks into a gas station alone..."

Did he just call me a beautiful woman?

I glance up. Maybe the sky really is falling or I'm hearing things that I shouldn't really want to hear. The bell over the door jingles and pulls my thoughts back. "Coming?"

"Yeah."

I walk past Liam and step up to the counter. The older gentleman behind the counter wipes his greasy hands on a rag and I glance at his nametag. I know most people in this town, but Joe must be new. "Hi Joe, I'm Abigail. I dropped my car off this morning. You called me about the muffler."

"Yeah, the part hasn't come in yet. Hopefully it will get here first thing tomorrow morning."

My chest deflates. I was really hoping it would be fixed. Liam moves in behind me, his body close as he puts his hand on my arm. "I can give you a ride tomorrow, Abi. It's not a problem."

I tap the counter. "Thanks, Joe. I'll check back in tomorrow after classes."

"Should be all fixed by then," he tells me with a nod.

Back outside, my steps are slow. "Damn," I curse under my breath.

Liam nudges me. "It's only one more day."

"But you have a game tomorrow night. You won't be coming back until late, and you probably want to stay in the dorm, and not drive for over an hour. You'll be exhausted."

"You could always drive."

Why is he being so nice to me? "That's true." Dammit, he probably wasn't even planning to drive back home. "I can find another way."

"You could always stay in the city if your folks don't need you back."

"I guess." We usually close early on Wednesdays. Business is usually slow mid-week. "I could check with Ocean. She only has a small bed, but we've shared it before. I was just really hoping it would be done, you know." I shade the late day sun from my eyes, and consider walking home. Liam has done enough for me as it is. "I hate being without my car."

"I can understand that, but I can take you where you need to go."

I frown, and I'm about to hike my bag up higher on my back when Liam takes it from me and tosses it into the back seat.

"Hey, it's not so bad, is it?"

Not so bad?

No, it's not so bad. In fact, it's quite nice. Too nice, and that sets alarm bells jingling in the back of my brain. I should gather up my things, walk away and never set eyes on Liam again. I make a move to go, but my legs seem to have a mind of their own and the next thing I know, I'm in the passenger seat again.

Stupid, traitorous legs. I shake my head. I guess as long as they stay closed when I'm around Liam, they can't really get me into trouble.

Ohmigod, where did that thought come from?

LIAM

I sit at my desk in my bedroom, my laptop open, and my calculus assignment staring me in the face. None of it makes sense to me, and I'm sick of trying. I exhale loudly, and rake my fingers through my hair as I glance out my bedroom window. My thoughts stray to Abi. Okay, that's not entirely true. She hasn't been out of my thoughts all day.

I kind of liked driving her to campus and home and I get to do it again tomorrow. I stand, and flop down on my bed as my dick twitches, memories of the sweet way she smelled teasing my cock.

Fuck, I shouldn't be thinking about her like that. It's wrong and we've only just created an uneasy truce. But it doesn't change the fact that I can't help but wonder what her lips would feel like pressed to mine, or better yet, her small body beneath mine...naked.

"Fuck." I groan and put my hand over my dick, giving it a hard rub. Maybe I should take it out and tug one off. That might help me get my mind off the girl I'm not supposed to touch. It's not like she wants me to touch her anyway. We're barely friends, and that frail truce could snap at any second. I almost fucked things up with the backpack.

I didn't think it was a big deal until I saw the humiliation on her face. The bag was a gift, but it represented much more to her—a reminder of those who have and those who don't. I didn't mean to make her feel small or less fortunate. I just wanted to do something nice for her. I only added the tutoring part in because it seemed like something she needed. I could easily hire a tutor, but she's all about tit for tat, and if that's how she sleeps at night, then I'm on board.

A seagull squawks outside my window and I push off the bed and stick my head out. The cool briny air washes over me, and off in the distance the sun is low on the horizon. I check the time and a plan forms. With any luck, Abi will be finished up in time to watch the sunset with me.

I probably shouldn't be hanging out on her dock, but fuck it. I do everything that is expected of me around this place. I don't go on the boats anymore, and I put all my time into hockey. I need to do at least one thing that makes me happy, for Christ's sake.

I tug on my hoodie and leave my room. Downstairs I find Dad in front of the TV, and Mom is beside him scrolling through her phone. Her head lifts and a smile lights her face. Charlie stretches and saunters over to me for a scratch, and I rub his ears the way he likes.

"Going out?" Dad asks.

"Thought I'd go for a run." I glance at Charlie. He's too old for a run now. He goes as far as the end of the driveway and turns back around.

"It's a lovely night for a run," Mom agrees.

Ember comes into the room. "When are you going to show me around campus?"

"Soon," I tell her. "Maybe over Christmas break."

"I want to see the sorority houses."

I almost stupidly blurt out that she should ask Abigail, or her friend Ocean, who lives in a sorority house.

"I wouldn't know anything about the sorority houses."

Ember laughs and punches my arm. "Right, like you're not sneaking in and out of them every weekend."

Jesus.

I grab her and put her in a headlock. "Really, Ember?" She laughs and pinches my side, and Dad turns the TV up to hear the game over our antics. "Is that what you think of me?" Last year I might have done that. This year, not so much.

"Maybe your sister would like to go for a run with you. Get her head out of a book once in a while."

My stomach tightens. Shit, if she comes, I won't be able to see Abi. I tug up my hood. "I don't need her slowing me down."

"Please, more like the other way around, and trust me, I'd rather get a root canal without painkillers."

"Jeez, love you too, sis."

She laughs and holds up the book she's been reading. "Just getting to the good parts. Hey," she says much more seriously. "How's Josh doing?"

"He's good, why?" I narrow my eyes on her. She's always asking about my best friend. She'd better not have a crush on him. He's too old for her. I don't think I have anything to worry about. It's not like Josh would break bro-code and go behind my back and do anything with my sister.

"No reason. I just miss seeing him around is all."

I glance out the window and the sun is sinking fast. "I'm out of here."

"Have a good run," Dad says absentmindedly as I open the door and step out into the breezy night. As cool air blows in off the ocean, I stretch my legs out, more anxious to see Abi than I should be. I kind of miss her, to be honest. Back when we were kids, before our parents poisoned us against each other, we used to have fun on the playground. This was when she was carefree, and didn't have to spend all her time at Boondocks. I honestly don't know how she handles all the responsibility.

I start running down the street. Lunenburg is growing quiet this time of year, with the tourist season dwindling, and many who come here and stay in their summer homes have returned to their winter residences. I kind of like it like this.

Dunn Fisheries don't really rely on a lot of foot traffic, like Boondocks does, so the lack of tourists doesn't hurt our bottom line. I make my way along the shore and look longingly at our fleet of boats on the dock. Many more are out at sea, fishing in the deep ocean.

My breath comes fast as I pick up the pace, and soon enough I see Boondocks in the distance. There aren't any cars around, and I slow my steps when I approach and peer into the window. The place is dark, which means Abi lucked out, and she was able to close up early. I glance over my shoulder, half expecting to see her walking up the hill to her house. That's when I hear my name.

"Are you going to stand there all day, or are you coming to watch this sunset with me?" Happiness races through me and I turn and peer down the long dock. I block the setting sun out of my eyes, and spot Abi standing beside one of the big Adirondack chairs. "It's not going to wait for you."

"I'm coming."

I jog down to where she's standing, and I can't seem to stop smiling as I take in her pig tails. I give one a little tug without thinking. Her mouth drops open, and I pull my hand away. "Oh, I'm sorry. I wasn't trying to hurt you. I'm not like those bullies on the playground." I shove my hands into the big pocket of my hoodie. "I shouldn't have done that. I just think your hair is cute like this."

Wait, why are her cheeks turning the color of the sky? The sun is reflecting off the ocean, turning it a gorgeous shade of orangey/pink, but is it reflecting on her cheeks too? Or is something else causing her face to heat? Something like...hair pulling? Fuck me.

"I know you're not like the bullies."

"I just think it's cute," I say again because I'm an idiot. "You used to wear it like that when we were kids."

"You remember that?" She drops into a chair, exhaling and stretching her legs out as she does. Her feet must hurt from being on them all night.

"I kind of had a thing for pig tails," I admit and she laughs.

"I didn't know that, and I only tied mine back because I was working." She kicks her shoes off, slides from her chair and dips her feet into the water. "That feels nice."

"Not too cold?"

"It might be for you. It's not for me."

I grin at the challenge hidden in her words. I tug off my runners and join her, trying not to wince as I dip my toes in. It's fucking freezing. She lays back, and stares up at the sky. I do the same.

"It is kind of pretty."

I turn to see her as the dock wobbles beneath us. Our legs briefly touch. "Yeah, pretty," I say but I'm looking at her.

"You don't mind me talking, right?"

I look back at the sky. "Nope."

"I never stay to watch the sunsets. By the end of the day, especially in the summer, I just want off this dock, you know. I want to go somewhere, anywhere else."

"I can understand that. What is it you do when you have free time?"

She gives a humorless laugh. "Study."

"These grants you want to apply for," I begin cautiously. "Hopefully they'll take you to Miami. Have you applied yet?"

"Working on it."

"If we both make it there, I bet we can see some amazing sunrises and sunsets." It's odd to use the word 'we' with Abi, but I kind of like it.

"I hear the sunsets in Santorini are spectacular." She takes a deep breath and lets it out slowly as the last of the rays disappear behind the hilly golf course across the water. "It's on my bucket list." She falls quiet for a moment. "What is it you like about the sunset?" she asks.

"I don't know. I guess it just signifies the end of the day, like a reset, and that anything is possible tomorrow. I guess it's a time for dreams."

"Deep."

I laugh. "You asked."

"I'm not making fun of you." She nudges me with her foot as she rolls to her side, and goes up on her elbow to rest her head in her palm. "When you think about tomorrow, what possibilities are you talking about?"

I have the world in the palm of my hands, and if I tell her what I really dream about, she'll likely laugh and think I'm nothing but a spoiled rich kid, which when it comes right down to it, I am. I've only ever had to work at hockey, and let's face it, hockey came easy to me. So, that's not much of a hardship. I like the game, I really do. Playing in the NHL doesn't suck. I think I'm just a homebody—probably another reason I don't stay in the city all that much—and I love being out on the open ocean.

"Playing in the NHL," I say, and reach into the pocket of my hoodie and pull out a jerky stick. I sit up and peel down the plastic wrapper, and the spicy scent mingles with the brine of the ocean. "Here."

Abi sits up and crinkles her nose like she just smelled something offensive. "Ohmigod, Liam. What are you eating?"

"This one is for you."

"What is it?"

I hold the stick out to her. "Beef jerky. Try it. I have another."

She waves her hand in front of her face. "Are you kidding me? It stinks. How can you eat that?"

"It's delicious." I take a big bite and chew.

"I doubt it."

I take another bite and she stares at me like I might have taken one too many hits to the head. "Have you ever tried one?"

"No, and I don't plan on it. Your diet has a lot to be desired."

"You're one to talk. Don't you remember all those snowballs you used to eat in elementary school."

She looks aghast, in the cutest way possible way when she counters with, "I was seven."

"So you're saying you don't eat them anymore."

"Well...no. I mean, I probably would. Coconut, chocolate and marshmallow. That combination is straight out of heaven, Liam. No one can resist that, but I don't think anyone makes them anymore. I haven't seen them in ages."

I laugh at that and hold the stick out. "This is good for you. It's a great source of protein..."

"Said no one ever," she adds, and we both laugh.

I try to read the ingredients, but can't see them in the dark. "Come on, it's good for you."

"If chemicals are good for you, sure."

I grab my phone and put on my flashlight app. "Beef, and something I can't quite pronounce..."

"Probably synthetic hormones. I wouldn't even feed my dog that."

"You a have a dog?"

"No, but if I did. Wait, are you sure that's not a dog's meat stick?"

I look over the label. "It's not. I don't think. I mean, I don't think I've seen Charlie eating them. Shit, maybe they are Charlie's." I stare at it for a second, shrug and take another big bite.

She laughs at that. "Your family runs a big fishing conglomerate. Why don't you snack on dried fish? It's probably better for you. Honestly, that thing is nitrates holding hands."

I tug on my pocket. "Not as easy to transport." I smile at her and she smiles back and there's something very nice and intimate in the way we're sparring.

"Your snacks need to have protein?"

I toss the last bite into my mouth. "Yup." She goes quiet, like she's thinking about that. "Did you enjoy the sunset?" I ask.

"I did until you stunk the place up with that meat stick." I tuck the wrapper away. "Good thing you don't have a girlfriend or boyfriend. No one would give you a goodnight kiss after that. That'd be the end of any relationship."

I pucker my lips playfully and kiss the air. "Are you saying if you were my girl, you wouldn't give me a good night kiss right now?" I'm joking of course, but now that she's put that idea into my head, I can't stop staring at her lips.

"Absolutely not," she shoots back. Her body stiffens but it's the way her tongue snakes out to wet her lips that has me thinking she might not really hate the idea.

Dammit, now I can't stop thinking about it. Should I act on it?

"You're happy this morning," Mom says, glancing up from her iPad as I stand at the counter, putting raspberry jam on my toast and take a big bite. Grandad flips the pages of the newspaper, and I'm not even sure he's reading. Maybe he's just looking at the pictures. Once again, the sight of him hurts my heart and reminds me how much my mother has on her plate.

"Abi?"

"What?" I ask, and turn my attention to my mom, to take in the fine lines around the corners of her dark brown eyes. Has she been looking extra tired lately? Things should be slowing soon at Boondocks soon enough and while that's great for taking a break and getting some rest, slower sales come with their own problems.

Mom stands to refill her coffee and bops me on the nose. "You're humming, and I haven't heard you hum since you were in middle school."

"Hmm, I didn't even realize I was." I chew my toast and follow it with a big drink of coffee.

"How was business last night?" she asks and I'm grateful she's not pressing my happy mood. I wouldn't have an answer for that. Or at least one I'd want to give her. "You didn't come in until late."

I brush my tongue over my bottom lip to catch a piece of jam, but my thoughts instantly go back to the way Liam was studying my lips like they were a prized possession—like he was dying for a taste. My God, for a minute there I really thought he was going to kiss me. That's crazy, of course. He was just looking at my mouth because we were talking about that disgusting meat stick and how he'd end up single if he were ever to try to kiss a partner after chowing down on one.

"It's slowing down. I...stayed behind to catch up on some things." It's true, I'm sort of leading her to believe it was schoolwork that kept me at the shop. But I guess technically I was 'catching up' with Liam. "I uh, had some paperwork, for the summer grants." I didn't fill it out. I'd only been thinking about it, and I'm not sure why I even brought it up.

"Oh?"

"Yeah, it's ridiculous. I probably won't even apply. It's for a program in Miami," I say and snort out a laugh like it's ridiculous. All the while, however, I gauge Mom's reaction.

"Miami, wow. That's so far away from home."

Guilt that I want more, that I want out of this small town, swamps me. I realize the store, the land, the boats and the fishing license has been in our family for generations and they probably wanted a son, because a son would continue the legacy. Dammit, is it so wrong to want to do something different?

"Yeah, I probably wouldn't be able to commute daily," I joke, and Mom gives a small smile.

"No, I suspect not." She turns her attention to Granddad. "More coffee, Dad?"

With the conversation over, I say, "I better get going."

"Have a great day," Dad pipes in as he walks into the kitchen, looking rather tired this morning, too. I thought he was home in bed when I got in last night. I turn back to Mom. "How did Granddad's appointment go yesterday?"

She puts on a smile but there's exasperation in her eyes when she says, "Good as can be expected."

How long can we all continue to care for him? I don't say that out loud, because when I do there's always backlash, so I brush crumbs from my hands, open the fridge and pull out the sandwich I made late last night, as well as a plastic container filled with healthy snacks. I sort of keep the snacks hidden as I slide the container into my backpack. I don't need questions. Not that Mom and Dad ever notice much when it comes to me. Heck, they haven't even noticed my car isn't outside. Or at least if they have, they haven't mentioned it. They're probably not worried about how I'll get to campus. I've been independent and solving my own problems for a very long time now.

"You don't need me back early tonight?" Boondocks closes early this evening, but I just want to double check. I'd never want to leave them shorthanded.

With her coffee cup halfway to her mouth, Mom pauses and asks, "No, why do you have something to do in the city?"

"Just some work," I say and shoulder my backpack. Wow, who knew I'd be lying to my parents so much? I spent my whole life following the rules and after a couple days hanging out with Liam, I'm telling half-truths all day long. I glance at the duffle bag I packed earlier. "I might actually stay overnight with Ocean."

"Okay, see you tomorrow," Mom replies and I walk to the porch.

I stand in front of the floor-length mirror and give myself a once over. I smooth my hand over my ponytail. I'd considered leaving it down, but this is much easier. I opted for my favorite skinny jeans over yoga pants, and a cute, frilly, short sleeve shirt. Not that you can see it under my hoodie. I take another second in front of the mirror. Honestly, I have no idea why my appearance is suddenly so important to me.

The screen door bangs behind me as I step out into the early morning sunshine. I didn't watch the sunrise this morning. I was up too late and needed to get a few minutes extra sleep, not that I had a restful night. I didn't. I spent far too many minutes—okay, hours—thinking about Liam. Speak of the devil. I spot him coming along the road, driving slowly along the narrow winding path, and my chest expands, filling with weird sensations that bring me...happiness. Lord, what is going on with me?

He slows, reaches across the seat and opens my door. "Morning," I say. I take in his big smile as I climb in and set my new backpack at my feet. Wait, is he staring at my lips again? His hand snakes out, and he rubs his thumb over the side of my mouth. "Oh, God. Jam," I tell him and grab a fast-food napkin from his console and wipe his finger. "I was in a hurry. I didn't want to miss you."

"I would have waited."

I toss my duffle bag into the back seat and glance over my shoulder, half expecting Mom or Dad to be peeking through the curtains, but they're nowhere to be found. As if sensing my unease, Liam starts driving, and I'm able to fill my lungs a bit easier when we round the corner, out of my parents' line of sight.

"Did you watch the sunrise this morning?" he asks and stifles a yawn. Did he have a restless night too?

"No. Did you?"

He shakes his head. "How come you missed it?"

"Because I was up late making these." I reach into my bag and pull out the plastic container. I open it and the smell of chocolate fills the car. It's not half as enticing as the aroma of his freshly showered skin, which is overwhelming my senses in the nicest possible way.

He narrows his eyes. "What are those?"

"Protein bars. Healthy. Have you eaten yet?"

"Yeah, but I can eat again."

I laugh and reach in to pull out one of the bars. "I wrapped them individually, so you can easily carry them in the pocket of your hoodie. That seems to be a real issue for you. Food on the go." I pull the plastic down and hand him the bar.

"This looks amazing."

"Try it."

He takes a generous bite, and the moan he makes pull a laugh from my throat, not to mention what it's doing to other parts of my body, parts a bit further south. "Good, right?" I ask, trying not to sound breathless...or aroused.

"Abi, this is delicious. It tastes like a brownie."

The excitement in his voice makes me laugh. "A brownie that is good for you."

"I can't believe you made these for me." The appreciation in his eyes when they meet mine, fills me with a strange kind of warmth. "I don't bake, so I don't know, but I'm guessing these took forever."

"Nope, just a few easy ingredients we had on hand." He shoves a big piece into his mouth, and holds the other end out to offer me a bite. "I'm good. I had breakfast, and I might have eaten my fair share last night when they were hot."

"A hot brownie is the best thing ever."

I had no idea I was going to get this kind of reaction from him, and I really like it. "You can warm it in the microwave."

"Oh my God, yes." I can't help but chuckle as he examines the treat in his hand. "You think this is good to eat before a game?"

"Better than a meat stick."

He laughs. "I'll have to hide these from the team." His tongue snakes out to lick the chocolate from the corner of his mouth, and I quickly tear my attention away before I lean in and help him.

I put the lid back on the container and set it in the back seat for him. "I can make more if you want to share."

He holds the last piece of bar close to his chest, like he's worried I might suddenly want a bite. "Hell no, I'm not sharing."

"There's enough there to last a week."

"Probably not," he tells me and I really like how much he loves his treat.

"Fine, I'll make you more. It's the least I can do for the drives."

"The least," he answers playfully. He finishes off the protein bar, and crumples up the plastic, setting it in the console to get rid of later. "Are you going to stay in the city tonight?" he asks, changing the subject.

I grab my phone. "Yes, I'm going to check with Ocean to see if I can stay with her." I shoot off a text and put my phone on my lap as I wait for her reply.

"Does this mean you're coming to the game?"

Is that hope in his eyes? Why would he care if I was there or not? I rarely get to the games, but I do like to support our college. "I think so. Ocean goes, so she'll probably drag me along."

"You make it sound like it's a hardship. Don't you want to see your *boi* kill it out there."

He grins at me, and while he's not my *boi*, I would like to see his plays. "Are you going to impress me with your skills, Liam? I hear you're quite tough on the ice."

"You know it." He jokingly lifts his arm to flex his bicep, and even through his big hoodie, it's impressive. Before I can think better of it, I reach out and give his arm a squeeze and now suddenly, I'm thinking about his plays and skills—just not the ones he uses on the ice.

"Impressed?" he teases, and there's a strange hitch to his voice. Did my touch mess with him as much as it messed with me? My God, what was I thinking? I shouldn't be groping him. It's overstepping boundaries and no better than the playground bully pulling hair.

Don't think about pulling hair.

"I'll let you know after I see you play," I say and he puts his hand back on the steering wheel. I take in his hard body that his big hoodie does little to hide. He gets his size from his father, but those muscles, I don't think they come from a gym. During the dog days of summer, when I would work the early morning shift or the late shift at Boondocks, I'd see him on the boats, working just as hard as the regular crew. I don't see that anymore. Then again, where would he ever find the time?

"Do you miss going on the boats?" I ask.

His head rears back, surprise in his eyes as he casts a glance my way. "Why would you ask that?"

I stare back, a little thrown off by his strong reaction. I was simply making conversation. I didn't expect him to go on the defense like this. "I'm sorry. If you don't want to talk about it."

"I didn't even know you knew I went out on the boats. You just surprised me."

Not an answer, but okay. "I used to see you," I tell him. "I'd watch the sunrise, and listen to all the men get their boats ready every morning." I smile.

"You have fond memories of those days," he states quietly, and the smile forming on his mouth tells me he does too.

I briefly close my eyes as the image forms in my brain. "The rising sun would be warm on my face. The seagulls would be squawking overhead, searching for breakfast. The port would be bustling with activity. It was different back then. My granddad was well and my parents were happier. I didn't hate it."

"You hate it now."

"I wouldn't exactly say I hate it. I love the ocean. I just hate the overfishing, and all the hours I put in at Boondocks, and the pressures my family seems to be under." He nods and I add, "You seemed happy on the boats. Do you miss it?"

"I used to see you too, Abi," he says quietly, instead of answering. "I didn't know you saw me, but when we headed offshore, I'd always see you on the dock."

"I didn't know."

"When did we start hating each other?"

"I think it was toward the end of middle school. Your father tried to buy our oceanfront property out from underneath us." That's when things started getting bad at home.

"He hated your family long before that, though."

"True," I agree. "But I think my parents kept me sheltered, and didn't say much around me, until that incident. It was then they warned me to stay away from you."

"Yeah, I remember the same thing. I'm sorry my father was an asshole."

I laugh at that and shrug. "Parents, what can you do?"

"I don't know." He goes quiet, but there's pain on his face. Does he not have a good relationship with his family? I always thought they were tight.

My phone pings and I snatch it up and read the message from Ocean. A moment of panic grips my chest. What the hell am I going to do now?

"Everything okay?" Liam asks.

I glance at him. "Ocean has plans for tonight. Apparently, she's seeing someone and her bed will be occupied tonight. She offered to check with one of her sorority sisters though, to see if they could put me up." I crinkle my nose. "I don't want to sleep in someone's room I don't know."

"Not a problem. I can give you a key to my dorm room. You can sleep there, and I can bunk with one of the guys."

"I can't ask you to do that."

"Trust me, Abi. There are a lot of free beds in the dorm after a game." He grins at me. "If you know what I mean." I nod. "I'll give you a key, and feel free to use it at any time. In between classes, or whenever. I don't mind."

"Like just show up whenever?" The idea of not hanging out in the library is appealing, and if he wants help with his calculus, his room might be a better place than the basement of the Ocean's science building.

"Sure."

"And I won't find...someone already there?"

He laughs. "I mean, I might be there. It is my room." He eyes me. "That's not what you're asking, though." I shake my head. "You will not find a woman in my room," he states, his voice taking on a serious edge. "I don't give my key to just anyone."

"Wow," I tease. It's so strange how he makes me feel important. No one has ever made me feel like I mattered before. When it comes right down to it, I'm a nobody. A nobody the guys on the team like to pick on, but a nobody, none the less. "Way to make a girl feel special."

"You are special," he says, not a hint of teasing in his voice. "Didn't anyone ever tell you that before?"

I glance at him, and when I find him staring at my mouth, a quiver rockets through my body and settles between my legs. My God, what is going on with him—with me? Maybe I shouldn't take the key to his room, or go to his game tonight. Maybe I should run all the way back to Lunenburg after classes, because if he keeps looking at me like that, I might put my hair in pig tails and tempt him to pull them.

8

LIAM

I tear my gaze away from the stands, away from Abi, and warm up with my fellow players. I might have been drafted but that doesn't mean I can let my guard down. Getting drafted and actually getting to play in the NHL are two different things.

I stretch out and try not to steal another look at Abi as she and Ocean, along with numerous other fans, cheer on our players as they come on the ice. I glance at the Islanders as they saunter on like they own the place, but no fucking way in hell am I letting them get a shot on net. I plan to kill it tonight.

And why is that, Liam?

Oh, I don't know. Maybe I want to impress Abi. Christ knows I've had a thing for her for many years, and up until the other day, she never talked to me—well, at least not since elementary school. Now that we're talking, I want to get to know her better, and she doesn't seem to be opposed to the idea either. When I offered her my room and my bed, I thought she'd tell me to go to hell, but she didn't. I have no plans to try to hook up with her tonight, even though the idea of her in my bed is making me insane.

Head in the game, dude.

Jesse comes skating over, and he bangs helmets with me. "Let's kick some ass tonight, Liam."

"You know it."

He skates back to middle ice and we all position ourselves as the ref prepares to drop the puck. Five seconds later, the puck is in play, with Jesse in control. The crowd goes crazy, and I quickly check on Abi to find her eyes on me and not Jesse racing down the ice with the puck. I like it. A lot. I turn my attention back to the play, my chest a little fuller as Jesse passes the puck to Alessandro, who passes it back after Jesse repositions himself, and within the first thirty seconds of the game, we score. Fuck yeah.

We all hug Jesse, and I get my head back in the game, stopping some pretty fucking hard shots that would impress even my biggest haters. But I'm on a mission tonight, and I plan to shut down the Islanders and send them the fuck home.

With minutes left on the clock, and the score two to zero, they pull their goalie and I prepare for the onslaught. We're bombarded, and the puck comes flying at crazy speeds, but Tanner and I are everywhere, intercepting each shot on net.

I dig it out from one of the players and get it to Jesse, who quickly carries it down the ice and shoots it into the empty net seconds before the buzzer goes off.

"Fuck yeah," I shout, and the guys pile onto me, banging helmets and shouting out congratulations. When the cheering dies down, we shake hands with the Islanders and bombard the locker room. We're all still high from the win, and I hurry to the shower, anxious to hang out with Abi. Will she go out for beers like the rest of us? She's not usually around for a game, so all the excitement might be enough for her for one night.

I catch Sebastian's glance after I shower and head back to the locker room. He looks like he wants to say something to me. I stand there with my towel wrapped around my waist and glare at him.

"What's up Sebastian?"

He scratches his head. "Uh...good game," is all he says. Did he spot Abi in the stands? Does he think there's something going on between us? I sure as hell hope not. His parents are friends with my parents, and I do not need a lecture from my parents. I'm sick of this bullshit.

"Thanks, you too," is all I say and tug on my clothes. Tanner throws his arms around me, and we head outdoors. I usually have one beer with the guys and head back to the dorm. Like I said, I'm a bit of a loner, so running off won't raise questions. I just hope the party doesn't spill back into Storm House.

Girls flood the streets, and jump on our backs for piggyback rides, but just thinking about that reminds me of Abi's pig tails, and my fucking cock thickens. I hope whoever is on my back doesn't see it, and think it's for them.

Inside our favorite watering hole, I do a fast glance around, but disappointment hits when I don't see Abi. I drop down onto the long bench seat, and girls pile in around me. Pitchers of beer are plunked down in front of us, followed by trays of nachos. My stomach is growling, but I'm not that hungry. I think I'm just anxious to see Abi.

I turn and that's when I spot her friend Ocean. She doesn't like me much. She of course sided with Abi back in the day, when Abi decided she hated me. What will she think when she finds out Abi is staying in my room. Wait, did Ocean just kiss Easton? Are they together? Is that's who's staying in her room tonight? Shit, I don't think I could have predicted that hook-up. Wait, if Ocean is here…

I turn and glance down the hall, and that's when I see Abi coming from the little girls' room. She's checking something on her phone, and that's when my pocket lights up. I pull out my phone and grin.

Abi: I'm impressed.

Me: You liked my plays.

Abi: You had some good plays.

I lift my head and find her walking to her friend's table. I'm holed up at the big center table, surrounded by puck bunnies. I'll need the jaws of life to get out.

Abi: I'm heading back to the dorm. I have some studying to do. Thanks for letting me stay in your room.

My heart jumps just thinking about her in my bed. *Get it together, Liam*. She is not your girl.

Me: I'll walk you.

Abi: No, enjoy your party. You deserve it. I have campus security coming. I used the app. Besides, we hate each other, remember. If anyone sees us together, they'll think the world is ending.

I stare at her as her fingers run over her phone, and I sip on my beer as conversation grows loud in my ears. The reminder of our feuding families is clearly her way of letting me know she's not in my room for sex. Hell, she doesn't want to be seen with me and while that probably is wise, it still kind of stings.

Small hands grab my face, and tug until I'm staring at the girl squeezed in beside me. The next thing I know a set of lips are on mine. I break the kiss in time to see Abi stand, her gaze leaving mine as she walks to the door, to where some guy from campus security is waiting for her.

She disappears, and the girl who kissed me starts pouting. "What's the matter, Liam?"

"Nothing."

"Why aren't you celebrating?" she asks, and then glances over her shoulder to the door—to where Abi just disappeared. "Are you waiting for someone?"

"No, I just…I think I'm getting a cold."

She backs up. "Eww, don't get me sick."

I reach for my beer again and take a big drink as one of the puck bunnies, Isla, turns her attention to Tanner.

I give it another fifteen minutes, and nod to Tanner, who was drafted by the Boston Bucks and is going there next year. "Tanner," I say as I try to slide from the bench. "Can I crash in your room tonight?"

He eyes me. I get it. I've never asked that before. "Yeah, sure," he responds and wraps his arms around the girl sitting on his lap. "I won't be needing my room." The girl giggles and kisses him and I practically dry hump them both trying to get out from around them. It's odd, really. Tanner Bang, known as Banger around the rink, only because of his last name, doesn't have a reputation like most of the other guys. In fact, he's a bit of a loner like me.

Tanner isn't much into puck bunnies, and I always wondered if he had his heart broken by someone, or if there's someone out there that he wants and can't have. That could be why he's so broody. But hey, we're guys, so we don't talk much about those kinds of things.

Once I'm free, I step outside, and the night air feels chilly now that my body has cooled down. I walk back to Storm House, which is pretty quiet right now, with the guys all out celebrating. It's crazy how fast my heart is racing as I hurry up the stairs and down the hall. I stand outside my dorm room for a second, and then I knock.

I listen to feet shuffle on the other side, and Abi is close to the door when she questions, "Hello?"

"Hey Abi, it's me," I whisper. "Just wanted to check to make sure you got back okay and have everything you need."

The door opens, and the second I set eyes on her, standing there in one of my T-shirts, and no pants, I nearly bite off my tongue. My gaze drops as my dick rises and Abi grabs the hem of the T-shirt and tugs it to her mid thighs.

"I'm sorry. I hope you don't mind. I forgot to pack pajamas."

"No, I don't mind at all." Nope, my dick is rather happy to see her in nothing but my T-shirt. Motherfucking prick that it is. Is she wearing *anything* beneath my blue T-shirt? Fuck. From the way her nipples are pressing against the fabric, I'd say she's not wearing a bra. What about panties? Goddammit, I really want to find out.

Walk away, Liam.

That's when I notice the pig tails. Jesus fucking Christ. Abigail Hart is in my bedroom in my shirt, her hair in pigtails, something she knows I like. Wait, is she doing all this on purpose? Did she know I'd come back to check on her, and wants me to ravish the fucking hell out of her, or is that just wishful thinking on my part? We both stand there, the temperature in the room skyrocketing as heat arcs between us. I get the sense she feels it every bit as much as I do. I take a few deep breaths, but filling my lungs is a chore.

"Is it..." Christ, I sound far too breathless. "...okay if I come in for a second?" I gesture with a nod over my shoulder. "I'm going to crash in my buddy Tanner's room."

"I feel kind of bad that I'm taking your bed." I resist the urge to ask her if she'd like to share it as she wraps one pigtail around her finger, and my palms itch, wanting to tug on it myself. "Your chair looks pretty comfortable. I could sleep in that."

"No," I say as she continues to stand there, looking so goddamn sexy I'm about to lose my fucking mind. "I'll just ah. I gotta go. I'll just grab some things I need."

She backs up to let me in and the T-shirt brushes over her thighs. I close the door behind me, not wanting any of the guys to see her half naked body should they come home.

"Of course. Grab whatever you need."

Grab whatever you need.

Of all the fucking things she could have said to me. I stand there and run agitated hands through my hair, and don't miss the way her chest is rising and falling rapidly too. I step into the room, and I glance at my mussed bedsheets as my body brushes hers. A groan I have no control over crawls out of my throat and my dick is so hard now, it's pressing against my unforgiving zipper and hurting like a son of a bitch.

Fuck me. I turn quickly.

"Liam?"

I go still, inches from her body, my back to her. Tension is so thick you could scoop it with an ice cream spoon. "Yeah?"

"If you're in a hurry, I can help. Just let me know what you need."

Is she fucking with me?

I turn abruptly and find desire reflected in her big blue eyes. As I take in her flushed cheeks, something inside of me snaps, and I know, what I'm about to do next is going to affect my balls in one of two ways. They're either going to be blue from rejection, or black and blue from her knee. No way is she going to let me touch her, yet here I am reaching for her anyway.

I put my hand on her hip, and grip as she sucks in a tight breath. Here goes nothing. "If you really want to know." My gaze rakes over her mouth. "What I need is you and what I want to grab is this."

I tug on her hair, and she swallows hard, her plump lips parting, much like they did on the dock and that's when my brain shuts down. "Abi," I murmur, and dip my head. The second my lips crash down on hers, she moans into my mouth and grabs at my hoodie. I fist the T-shirt she's wearing as we turn around, and I back her up, until she's pressed against my door.

She's not rejecting you, Liam.

I kiss her like a man starved and she takes every bit of it, giving as good as she gets. It's like we've both gone mad, insane for one another, which is crazy, considering our history.

"Still hate me, Abi?" I tease as I break the kiss.

"Yes," she answers, and I chuckle.

"I guess you'd hate it if I did this." I grab the hem of the T-shirt and slowly lift it as I gauge her reactions.

She moans in delight and leans into this game we're playing. "Hate it," she murmurs, and I nearly bite off my tongue when I find her in lace panties and nothing else.

"Jesus," I groan as I take in her perfect breasts with the most gorgeous pink nipples I've ever had the pleasure of setting eyes on. "Abi…" I toss the T-shirt away and go straight for her breasts. I lightly run my palms over the outer edges, reveling in the softness of her skin, and her nipples tighten even more.

"Liam…" Her head falls back as I admire her gorgeous body, completely in awe of her perfection, and while there are so many things I want to do to her—with her—I can't seem to stop looking, or touching. "Please…" she murmurs.

I swallow against a dry throat, loving the need in her voice, the way she's not afraid to ask for what she needs. "Would you hate it if I put my mouth right here?" I brush my thumb over her puckered bud, and reach down to adjust my dick before I rupture something.

"Hate," is all she murmurs, and I bend forward and her fingers go to my hair as I take her perfect pink nipple into my mouth. Heat flashes through my body, every nerve on fire as I suck her in deep and run my hands down her back until I'm cupping her ass through the barely-there lace.

"These," I whisper around her plump globe as I tug on the flimsy band.

"Hate them?" she asks, her voice laced in need and want.

"Yes."

"Never want to see them again?"

"Never," I grouch.

She rocks forward, and wiggles, her sweet sex teasing my cock. "Maybe you should take them off me then."

I lift my head and the pure desire in her eyes prompts me into action. I fist the material in my palms, and in one quick jerk, rip her panties clear from her hips. Her gasp of pleasure wraps around me and for the briefest of seconds, I can't believe Abigail Hart, my sworn enemy, is naked in my bedroom. But she is, and dammit, I'm going to show her exactly how much I hate that.

9

ABIGAIL

What the ever-loving hell am I doing? Well, okay, I guess I know what I'm doing, but really did I come to his room, and forget my pajamas on purpose so I could hook up with the guy I've hated for years?

Yes, yes you did, Abi, and if your best friend Ocean ever found out what was really going on, she'd no doubt think you might need a brain scan.

I didn't get a chance to tell her much, other than Liam had given me a lift and had offered me his room while he bunks elsewhere. I'm assuming she suspects more is going on, but with the hockey game and being surrounded by people, we couldn't really talk. Will I tell her? Then again, what exactly would I tell her? The facts are the facts. Liam helped me and has offered me his room. Nothing else is going on here, right?

Yet...

Okay, it's true. I want more.

Maybe Ocean would be right. Maybe I do need a brain scan. My body momentarily freezes at that realization, because let's face it, this is so not like me. But maybe I'm a little tired of being me, of taking care of everyone and everything all the time. Maybe just once I want someone—and that someone happens to be my nemesis—to help me forget about life for a while and just enjoy each other's bodies.

"Abi?" he asks quietly, inching back to see my face. His eyes hold one question, and that question is—second thoughts?

I grab his hoodie and haul him back to me, and without any hesitation, I press my lips to his, letting him know exactly where I stand. Hot sex with the guy I hate, no regrets come morning. He groans into my mouth and I love it. Love that I —a girl half his team calls names—can make this man moan with want.

I slide my hands under his hoodie, dying to feel his hot skin and muscles beneath my fingertips. His entire body quakes and he steps back. Now it's my turn to wonder if he's having second thoughts. I swear to God, I'll sink to the floor and die of embarrassment if this half-cocked plan backfires on me.

"Doesn't seem fair that you're naked and I'm not."

I grin, heat racing through me as he grips the bottom of his hoodie and peels it over his head. The strangest noise crawls out of my throat and he grins in response. He also clearly likes the way he affects me. I guess that's one more thing we have in common.

His T-shirt follows, and I can't stop staring at his gorgeous body as he pops the button and unzips his jeans, and quickly shoves them to his feet. My gaze drops, naturally to take in his boxers and the lovely way his erection tents them. I swallow, and lift my eyes to his as he pushes against me again, pinning me to his bedroom door.

I run my hands down his back and into his boxers to grip his hard ass. He groans into my mouth and tears his lips away to bury his face in the crook of my neck. Like a man on a mission, he nudges my feet apart. My sex opens for him and I grow wetter with excitement.

"Abi, fuck..." he murmurs and inhales my skin. "I need to taste you."

"Yes," I manage to get out as I shift and slide my hand around his body to the front of his boxers. I grip his cock as he slides a finger into me. As he pushes into me, he uses the heel of his palm to apply pressure to my clit. "Oh."

"Hate that, do you?" The gruffness in his voice arouses me even more.

I move my body, grind against him. "Hate it so much."

He moves his finger in and out of me with skilled precision, and I dip into the pre-cum spilling from his crown.

"Fuck me," he growls.

"Hate it?"

"It's the worst," he laughs and jerks forward to slide his long length into my palm. I stroke him and he grunts, but his cock falls from my hand when he sinks to his knees. He grips my thighs hard and glances up at me with those dark eyes that hold so much need. My entire body quakes hard and the second he turns his attention to my sex, and runs his tongue from bottom to top, my legs nearly give out.

He braces me against the door to keep me upright as he buries his face between my legs, eating at me like he's discovered a prized delicacy, and wants to keep it all to himself. I rake my fingers through his hair, and move my body, bumping into his mouth. His tongue centers on my clit, and the room closes in on me.

"Liam...God, that's the worst." As I use his words, he chuckles, and it vibrates through my body. I take my breasts into my hands, and he glances up. His eyes darken even more as I run my thumbs over my nipples. He goes back on his heels, and slides a finger deep into my quivering sex as he watches me. I guess he must *hate* what I'm doing, because he looks like he's about to go off like a rocket.

"Yeah," he murmurs, and wets his lips as I touch myself. I sag against the door as his finger takes me higher and higher, until I'm crying out in bliss. I glance down at him, a desperate need to taste him overcoming me. I cup his face and he glances up at me.

"Stand," I demand, and he doesn't ask questions. He stands, and groans as I sink to my knees, tugging his gorgeous cock from his boxers. "Oh my," I murmur as his appendage jumps in my hands.

"Fuck, Abi."

"Would you hate it if I put this in my mouth?"

He stares down at me, a growl in his throat as he wraps my pigtails around one hand and tugs, forcing my mouth open, thus answering my question, and ohmigod, him tugging on my hair like that has to be the hottest thing I've ever felt.

I inch forward and take his cock to the back of my throat. I gasp as it hits and he tugs my hair again, this time to move my head back to prevent his cock from choking me. I moan around his thick cock, and lick the pre-cum from his slit, and his hands tighten even more around my pigtails. At first I wasn't sure if I should braid them or not, but now, it's clear I made the right decision. Who knew having my hair pulled during sex could be so arousing?

I wrap one hand around his pistoning cock as it slides in and out of my slick mouth, and his moan of pleasure as I grip his cock interrupts his litany of grunts. I secretly grin, loving the way his body is trembling under my ministrations. He thickens even more and curses erupt around me. The next thing I know, he's picking me up and carrying me to his bed. He lays me down, kicks off his boxers, and uses his thumb to wipe the corners of my wet mouth as I push my books away until they fall onto the floor with a thud.

He's practically growling as he climbs over me, kissing my mouth with such heat and hunger that it sears me from the inside out. I touch him, loving the way his muscles quiver beneath my fingers. His cock presses against my leg as he shimmies lower to take one hard nipple into his mouth.

"Liam," I moan. "Yes."

He nibbles on my nipple as his big hand closes over my other breast, giving it a firm massage that stimulates the needy spot between my legs. I have never been so needy in my entire life. He growls like a wild animal, and moves his mouth to my other breasts. I lift my head, watching the way he sucks. As if sensing my eyes on him, he lifts his head and his mouth is wet.

God, I hate that. I hate it so much, small tremors begin deep in my body, and my sex clenches, needing something to cling to. I bite my bottom lip, wanting this to last longer. As if sensing my struggles, he keeps his eyes on mine and adjusts his body until he's between my thighs, his hands under my legs, lifting my sex to his mouth.

He buries his face in my sex, and takes my clit into his mouth, sucking until I'm a hot trembling mess. I grab the bedding and fist it, as the world shuts down around me, pleasure being the only thing that exists in my universe. He balances me with one hand and slides a thick finger into me.

"So...so...horrible," I mumble, as my orgasm takes hold and catapults me into outer space. I clench and he pushes a finger high inside me, holding still so I can grip it tight.

"Fuck," he bites out as I squeeze him tight. "My cock is going to hate being in here."

That pulls a chuckle from my throat as the quakes slowly subside. "I'm going to hate it, too," I groan and my words come out harsh and rough. I go up on my elbows, my chest rising and falling quickly as I try to swallow against a dry throat. Liam goes up on his knees, grabs the water bottle from his nightstand, one I'd been drinking from earlier, uncaps it and puts it to my mouth. I take a drink, loving the way he's taking care of me. I'm used to doing everything on my own, so it's surprising how quickly I could get used to someone caring for me. He takes a swig, and sets it down, not bothering to recap it and that's when I notice his hands are shaking. He's not as in control as he appears.

I turn my head at the sound of the drawer on his nightstand being pulled open, and Liam pulls out a condom. "Tell me how much you're going to hate having my cock in here," he pleads as he lightly pets my sopping wet pussy.

"I'd rather jump onto the roof of a burning building."

He makes a hissing sound as he rips into the condom and I stare, mesmerized as he rolls it down the long length of his cock. "That's a lot of hate."

"Right," I agree, as he finishes sheathing himself, and falls over my body, lightly running the back of his finger over my breasts and stomach. "Tell me more."

I quiver as he touches me, and while there's a sense of urgency in him, I get the sense he wants to prolong this night as well. My guess is we both know this is a one-time thing. We can't be together. We shouldn't be together. Our families would disown us, but dammit, I can't think about that right now, not when he's touching me with such delicate precision.

He slides lower and presses hot, open-mouthed kisses to my flesh. Goosebumps form as my arousal builds again. "Well," I begin. "I'd probably prefer a thousand paper cuts, then have you put your cock in me."

He hisses again, and the sound feathers over my flesh. "Wow, a thousand, huh?"

"Make it a million." I move my body, trying to force his cock inside me, a new kind of desperation gripping me.

He pushes my legs open and runs his fingers along my inner thighs, which are damp from my climax. Shifting, he puts his hands on either side of my head, and hovers over me, his cock rock hard and pressed against my opening. I lift my hips, wanting more, and he groans as he inches forward, breaching me with only his crown.

"Tell me how much you hate that."

I swallow and try to get my brain to work as warm and needy sensations rocket through me. "I'd rather skydive with a broken parachute than have you inside me." He offers me another inch, and I briefly close my eyes. God, that feels so incredible.

"Babe," he says and my lids open. I take in the seriousness on his face, and sense he's ending our playful game. "There's nothing in this world I'd rather do right now than put my cock in you."

My heart jumps at the need and tenderness in his tone. I put my arms around his shoulder, needing to touch him as my body opens for him. "Same," I whisper, as he slides all the way in, taking my breath away as his thickness parts me, and his crown hits my cervix. "Liam," I cry out.

"Yeah, Abi," he murmurs. "I know. I know." He grunts, pulls out, and slides in deep again. His face twists. "Jesus, you're so hot and tight."

I move my body, and the friction takes my pleasure to a new height. "I...I...Please..." I stammer, my brain too mushy to even know what I'm begging for. He must know, though, because he starts moving his body, pushing deep, and pulling out. He angles his body for deeper thrusts, hitting me in places I didn't even know existed. His breathing becomes rough and harsh, and he clenches his jaw.

I concentrate on pleasure points as his cock swells inside my tight channel. He powers into me, his grunts and my moans are the only sounds in the room. I scrape my nails over his back, reveling in the feel of his hard muscles tightening and loosening as his pelvis teases my clit with each downward thrust.

He powers in deep and rotates his hips. "Oh," I cry out, as he hits me in the perfect spot. "Liam..." I cling to him as another orgasm catches me by surprise and takes me over the edge. He goes still and curses under his breath, like every clench around his cock is about to become his undoing.

He inches out a bit as my body vibrates and that's when I take over, moving my hips as he stays still. I slide his cock in and out of me, and he takes gulping breaths as he watches.

"That is so fucking hot," he grunts out, and puts his hand under my ass to aid me. I glance down at his wet cock, and moan. I look back at his face, and sheer pleasure radiates from his eyes as I fuck him. "Abi..."

His cock thickens even more, and he powers forward, driving me into to the mattress as he falls over me, his lips finding mine as he lets himself go high within me. He grunts into my mouth, and our hearts pound together as his body goes tight, ecstasy overtaking every muscle in his body.

He collapses on top of me, moisture sealing our bodies together as we both gasp for breath. Loving the weight of him pinning me to his bed as my body melts from post-orgasmic bliss, a laugh I have zero control over bubbles out of my throat.

His head lifts and there's a playful glimmer in his eyes as they meet mine. "Not the normal reaction, but okay."

"I just..." I shake my head in awe. I just had sex with Liam Dunn. "How did we get here, Liam?"

"Well," He begins as he toys with one of my pigtails. "You walked here with security after a game, and I—"

I whack him, and he feigns hurt. "You know what I mean."

He chuckles. "Yeah, I know what you mean, and I don't know what to tell you." He rolls off me, and we both exhale as his cock slides from my body. I already miss it. "All those years we didn't talk, and now...this."

I laugh. "It's not like we did all that much talking tonight. Well, except for me to tell you how awful this all was." I make a face like I'd just eaten something sour.

His grin curls around me and I shift, needing to be closer. He lightly touches my arm and I quiver as he trails his finger over my flesh. It's the weirdest thing, but I really like when he touches me like that.

"It wasn't at all awful, was it?" he asks quietly his voice so tender and soft, it wraps around me, hugging like my favorite hoodie.

"Not at all."

"You're saying you liked it, Hart."

"I'm saying I liked it, Dunn."

His brows lift, and I spot hope in his eyes. "Enough to do it again?"

10

LIAM

My buzzing phone pulls me awake, and I turn to find it on my nightstand. Shit, I was supposed to meet Tanner at the gym this morning and I'm late. I reach for my phone, and memories of why I'm late rush into my sleep fogged brain and pull me wide awake. I turn quickly, and a stupid grin spreads across my face when I find Ali spread across my bed, the sheets around her knees. Naked and on full display, everything about her is warm and soft, and that pretty shade of pink on her cheeks makes me want to get back between her legs—with my mouth.

Fuck, she's gorgeous. I snatch up my phone and shoot a quick message to Tanner. He's not much of a party guy either, which is why it's usually only the two of us in the gym on the morning after a game. Why again did I make plans? Oh, right, because I had no idea I'd be up all night having sex with sweet Abigail Hart, the girl who's supposed to hate me.

I quietly set my phone down and take in Abi's mussed hair. We took out her pigtails when we showered together and now her hair looks like a bird's nest because she went to bed with it wet. My heart thuds against my ribs. Jesus, she's the most fascinating woman I've ever set eyes on and I still can't believe she's in my bed.

While she probably needs to get up and get ready for classes, I don't think I'm quite ready to let her go as my brain goes back to the way she moved her body and worked her hot pussy over my cock. Christ, it was mind-blowing hot. I shift, until I'm over her, balancing my weight on my knees as I put my hands on either side of her body, and bend to take her perfect pink nipple into my mouth. Pink is quickly becoming my favorite color.

As I lightly kiss her breast, and use the soft blade of my tongue to tease her bud erect, a moan fills the silence of the room and I glance up to see her smiling at me. She runs her fingers through my mussed hair.

"Good morning," I whisper.

"Yeah, great morning," she responds, her voice groggy and low, and arches her back. Her nipple hits my chin, and we both moan as we experience different sensations. "A girl could get used to waking up like this."

"Stay with me again," I blurt out without thinking. "Tonight. Stay tonight, Abi."

Her smile fades as her eyes clear. I slide up her body and press my lips to hers, wanting to kiss her before real life sets in for both of us. She puts her arms around me, and holds me to her warm body. I bury my face in her neck and breathe in the enticing smell of her skin.

"I can't," she finally answers.

"It was just a thought." I try not to sound as disappointed as I feel.

"I have to get back home tonight and check on my car, and do a shift at Boondocks."

"Right," is all I can reply.

"If you want to stay in the city tonight, I—"

I press my lips to hers again to stop her. I kiss her deeply, until we're both a hot mess. "I'm driving you," I state as my cock presses against her thigh. She turns her head, and checks the time on her phone. "Right, I get it. You have to go." I guess it was fun while it lasted. Honestly, did I expect we could keep doing this? Not really. We both live different lives and we need to get back to them. I make a move to climb off her, but her hand on my arm stops me. "What?"

Her grin is playful and sexy. "I do have to go." I nod, and shift, but she stops me again. "But I have a few minutes."

I grin at her. "Are you looking for a quickie, Hart?"

"Does that mean you can be quick?"

"That was pretty much my middle name when I was a teenager." That makes her laugh.

"Liam Quickie Dunn." The pink in her cheeks darken with arousal and it's so damn sexy.

I tug her hair and heat moves into her eyes. "No need for name calling."

Her eyes open like she had a lightbulb moment. "Ohmigod, Quickie Dunn. Quickie *done*, get it."

"Yeah, I get it. I'm not totally dense."

"Did people call you Quickie Dunn?" she asks. "It definitely has a ring to it."

"No one called me that and hey we're not on the playground, Hart, and I've learned restraint since my teenage years."

"No, we're not on the playground, but there's definitely a need for hair pulling," she responds, her voice a little deeper and far more breathless than it was seconds ago.

I laugh and reach into the nightstand and snatch a condom. "A quickie it is, no restraint."

"I liked your restraint last night." She widens her legs and I nearly shoot off as I take in her glistening pink softness. "But I don't want that this morning."

"You want a straight up hard fuck, Abi?" I ask and her chest rises and falls quickly at my bluntness.

She nods and I rip into the condom and roll it on. "Uh huh," she murmurs.

"Then I don't have to do math?"

Her face scrunches. "Math?"

I laugh. "Didn't you know? Doing math helps with restraint."

"I thought you weren't very good at math."

"I'm not."

"Then how does it help with restraint?"

I kiss her, and slide a finger into her body to prepare her. She moans and clenches around my index. "It doesn't really, especially when it comes to you. I was a fucking mess last night. I could barely keep it together." She grins, and bites her bottom lip. "Oh, you like knowing that, do you?" She gives a small nod, and I pull my finger out. "Fine, let's see if you like this too."

In one hard thrust, I push my cock all the way inside her, hitting her cervix and driving her deeper into the mattress. She gasps, pleasure flashing in her eyes as she reaches up and grabs onto the headboard.

"God, Liam...yes...just like that."

She begins to move, and I press my hand on her stomach. Her eyes meet mine. "Like this?" I ask, and pound into her as I hold her down. Her eyes darken with desire as she lays there, letting me give her all she needs. I fuck her hard and grind against her clit, and her head goes from side to side as her little whimpering noises tug on my balls in the best kind of way.

My dick aches for release, and I know this is a quickie, but dammit, it can't be that quick. She just takes me to the edge fast, faster even than when I was an inexperienced teen. Quickie Dunn. I chuckle at that. Thank God that's not my nickname on the team.

She lets go of the headboard and her hands land on my chest. She splays her fingers, scraping them over my hard nipples. I moan and bend and press my lips to hers as I fuck her like a wild animal in heat. My balls tighten, and I rub her clit, desperate to take her over the edge before I explode. Knowing what she needs, I balance on one hand, rake my other through her hair and tug until her mouth is wide open. I suck on her bottom lip, drag it between my teeth, knowing I'm going to leave her tender and kiss swollen and liking the idea that every time she wets her lips, she'll think about this.

"Liam," she cries out, her voice harsh and dry and full of desperation. Hot wet heat rushes from her body as a beautiful keening cry curls around me. Fuck, I love making her come.

A hard quake goes through me as my body tightens, needing to last just a bit longer to draw her pleasure out. She clenches, massaging my dick, and I'm far too gone to even do the simplest of math.

"Yeah, Abi. Come all over my cock."

She wraps her arms around me, and her mouth is near my ear as she hugs me. "No restraint, Liam. I want all your cum."

"Jesus," I murmur, her sexy words becoming my undoing. I throw my head back and fill her with my cum. Technically, I'm filling a condom, but I'm doing it while deep inside her and that's pretty fucking good if you ask me. I grunt and push harder, deeper, wanting every inch of myself in her.

As my body comes down, I chuckle, and she pushes on me until she can see my face. She's smiling too. "Crazy, right?" she says and shakes her head.

"Really fucking crazy." Crazy good. Crazy awesome. Being with her is every kind of crazy and I want more.

I press a soft kiss to her mouth. "I guess we should get moving, huh?"

"Yeah," she says, and runs her fingers through my hair, looking like she's going to laze in my bed all day. I could get behind that. But I can't let her miss her classes. She's on scholarship and can't do anything to jeopardize that.

"Do you want to shower first?"

She frowns. "Didn't enjoy showering with me last night?"

I snort out a humorless laugh. "You did see how hard my dick got when you soaped it up, right?" Her grin is mischievous. "Which means, if we want to make it to class, we shower separate or I'm going to spend the next hour in there fucking you properly."

"I think you fucked me properly already, Liam."

I stare at her. She's saying so many things I never thought I'd ever hear leaving her lips, it has me shaking my head in bewilderment. I pull out of her, give her a slap on the side of her ass and command, "Go. Now."

"Fine." She climbs out of bed and I growl as I take in her perfect ass. I try to get my brain in gear. "What time does your last class finish?"

"Four," she tells me. "But we can leave after you finish."

"Pick you up outside the Ocean's institute?"

She nods and stops halfway into the bathroom. "Sorry about not getting around to tutoring. Later tonight maybe. After sunset?"

My heart pumps a little faster, happy that she wants to watch the sunset with me again. "Yeah, sounds good."

She disappears and the shower turns on. I go to work on making coffee in the microscopic kitchen, if one could even call it that. My meals are in the communal kitchen downstairs but at least I have enough here to get caffeinated. I'd like to move out my senior year, even though Dad thinks I should stay in the dorm. Maybe I should stay, especially since my kid sister will be on campus next year. No way am I letting any of the players near her. Although they all know better than to lay a hand on her. Yes, I'm overprotective. Sue me.

I toss a pod into the machine and grab one of the protein bars Abi made. I don't have any milk on hand, but make a mental note to get a small one for when she stays over. I wish

I could make her something to eat, and for a brief second, I consider running out to grab breakfast sandwiches. She'd likely scold me for my bad choices and I kind of like that she worries about my health.

As the coffee drips, I shoot a text off to my best friend Josh. Josh and I have been friends forever, so he knows Ember. It shouldn't bug me that she asked about him. Even if she does have a crush on him, Josh would never break bro code.

Once the coffee finishes, I grab the mug, walk to the bathroom, and open the door. I don't think Abi is going to protest if I walk in on her naked, not after everything we just did and I kind of like that I can just walk into the room, like we're long-time lovers. We aren't but the intimacy from last night and this morning, sort of shot our relationship to a new level.

"Hey, Abi, I made you a coffee. It's on the sink. Sorry there's no milk."

She opens the glass door, and peeks out. "I can drink it black when I need to."

I nod and smile. Isn't that just like her? She doesn't complain about much, or even ask for much in return. She takes what she's given and makes the best of it, and I admire that about her.

She goes back to showering and I stand there for a second, admiring her through the steamy glass. I grin, and head back to the kitchen to get another coffee when something bangs against my door.

I inch it open and find Sebastian and Conner. They both look hung over, so do the two girls walking ahead of them.

"Need something?" I ask.

"Sorry, accident," one of the girls says, turning around. "I didn't mean to bang into your door."

"It's fine." I'm about to close the door, when Sebastian stops. "Hook up last night?" he asks, and my body goes stiff.

"Not your fucking business." I resist the urge to glance over my shoulder, as I block the doorway, praying Abi doesn't come out from the bathroom.

He grins. "Heard some noise is all." He tries to see over my shoulder but I'm taller. "Who'd you hook up with?"

"No one you know."

He stares at me for a second, and I swear to God if he says Abi's name or calls her something else, I'm going to knock his front teeth out. One of the girls stumbles again and as the other grabs her, they both start laughing.

"You'd better help your friend before she hurts herself."

"Yeah," is all he answers, and I shut the door just as Abi comes from the bathroom. Her eyes go wide when she sees me.

"Everything okay?"

"Everything is fine." I don't want her worrying about Sebastian, and maybe hooking up like this in my room might not be our smartest move.

She takes as sip of coffee and I toss in another pod. I watch her from the corner of my eye as she reaches into her duffle bag and pulls out clean clothes.

"Don't need a T-shirt?" I ask playfully.

She grins and tosses the one she wore last night into the bag. "I'm good, and I'll wash this one for you."

"No need." I take in her gorgeous body as she pulls on her panties and bra, followed by tight jeans and a shirt. "I think maybe you're keeping the shirt as a reminder of last night."

"I guess now I know what you're doing with these." She opens my nightstand and pulls out her ripped panties, and I give her a sheepish grin.

"I don't know how they got in there."

"They might have fallen in when you ripped them off my body."

"I can replace them."

"It's okay. I have plenty." She tosses them back into the drawer. "I'll just put them back and you can toss them out later."

I step up to her and pull her into my arms. She cranes her neck to see me and I dip my head and kiss her. "Contrary to what you might believe about me, I'm not a weirdo panty thief, Hart," I say, and she chuckles.

Her eyes are warm, full of playful disbelief when she answers with, "Sure whatever you say, Quickie Dunn." I laugh as her eyes narrow and her gaze drops to my chest. "Honestly, I'm not sure what I believe anymore."

My mind instantly goes back to my father, and how he wanted me to snoop on the Harts. Jeez, if she were to ever believe that the apple doesn't fall from the tree, I can kiss my balls goodbye. Why does everything have to be so fucked up and twisted when it comes to Abi and me?

My body is sore in the most awesome ways as I stand on the curb and wait for Liam to pick me up. I hope I don't run into anyone I know, seeing as I'm standing here with a smile on my face that would rival the village idiot's. At least we won't run into anyone from the team. Liam took me out the back way this morning so I wouldn't run into any of the guys. No walk of shame for me.

None of the team members have classes near this building. Liam would have some explaining to do. It's also a good thing I haven't seen Ocean in a while. I have some real explaining to do when I do see her, just not today, considering the freaking chafe marks on my face.

Did I really tell Liam I wanted a quickie, and then tell him I wanted his cum. A wave of embarrassment comes over me, even though Liam wasn't embarrassed at all in the heat of the moment. I think he kind of liked when I talked like that. Believe me, I've never told anyone what I wanted before, in or out of the bedroom. I basically just go through life, doing what needs to be done and expecting nothing in return.

But oh God, did Liam ever give a lot in return. My body quivers as it remembers his every touch with his fingers and tongue. In the distance, I spot his car, and I square my shoulders. I wave to him, even though I already know he saw me.

Shoot, are things going to suddenly be awkward? They weren't last night, or this morning after we showered, drank coffee and ate protein bars. Everything between us was easy and natural, and I can't deny that I like a lot of things about the man who's been my enemy for years.

As he approaches, I playfully stick my thumb out and he grins as he pulls up beside me. He pushes open the door, and I bend to see him.

"Hey there, stranger. Going my way?"

I check the back seat to see if he brought my duffle bag. I spot it on the seat. I'd forgotten it this morning and texted him. A part of me thinks I might have done it on purpose, just so I could send him a message. God, what have I become?

He taps the steering wheel and tugs down his sunglasses, acting like a real-life creeper, which is kind of funny. "It's dangerous for a young woman to be hitchhiking all alone."

"Dangerous for you, maybe," I as I study my nails like they might be lethal weapons, and he laughs.

"Oh yeah. You going to hurt me?"

"If you try something." He arches a brow. "I've got moves." I slide into the car, drop my backpack and the next thing I know his hand is cupping my neck, bringing my mouth to his.

He kisses me, and our lips linger, our breaths mingling. I stare into his dark eyes, and my heart jumps at the needy way he stares back.

Don't fall for him, Abi.

I shut that voice down, because it's a ridiculous thought. I might have known Liam since we were kids, but I don't know him now. Sure, he seems sweet and kind, driving me back and forth when I'm in a pinch. Other than the fact that he's an NHL draft pick and likes to work on the fishing boats, knows how I like my coffee, doesn't party with the team much, is kind of a loner, and keeps panties as souvenirs, what do I really know about him? Heck, he could be spying for his parents, for all I know. Do I really believe that? No, not really.

He moans, and licks his lips like he's savoring the taste of me, he inches back, his hand still around my neck. "What do I have to do to see your moves?" He tugs on my hair, fully aware of what he's doing.

That...yeah, that.

I lift my chin. "Excuse me, I just met you. I mean, you'd at least have to buy me a drink or something."

I love the way he's grinning, so innocent and adorable. He pulls a paper cup from the console and holds it out to me. "Chocolate espresso from your favorite coffee shop."

"How did you know?"

"I know you think I'm stupid, but I know things."

"I do not think you're stupid." Why does he always say things like that? My eyes widen in delight and I breathe in the delicious scent. "Ohmigod, this smells amazing." I wrap my chilled hands around the cup. "All the moves," I blurt out. "For this," I hold my cup up. "You get to see all the moves."

His laugh fills the car as I pull the tab back and take a sip. "That's all it takes, huh?"

"I had no idea I was so easy, Dunn."

"I don't think you're so easy, Hart. It's been what, like ten years since you looked my way?"

"Twelve," I say without hesitation.

"Twelve and a half," he states flatly. "It was halfway through the year in middle school when the shit hit the fan."

I cast a quick look at Liam and take in the frown on his face. Shit hit the fan all right. Our traps and storage sheds were messed with, and his father tried to destroy us. As kids, we should have been kept out of the family rift, maybe protected from all the hatred. But how could I not be affected when I could have ended up homeless, how could I not hate Liam just a little bit for that?

"Hey," he says quietly bringing my thoughts back. His big palm lands on my leg and I like his touch a lot. "I was going to get us big juicy hamburgers to eat on the way home, but I knew you'd lecture me." I open my mouth to protest, and he holds his hand up. "I mean that in the nicest way, Abi. It's nice that you care."

I care about Liam Dunn.

Wow, who would have ever thought. I take a sip of my delicious espresso. "You can have a cheat day, you know."

He glances over his shoulder and pulls onto the road. "How about we hit up that café in Hubbards on the way home? They have healthy food."

"The Trellis?"

"I don't think anyone will recognize us there." I hesitate for a moment, and as I consider getting caught together, he adds, "Dinner is on me, payment for helping me with my calculus."

Instantly feeling bad for not getting to his tutoring, I groan. "We really need to get on that. We probably could have done that after the game last night."

"I liked what we did after the game, better."

"Wait, is this meal about getting into my panties again?"

"I actually still have your panties," he informs me, and my body warms.

"Wait, I thought these rides were also for helping you with calculus?"

"Okay, then." He wags his brows playfully and suggestively. "You can owe me something else for dinner."

My mouth drops open and I square my shoulders. "So dinner, and this espresso are really about trying to get me into your bed again?"

"Come on, Abi," he shoots back. "You already told me you were easy. You straight up admitted it, which means there's no way I'd have to go through all this effort."

"Hey," I yell, and whack him. "Maybe a girl likes the effort."

"And maybe a guy wants to put the effort in, because he wants to spend more time with you."

God, when he says things like that...

I sink back into my seat and enjoy my drink but feel his eyes on me. "What?"

"Did you get your grant paperwork done?"

I turn my head and look out the window. "No."

"Are you going to do it?"

"I don't know, Liam." I stare at the houses as we drive past them, most of which are owned by the college. "I'm not sure I can just up and leave, you know. My parents…"

"Can't they hire someone?"

"Apparently, they don't trust anyone."

I listen to his throat as he swallows, clearly knowing where that distrust comes from. "You can't work there forever. If you're planning on staying, why bother with a marine biology degree?"

I take a big breath, and let it hiss out of my lungs. He's got a point there and it's not like I haven't been giving it a lot of thought. After I graduate, I can get work here in Halifax, but it's not what I really want. Driving back and forth from the city every night to help out at Boondocks isn't what I want, either. My stomach cramps, because I can't just up and walk away from the family business when my parents need me, right?

"I probably won't get the grants anyway."

I turn to look at him, and he knows as well as I do that I have a pretty good chance of getting the funding. Those grants could so easily lead to a master's degree and that's a dream come true for me.

"You should at least apply," he says. A beat of silence and he adds, "At least promise me you'll apply."

"If I promise you that, then you have to promise me something in return."

"Fine, what do you want me to promise you?"

"I don't know yet." He laughs at that. "I'm going to need to think on it."

"Should I be afraid?"

I grin at him. "Probably."

With that, we fall into easy conversation as he pulls onto the highway and we head back home. We talk about hockey, and school and our friends, and keep the topics off our home life and the conflict between our families. After about a half an hour he pulls his vehicle between two SUVs at The Trellis.

"I've never been here," I tell him.

"I've been a few times. Food is good."

We head inside the cute restaurant, and I sit. It's actually nice to be served instead of serving everyone else all the time. I glance at the menu. "They have hamburgers." I look at him over the menu. "Probably not as bad as fast food."

"Want to do it?" he asks, hope in his eyes.

"Sure, why not? I usually eat seafood off our own boats as I've vetted the fishing practices, but I can eat beef here. It's a treat once in a while." The server comes and we both get drinks, and when she leaves, I lean into Liam. "The NHL, Liam. That's kind of a big deal."

He nods, but his voice doesn't hold a lot of enthusiasm when he says, "I'm a lucky guy."

"Luck didn't get you there. I've seen you play."

His chest puffs up at the compliment. "Maybe," he snorts. "Or maybe my father paid for a spot on the team."

I shake my head. "You don't think that, do you?"

"No, I don't think that. I just...he really wants this for me, and well, when he wants something, he gets it." We stare at one another for a moment. "Not always, I guess," he adds and doesn't need to elaborate. He's talking about my family property.

"Are you looking forward to going to Miami?" I ask.

"Yeah, sure."

"Wow, way to sound excited."

"I am. It's just a long way from home." The server comes with our drinks, and after we put in our order, I lift my glass and hold it out for a salute.

I consider our futures. "What should we drink to?"

"Miami?" he mutters, but it's more of a question. Does he not want to go? God, I'd give a kidney to do a master's in marine biology in Miami. We both drink to that and I set my glass down.

"It's funny though, Liam. Seems like you want to stay here and can't, and I want to go and can't."

"You can go. You just have to fill the forms out for the grants and it's not that I don't want to go." He shrugs. "I don't know what I'm saying. Jesus. Do you know how many guys would kill to be in my position? I sound like a whiny fucking baby."

"Quite a few, I suppose." I eye him as he shakes his head, like he might be disgusted with himself. "Why do I get the sense being in your position is not all it's cracked up to be, Dunn?" Does Liam not have the perfect life I always assumed he had?

"Family pressure." He snorts. "You get it."

I nod. I get it all too well. But he has a lot more to prove than I do. I never stopped to consider that before.

"Abi," he whispers. "Hockey is pretty much the only thing I'm good at. I have to make it work."

My heart pinches tight at the worry on his face. "You're good at other things, Liam."

He laughs, but it's humorless. "No, I'm not. I'm barely passing calculus. Sure, the professors give me a lot of leeway, but that just nails home the fact that I suck at everything but hockey."

I take in the pain in his eyes, and I reach across the table and put my hand over his. "Liam, you know people have different strengths. Hey, you knew what was wrong with my car, just by hearing the noise, remember?"

He nods and holds his hands out. "I am good with my hands."

I smile at him. "I'll vouch for that."

"That reminds me," he jokes. "When are you going to show me your moves?"

12

LIAM

I sit in the back office at Boondocks, out of sight. There's an emergency exit door right behind me, so I can disappear if her parents show up, not that Abi thought they would. Still, this is risky, and we shouldn't be taking chances. I don't want to get her into trouble, but when she offered to help me with my calculus between customers, and offered to watch the sunset with me, how could I say no?

I lean back in the chair and stare at my laptop, going over the way Abi taught me to solve the equations. She has a knack for explaining things the way my professor can't and hey, maybe I'm not that stupid after all. Whether I am or not, I'm not a stellar student, and have to stay on the straight and narrow for hockey. It's my ticket in life, and I swear my father would cut me off in my college years if I did anything to screw that up.

Abi's voice trickles to the back room as she speaks with her customers, and the sound fills me with happiness. We had a nice drive home and it was fun having a quiet dinner with her. I enjoy talking to her. She's smart and beautiful, and honestly, completely out of my league. But until she realizes that, I'm going to hang around. I can't even imagine what life would be like for us if we both went to Miami. We could see each other without sneaking around. Yes, okay fine, I'm getting way ahead of myself.

A piece of paper sticks out of one of the drawers, and my father's words come racing back to me. Jesus. Does he really think I'm going to snoop and get dirt on the Hart family? He must be out of his mind. I try to study some more, but the paper keeps pulling my attention. I shouldn't touch it, but maybe I'll just tuck it away so it's not a distraction. I pull on the drawer and reach for the paper, drawing my hand back fast when I spot movement at the door.

Abi's gaze goes from me, to the paper falling to the floor, back to me again. "What's going on?"

"Nothing," I add quickly. Why do I sound guilty? "There was a paper sticking out and I was going to put it back. It was distracting me. Then I saw you and you startled me, and I pulled my hand back and it fell." Okay, way to ramble and make it sound like I was snooping.

"Okay," she says and crosses the room. She picks up the paper, glances at it, and puts it back in the drawer, closing it tight. "Good, not distracting you anymore?"

I tug on her until she's in my lap and my cock instantly thickens. "It's possible something else is distracting me now."

"You're not going to drop me on the floor too, are you?"

"Depends."

She angles her head. "Oh, on what?"

"Whether you'll kiss me or not."

Her eyes widen. "Are you saying you'll drop me onto the floor if I don't kiss you?"

"No, never, but I might be saying it's possible I'll clear this desk and drop you on it, and have my way with you if you do?"

Desire fills her eyes, and she glances at the desk. "I never knew you were such a risk taker, Dunn," she says.

"Actually, I'm not. When it comes to you, I can't seem to help myself." I put my hand around her head and bring her mouth to mine. I kiss her deeply, and I'm seconds from laying her out when the bell over the door jingles, knocking some sense back into the both of us. She jumps up, and glides her hand over her hand to straighten it, her cheeks a pretty shade of pink. "Sorry," I apologize quickly.

She hurries to the front of the store, and when I hear a man's voice I push to my feet, and walk quietly into the hall. Is it her father? My heart jumps. Shit, I don't want to get her into trouble and I shouldn't even be here.

I spot Danny from the gas station standing on the other side of the glass case, smiling at Abi. He's asking about her car, and I think he's flirting with her. I inch back, and walk into the small kitchen where they prepare sandwiches and other kinds of goods. Everything is clean and wiped down as Abi tries to close the place for the night. She laughs at something Danny says, and an instant wave of jealousy grips my gut. Shit, I had no idea Danny was interested in Abi.

I walk back to the office and trip over a damn cord. I curse, and bang against the wall, and that's when I hear Danny ask if someone is in back.

"No," Abi says quickly and I don't miss the panic in her voice.

"I can take a look back there if you'd like." Danny offers, and I shake my head at my own stupidity. I quickly close my computer, slip it into my bag and go out the back door. I make my way to the dock, and drop down into one of the chairs, obscured by the shadows. The store was busier than usual tonight, so we missed the sunset, but it was nice to hang out with Abi.

The bell over the door jingles and the sound carries into the night. I grab my phone and shoot Abi a text to let her know I slipped out the back. Fuck, this sneaking around is total bullshit. Maybe I should just leave. What we're doing here isn't good for either of us.

"No, it's fine. I can walk," I hear Abi answer, and I turn to see her lock the door as Danny hovers close.

"It's on my way, no problem," he says, and I resist the urge to tell him to get the fuck away from my girl. Except she isn't my girl. He takes her backpack from her and hikes it over his shoulder, in much the same manner I would have and I guess I like that he's thoughtful like that. I mean if she's going to be with any guy I want it to be a decent one. Still, I hate everything about this. I see her look back at the dock before she disappears into the night.

I stand there for a few moments, my chest tight as the street grows quiet, I go back to my car, and drive away, leaving Boondocks and Abi—and Danny—in my rearview mirror. Sneaking around with her is wrong, and I need to end this thing, whatever it is, and get my focus back on my studies and hockey. She's much better off without me.

Instead of going home, or even back to the city, I drive to the docks, where our family keeps a few small fishing boats. The big commercial ones are further down, anchored near the sorting facility, which can go all hours of the night. Here, it's quiet, and that's what I'm looking for.

I park, and my steps echo around me as I walk along the wooden dock and jump onto a recreational boat. I move inside the cabin, and pull out my phone, hoping Abi responded, even though I just vowed to stay away. I read a message from my buddy Josh and shoot off a reply. I can't even imagine what he'd think if he knew what was going on between Abi and me. Life is funny, though. I never thought she'd speak to me, let alone find her in my bed. But he'll never find out because it has to be over between us.

The boat rocks and I close my eyes, a wave of exhaustion overtaking me. Maybe I'll sleep here tonight. It's not like anyone at home is going to miss me, or even know I'm not in the city. I stand, and I'm about to grab a blanket, when the sound of footsteps on the dock draws my attention.

"Hey sailor," I hear, as I poke my head out from the cabin, and find Abi walking toward me. My heart jumps, higher and harder than it really should, considering I'd just given myself a lecture to stop seeing her. I stand there for a second, and her steps slow. "Hey." She glances behind her. "If you're busy...I can go."

Let her walk away, dude. End this now.

"I'm not busy." I jump off the boat and glance into the night, half expecting to see Danny behind her. "What are you doing here?" Okay, maybe that came out a bit harsher than I intended.

"Sorry, I didn't mean to trespass." She takes a step back, and even though it's not in our best interests, I take a step toward her and capture her hand. My heart thunders.

"I'm sorry. I didn't mean to say it like that." My glance falls over her small body. It's cold. She should be in a coat, not a hoodie. "What did Danny want?"

"He walked me home and asked me out."

I nod and fight to ignore the jealousy tightening my gut. "What did you tell him?"

She angles her head. "You sound like you're jealous, Liam."

"I'm just..." I don't know what I am. "He doesn't seem like your type," is all I say.

"He's a nice guy, and I'm not sure I have a type." She goes quiet for a second as waves lap against the dock. "I told him I was too busy to date." I exhale, and rake my hand through my hair. "I can't do a relationship right now," she adds, and I can't help but think that last part was a warning to me. Does she think I'm getting serious here, or something?

I step up to her, put my hands on her shoulders and rub to create heat as she hugs herself. "You should get home. It's cold out. Come on, I'll walk you."

She nods, but instead of turning, she moves in closer, her body bumping mine. "What's my type, Liam?"

"I don't know. Just not Danny."

"He's nice. He fixed my car and gave me a great deal. He also stopped to check on me and walk me home. Do you think I like assholes or something?"

I laugh. "Didn't you date Brennan Langley your first year at the academy?"

She groans and covers her face. "Ohmigod, I do like assholes. Wait, how do you know about Brennan?" She pokes my chest, and I snatch her finger and bring it to my mouth to kiss it. "Keeping tabs on me, Dunn?" she asks, her voice not quite as steady as it was moments ago.

I make a fist and lightly nudge under her chin. "You know what they say, Hart. Keep your enemies close."

She smiles, and glances over her shoulder when a dog barks. "I don't want to go home."

"No?"

She glances down, turning her eyes from me. "Not yet."

"How come?" I put my thumb under her chin and lift her face to take in the hurt lingering there.

"I just…my parents."

"Ah, parents," is all I say, sensing she doesn't want to talk about it. The need to protect her washes over me. "I don't want you to go home either, Abi." I put my arm around her and lead her onto the boat. Inside the cabin, she glances around and sits on the padded bench. I grab a blanket. "Stand." She eyes me as she stands and I pull on the bench, turning it into a small bed. "Can you stay with me, Abi. For a little bit?"

She nods, and I lay a blanket down. She takes her phone and keys from her pocket, sets them on the small side table, and stretches out on the makeshift bed. I lie beside her, covering us both with a heavy comforter. She lets out a slow breath as I put my arm around her.

"This is nice." She snuggles into me. "Being here with you, Liam. It's nice."

"Yeah, nice," I agree, loving it more than I really should. She basically told me straight up we have no future, and I know that too. I don't need the constant reminder, and it's bugging me.

After a long moment of silence, she asks, "So what's your type?"

I chuckle. "You, Abi," I admit. "You're my type. Didn't last night prove that?"

She grins. "Yes, I guess so. But I think you have a lot of types."

I get it. She's referring to all the girls who hang out after the games. What she doesn't realize is that I rarely go home with them. I've never even had a steady girlfriend.

"I'm with you, Abi."

"I see you guys with lots of different women."

She should look closer, because *I'm* not with a lot of different women. "I lied to you when I said there wasn't someone special."

She stiffens and I press my lips to hers to stop her from retreating. "I'm talking about you, Abi."

"Oh." She laughs. "I'm not special, Liam. Besides, this." She points back and forth between the two of us. "This probably shouldn't be happening."

She's not fucking wrong. "But it is."

She goes quiet for a long time, and for a second, I think the rocking boat has lulled her to sleep, until she breaks the quiet and explains, "Danny is a nice guy, but I'm not going to date him. I'm not going to start up anything serious with a local when I might be going to Miami for my summers and maybe for my master's."

I inch back to see her. "You're applying for the grant?"

She gives me a small, almost sheepish smile. "I promised you, didn't I?"

I smile back, so damn happy she's going to apply, and while I want to ask what changed her mind, I don't. "Right, and you've yet to let me know what I had to promise in return."

"Still thinking on it." Her fingers go to my chest, and she lightly traces the words on my hoodie.

"What are you doing this weekend?" I ask as she yawns.

"Work, study, sleep, eat. Rinse and repeat. You?"

Fuck, I hate how she has no time to herself and when she does, she's completely exhausted.

"This weekend is the big beachside blowout. It's kind of a team bonding event. A lot of people come out for it. We have pumpkin races."

"Pumpkin races. I read about those. That sounds fun."

I laugh. "I'm asking if you want to come."

She lifts her head, her eyes on me. "I don't think I can, Liam. People will think the world is ending if we're seen together, remember?"

Before I can stop myself, I blurt out, "What if we didn't give a fuck what others think?"

13

ABIGAIL

Seagulls squawking overhead pull me awake, and I try to move my body, but I can't. Something big is pinning me in place and why am I hearing birds? Did I fall asleep with my window open last night? I peel one eye open, having no idea where I am, and then I open the second eye and the room comes into view, I quickly turn my head and find Liam beside me.

My heart does a little wobbly dance as I take in his handsome face. He looks rather boyish this morning. His hair is a tangled mess, and the hard lines of his face are softer in his sleeps. If I could, I'd shift closer and give him a good morning kiss, but his big, heavy arm is across my chest, pinning me to the makeshift bed. That's when I realize I slept here all night. Will Mom and Dad be worried about me?

I carefully lift his arm, shimmy out from beneath him and check my phone for messages. I find one from Ocean, asking if I want to meet for lunch today. Will she be going to the beach party Liam invited me to? Not that I can or should go. He might not care what others think but I'm not sure we should be seen together, and when it comes right down to it, my car is working now and we have no other reason to be around each other.

Other than the fact that you really like him, Abi.

In need of coffee, I check the pantry and find a couple of pods. The boat isn't fancy. In fact, it's much like the one we own, handed down from Grandad to my dad, and has all the essentials, like a coffee maker. I put a pod in, and as it brews, I step outside, pull my sleeves down to cover my hands, and hug myself as the sun begins to climb over the hilly golf course.

"Hey." I'm about to turn at the sound of Liam's voice, until he wraps his arms around me and tugs my back to his chest. I let my head fall back to rest on him, and he puts his mouth near my ear. "I'm glad you're still here."

His warm breath falls over my neck and warms me from the inside out, and when he holds me tighter, like I really am special to him, my throat tightens. "I can't stay long. I have to get home before Mom and Dad send a search party." I laugh, but it's fake.

"Yeah, okay." His voice is low, wounded as his hold loosens. "Did you want to have coffee first?"

I turn to him, and the second I take in the vulnerability on his face, the warmth in his eyes, it takes me back to the time when we were kids, and there was no hate in our lives. He was just a sweet boy on the playground, who didn't pull hair.

Do not fall for this guy, Abi.

"Yes, I'd love a coffee." He nods, and is about to turn. I put my hand on his arm, and he dips his head. This man took such good care of me last night. I was exhausted, and didn't want to go home and he gave me a safe haven on this boat, tucking me in and keeping me warm. "Liam, I'm glad I'm still here this morning." The smile he offers me curls around my heart and it pounds a little harder against my ribs.

"We don't have fresh milk."

"Black is fine."

He nods, and adds, "I'll have milk for you next time." His words tug at something inside me. A reminder that we can't have a next time perhaps. With sadness invading my heart, he steps into the boat and I'm about to follow when a strange sensation raises the hair on my neck. I turn and glance down the dock, and have the oddest sense that someone is watching us. I scan the dock and street, only for my search to come up empty. I step onto the boat, and Liam hands me a mug of coffee. I take a big sip and moan. He tosses another pod into the machine, and I hand him my cup to sip until his is ready.

"Liam, I don't think there can be a next time," I state, working to keep my voice even.

"Didn't sleep well?" he asks, not really getting what I'm saying.

"I actually slept really well." I check my phone, and take one more sip of coffee. "I should get going." I set my mug down. "Thanks for all the drives back and forth, and the...well, thanks."

He gives a tight nod as realization sinks in. "This is it, Hart?"

"Yeah." I go up on my toes to give him one last kiss, even though I really don't want this to be over, it has to be this way. We might both end up in Miami, but we're different people going different ways, and I can't do this sneaking around much longer. "See you around, Dunn."

"Bye, Hart," he responds.

As my insides quiver, I hurry off the boat, and swallow past a tight throat as I practically run up the hilly path leading home. I slide my key into the lock, expecting to find Mom, Dad and Granddad in the kitchen. They'll think I was out watching the sunrise, and they wouldn't be wrong. Except the kitchen is empty, and the coffee isn't even made. I grab my phone again and check for messages, and find a new one from Mom.

I read it quickly and fight down the panic as I run back outside. I glance around, searching for my parents, who are searching for Granddad. Where could he have gone and how long has he been missing? I check my phone again and reread the message. But all it says is they need help finding Grandad, and nothing else.

The last time he went wandering, he ended up at the dog park. It's been years since he had a dog, yet sometimes he forgets that. The car is gone from our driveway, so I'm sure that's where my parents started looking. I jump in my car and drive the short distance. I spot Mom and Dad near the tree line, and I hurry from my car. I'm breathless when I catch up to them.

"Abi, where have you been?" Mom asks, the anger in her voice hitting like a slap to the face.

My entire body stiffens as she directs furious eyes my way. "I was out."

Dad is just as upset with me as Mom, when he says, "We checked the dock. You weren't there."

I don't miss the accusation in his tone. I jerk my thumb out. "I was down further."

"You can't just go wandering off," Mom begins as Dad eyes me. "We have enough to worry about with your granddad as it is. We can't be worrying about you too."

"No, of course not." My stomach knots, and the coffee I'd just shared with Liam sloshes around inside. I swallow before it comes back up and spills over my shoes. "I'm sorry."

"Don't be sorry," Mom quips. "Help us look."

"Okay," I manage to get out around the lump in my throat. We spend the next twenty minutes calling out to Granddad. "Why don't you drive around the neighborhood, Abi?" Mom eventually suggests. "We'll head out to the road to make sure he's not headed to the old lobster compound."

The old lobster compound no longer exists. Granddad's father owned it but sold the parcel of land to the Dunns many years ago, when the families were still friends. Why and when did all that change? I know Liam's father wanted our land, but where did the hatred come from?

I'm not sure and my parents don't talk about it, and I can't ask Granddad, because sometimes he forgets he forgets most things now. I nod, and hurry back to my car. I check the time and guilt swamps me as I consider the early morning classes I'm going to miss. Another wave of guilt grips my throat. I shouldn't be worrying about myself when my granddad is lost.

I love him so much and care about his well-being, which is why I once asked about putting him into long term care, but that idea was shot down. I'm not saying I don't think we shouldn't care for him. I'm saying I don't think we're equipped to care for him. None of us have the tools. If driving around first thing in the morning searching for him doesn't prove that point, I don't know what does.

I drive along the water and just as I'm about to go up the hill and head home, since maybe he went back, I spot movement on the dock. I pull my car over, and hop out, running so fast toward Boondocks I nearly trip over my feet. Running is not my strength.

"Granddad," I blurt out when I spot him trying the front door. Tugging and pulling and nearly jerking the knob right off. There's a rip in his shirt, and fear tightens my chest. Did he hurt himself? When he doesn't turn toward me right away, I call out to him again. "Granddad, it's me, Abigail. We need to get you home."

"I have to open," he snaps, and stares at me like I'm a stranger he just met on the dock.

I walk up to him slowly, and reach for his hand but he tugs his arm away. "You don't have to open today. It's Friday. On Fridays we open later in the morning, because we stay open later at night."

He frowns and his hand slips from the knob. "Oh, right," he murmurs, and this time he lets me take his hand.

"Let's get you home." He allows me to lead him to the street, and I spot Liam's car slowing down. My stomach tightens. I'm not sure whether to cry out from relief, or recoil. Wouldn't his family love to see this chink in our armor. Then again, Liam is not his father, and wouldn't try to use weakness in our family against us. He rolls his window down, and I'm so shaky, I'm worried I might cry and that's when I realize I am happy to see him. But this is not his problem, so I lift my hand and wave him off. He sits there for a second, like I somehow knew he would, and there's a part of me that's very grateful for his care.

Granddad slows, and starts getting agitated again. "I don't think I turned the oven off," he says and pulls away from me. "We don't have fire insurance."

"The oven's not on," I blurt out as Liam steps from his car, overhearing the exchange. "Everything is okay." I reach for Granddad again, but he waves me off, and while he might have mental decline, there is nothing wrong with his strength. His hand connects with my cheek, hard, and I gasp and stumble backward as tears sting my eyes.

"Shit," Liam swears, hurrying across the street. "Abi, are you okay?"

I nod, even though I'm not. I just ended things with a guy who continues to help me anyway, my parents are mad at me, and I can't get my granddad to go home. The perfect trifecta to bring on tears, which I must fight. I don't cry in public.

Never show weakness in front of a Dunn.

As my Mom and Dad's words rattle around in my brain, Liam turns his attention to my Granddad and my heart lurches. I don't want him to get in the middle of this, and if Granddad recognizes him and thinks he's trespassing, things could really turn ugly.

"Hey Mr. Hart," Liam calls, and Granddad turns.

"Who are you?"

"I'm a friend." He jerks his hand over his head. "Did you want to check the oven?"

"What are you doing?" I ask him.

"Can I have the keys to the shop?" I fish them from my pocket and hand them to him. He puts his big hand on Granddad's back and leads him into Boondocks. I follow behind, and Liam starts talking about the fishing industry, something Granddad always loves to talk about. He might be mentally declining, but he does love to tell old stories.

They get inside and Granddad glances around. "What are we doing here?"

"We were just closing up and heading home," Liam informs him. "What was that you were saying about that big bass you caught?"

Granddad laughs, steps outside and Liam hands me the keys to lock up. I do it quickly and my heart is pounding as Liam walks Granddad to my car and gets him into the passenger seat. He shuts the door and stares at me over the hood.

"Thank you," I murmur, and fight the urge to cry.

"You good, Hart?" I nod and he taps the roof. "See you around."

I drive the short distance home, and Granddad gets out of the car and shuffles into the house. I shoot Mom off a text to let her know I found Granddad and he's safe. I follow him in, and he plunks himself down at his favorite seat.

"Coffee?" I ask, doing my best to keep my voice from shaking.

He frowns and looks toward the door, and it hurts my heart to see his struggles. The grandfather I remember was larger than life, and robust and the kindest man in the world. "Who was that nice boy again?"

"Just a friend," I tell him. If he knew it was Liam Dunn, the son of the man who started the rivalry between our families, he probably wouldn't call him nice. For a brief second, I worry that he'll tell Mom and Dad that Liam was on the premises. But I'm sure in two seconds, Granddad will forget all about the encounter. "Toast?"

He nods and reaches for yesterday's paper, and starts flipping through it. By the time Mom and Dad come in the front door, Granddad is settled and having his breakfast. I brace myself as Dad sits across from Granddad, frustration all over his face. But it's not Granddad's fault. It's the disease.

"There was this nice boy," Granddad begins, and my father sighs, thinking Granddad is simply rambling and he's not really interested in hearing it.

"Where was he?" Mom asks quietly, and I explain that I found him at Boondocks. She eyes me. "What happened to your face?" I put my hand to my cheek and it stings.

"He didn't mean it. He was trying to get into Boondocks, and pushed me away."

A beat of silence and then, "You should put some ice on that."

"I actually have to shower and get to the city. I have classes." I work to keep myself steady after the commotion of the morning, and hurry to my bedroom, which is located at the back of the house, far enough away that I can't hear the conversation going on in the kitchen. I grab clean clothes and make my way to the shower. I can forget about making my first class, but I shower and get ready quickly, anyway, simply needing some alone time.

I tie my hair back and once I'm ready, I square my shoulders and walk into the kitchen. "You'll be back in time for your shift tonight?" Mom asks.

"Yeah."

She looks at me like I've done something horrible, and guilt swamps me. Maybe if I was watching the sunrise on our own dock, none of this would have happened.

"We're going to take your grandfather to visit his sister in Shelburne tonight. We might not be back early enough to open tomorrow. You can take care of things?"

Saturday openings are at noon, so that means I can sleep in a bit. "Not a problem. See you later," I say, and grab my backpack and head out the door, happy that I have the place to myself tonight.

I get in my car and start driving. I'm never going to get out of this town, and I feel so bad that I so desperately want to. The next thing I know the road is blurry before my eyes as tears start spilling. I pull into the carpool lot just before the highway. I lean forward, and brace my forehead on my steering wheel. I take deep gulping breaths to pull myself together, and nearly jump out of my seat when knuckles rap on my window.

I turn and see Liam standing there, gesturing for me to roll down my window. I do, and he bends, bracing himself on the door. "Come on. I'm driving."

14

LIAM

I remain quiet, letting Abi sort through her thoughts as I drive us into the city. Every now and then, I cast a glance her way, just to make sure she's okay. She continues to stare straight out the front window, and I resist the urge to reach over and take her hand.

"How did you know?" she asks quietly.

"What do you mean?"

"You were good with my granddad. How did you know how to handle that situation?"

"Do you remember my grandmother?" Grandma use to volunteer on the playground when we were in elementary school.

"Vaguely."

"She passed away a couple of years ago. She was only sixty-five, but she had early onset dementia."

"I'm sorry, Liam. I didn't know."

"Thanks. It was a tough time. We put her in a nursing care facility, and we took a few classes."

"Maybe I should take some classes."

This time I do reach out, and put my hand over hers. "When would you ever fit them in?"

She snorts out a laugh. "You're right."

"I can give you some pointers, and this is not my business, but maybe your granddad should be in a facility too."

"I know," she says quietly, her tone low and deflated. "Are you sure you don't mind driving me back tonight? It's Friday. You must have something better to do."

"I don't," I admit. There's nothing I'd rather do than spend time with her. I don't say that though. Even though she accepted a drive and is letting me hold her hand, she ended things this morning.

"I'm sorry you're missing your first class." She shakes her head, shame on her face. "I'm letting everyone down today."

I grip the steering wheel tighter. "Tanner will take notes for me, and you haven't let anyone down, Abi."

"You didn't see my parents this morning. They were pretty upset when they couldn't find me. They looked on the dock." Her lips tighten as she stares out the window.

"What did you do wrong?"

"I was born a girl."

That stops me cold. Holy shit, is that true? I go quiet, and she practically whispers, "A boy would have taken over the business, maybe even made their business bigger and better. I want to make the world better, the ecosystem better, and I don't think I'm hurting their business by doing that. But I don't think they see it the same way."

"I'm so sorry." Jesus, what else am I supposed to say? She's following her passion and we should all be supporting that.

"What I did wrong goes deeper than just not being on the dock this morning."

I don't usually give pep talks. I'm usually on the receiving end of them from the team. I can't let her hurt like this, though. I have to say something, anything. "Your grandfather went wandering and you found him and brought him home. You didn't do anything wrong, Abi." As my voice rises, I try to keep my anger in check. What goes on in her home isn't my business. That doesn't mean I have to like all the responsibility and the blame they pile on her. To lighten things, I add, "And if you had been born a boy, that might make what we've been doing a bit difficult for me, since I like girls."

She gives a half laugh, and plucks at the hem of her hoodie. "If I hadn't slept on the boat."

"Don't you have a right to a life?" I blurt out and she pulls her hand out from under mine and hugs herself. "I'm sorry." Fuck. "I'd just like to see you have some fun. Do something just for you. Something that brings you happiness."

She gives me a small smile. "I kind of did something just for me the other day. Something that made me happy."

I grin back at her and point downward. "Don't think it didn't make someone else happy."

Her laugh lightens the tension between us. "I just feel like the world is conspiring against me sometimes, and maybe I should have watched the sunset longer to remind myself I'm pretty insignificant in this world."

"You're not insignificant, Abi."

"Oh, God," she groans and puts her hand on her forehead. "I should not be whining or complaining."

"You're venting. There's a difference. You're allowed to vent."

"I feel guilty about that, though. My parents have a lot on their plate."

"You do too, Abi, and you don't like to ask for help."

"Oh, you think you know me now do you, Dunn?"

"Maybe more than you think, and I know what happened between us before isn't going to happen again, but I'd like it if we could still be friends."

She wraps her finger around her ponytail. "I think we can be friends."

"Friends with benefits?"

"Hey," she bites back, but it doesn't hold weight. I don't think she wanted to end things this morning, I think she needed to, and if I was smart, I'd walk away from this.

"What I mean is when you need help, you ask me." I stop and poke myself in my chest. "When I need help, I ask you. That's what friends do."

She thinks about it. "I think I could do that. I really only have Ocean and it's hard for us to even have time together with her living at the sorority. You must have a lot of friends on campus, though."

"I don't really. I have teammates."

"Josh was really your only friend, wasn't he?"

"Yeah."

She makes a fist and nudges my chin. "You're kind of a lone wolf, Dunn."

"You sound like you like that."

"I like you." My gaze jerks to hers and pink colors her cheeks, like she'd given away too much of herself. "I wouldn't agree to be your friend if I didn't like you."

"Right. Friends."

"The lone wolf thing can be a bit of a problem for you in Miami, though."

"How so?"

"Lunenburg, it's a small town. Miami." She stops and attempts a whistle, which comes out sounding like a wounded animal and makes me laugh. "Miami is full of beautiful women," she continues. "And you're going to be a big deal, Liam." I roll my eyes at her. "They'll be throwing themselves at you. It will be hard to get away from that."

"What do you suggest?"

"Find yourself a woman and fast. That should hopefully help."

"I'll think about that." I turn the air up as a wave of uncomfortable heat hits me. "Then again, if I don't pass calculus, I won't have to think about it."

"I'm sure your professor will cut you some slack."

I frown, hating that I get an easy pass because I'm academically challenged.

"But I can help you if you'd like, Liam. Friends help friends, right?"

"Thanks."

And just like that...we fall into an easy conversation for the rest of the drive to campus. She's easy to be with, easy to talk to, and she doesn't check out mentally when conversation turns to hockey, and I don't check out when she talks about the grants she can apply for—with less enthusiasm this time, which scares me a little bit. I eventually tell her about the training I received at the nursing home, and how to redirect conversation when you can. We even go over a few scenarios.

I check the time as we approach campus. "What time is your next class?"

"I have an hour to spare."

"Want to hang out in my room? Hang out there instead of the library or cafeteria?"

Her stomach takes that moment to grumble and she puts her hand over it. "I didn't have much of an appetite this morning after...Granddad."

"I'm hungry too. Come on. I'll make you something moderately healthy."

I grab our backpacks from the back seat and shoulder both of them. Storm House is pretty quiet this morning, with everyone in class. We walk into the big kitchen, and I open one of the many fridges. "This is my section," I tell her.

She bends and peers in and I try to ignore the gorgeous sight before me, and how my dick is standing up for a better look.

She glances back and I lift my head quickly, although I'm pretty sure she caught me checking out her ass. Man, I need the tutoring but it's going to be brutal being around her and not touching.

"I see eggs, and cheese," she informs me.

"Enough to make an omelet." I reach around her, pull the carton of eggs out and look for a best before date. "That's healthy." I point to the shelf above mine. "That's Jesse's shelf. He won't mind if we borrow some of his bread."

"How do you borrow bread?"

I laugh. "I'll buy him a loaf next time I'm at the store."

"What's in here?" She opens the vegetable drawer and pulls out what I think was a red pepper, and it drips into her palm. "Eww, Liam. What is this?

I grab the garbage can and she drops the pepper into it. "That drawer," I tell her. "That's the veggie hospice."

"What?" she asks laughing as I turn on the kitchen faucet and squirt soap into her hand.

"It's where veggies go to die."

"Ohmigod, Liam." She laughs hard, and it's so contagious I laugh with her. She turns the water off. "You're crazy."

In that moment, and even though she ended things between us, I can't help but pull her into my arms. Her laughter dies abruptly and she puts her wet hands on my chest. I expect her to push me away, and I'm a bit surprised when she sinks into me, like she's desperate for my touch.

"Abi," I whisper, my heart pounding as her head lifts. My gaze drops to her mouth, and she parts her lips and wets them. "I want to kiss you."

"I...want that too. This morning...I just..."

I'm desperate to kiss her, I just don't want her doing something she's going to regret later. "It's not a good idea, I know." I cup her face, and take in the bruise forming beneath her eye. Christ, she had a hell of a morning and if she'll let me, I want to take care of her.

"I'm not sure I care right now," she answers.

I bend, and press my lips to hers. Softly. A tender joining of lips. As her hands hold my chest, I close one of mine over both of hers and hold her to me. We trade kisses, and hold onto one another until someone clears their throat. Abi jumps back, and I turn my head to find Sebastian staring at us, a smirk on his face, like he caught me with my hand in the cookie jar, and in a way, he did.

"So, you *are* fucking fi…"

I take a threatening step toward him and his words fall off. "Watch your fucking mouth, Sebastian." Sebastian turns his gaze to Abi, and I step closer to him, blocking her from his sight. "You said you weren't fucking her."

"What Abi and I are doing is none of your business."

"Maybe not. Does your father know?"

I stiffen, and he notices it. Fuck. "It's not his business either."

"I think he'd probably like to know you're fucking the daughter of the man he hates."

"Not that it's any of your business, but he knows I'm with Abi." It's a half truth. I told him I gave her a ride and he told me what I needed to do if I insisted on driving her around. "So why don't you fuck off out of this kitchen."

He offers me a look that suggests I'm full of shit. "My kitchen too." He walks around me, goes to his fridge and pulls out a bottle of water. I stand still, my hands fisted at my sides. While I'd like to punch the smug grin off his face, I don't want to get into trouble with Coach. He saunters past me and out the front door. I focus in on Abi. She's standing there with a stricken look on her face.

"Abi." I hurry to her and pull her into my arms. "Don't let anything that asshole says get to you." Her body is stiff, and I search her face.

"I shouldn't be here."

Fuck.

"If you want to go, you can go, but don't go because of Sebastian." I put my hand on her upper arms, and watch her dark lashes fall over her big blue eyes. "Look, it's been a crazy day and it's only ten in the morning. Let's make some food and eat it in my room. Then I'll drive you to class." She hesitates. "The day can only get better from here." She huffs out a laugh and her shoulders sag. "Let's hope." The fridge beeps from being open too long and I grab the cheese and bread. "Why don't you sit and watch my culinary skills?"

"I thought you said you were only good at hockey."

"And sex, don't forget sex," I joke, wanting to keep the smile on her face.

"I don't recall you saying you were good at sex."

"I didn't say it. I showed you, remember."

She laughs. "Okay, so hockey, sex and cooking."

"You agree then. I'm good at sex?"

"Keep your fishing to the boats, Liam."

I laugh, and scrunch up my face. "I wouldn't go so far as to say I was skilled at 'cooking'." I do finger quotes around the word. "I would probably say I can make a mean egg and cheese sandwich."

"Let's see it, Dunn."

I grab a pan, and set it on the stove. I drop four slices of bread into the toaster. "Know what makes my sandwiches so good?"

"You make them with love?"

"No." I reach into the fridge and pull out a big tub. I hold it out and say, "Butter." I grab a spoon and put a big dollop in the pan. She laughs hard, and my heart swells. I take in her smile, liking everything about this girl. She might be right about one thing. I might need to find a woman and fast in Miami. Now, how do I get her to fill out the grant forms so that girl is her?

But I can't have that, right? We're not supposed to be together.

While this Dunn might be done giving a fuck, there's one Dunn in the family that could ruin a lot of things—including my future in Miami—if I do.

FML.

15

ABIGAIL

"Any more thoughts on the beach?" Liam asks.

"Can I give you an answer in the morning?" I say as I shift closer to him, our legs touching as they dangle off the dock. Before Liam can answer, I look over my shoulder. I don't know what is wrong with me. I keep getting the strangest sense that I'm being watched. Maybe the incident with the Storm players spooked me more than I want to admit.

"What's up?"

I look back at Liam. "I just want to make sure Mom and Dad don't need me in the afternoon." I don't usually work Saturday, it's a time for my schoolwork mostly, although I promised to open tomorrow. If they don't get back early, I'll be stuck working all day. I don't miss the way his body physically tightens. He doesn't get it. He doesn't have pressures on him like I do. Okay, maybe that's not a fair statement. He has pressures on him, they're just different from mine.

"No, I mean, what's up back there?" He turns around and searches the dock. "Is there someone there?"

"No, I think I'm just getting paranoid or something," I explain trying to make light of it.

He lightly touches my face, brushing my blowing hair back. "I'm here."

My knight in shining armor. I don't believe in fairy tale endings, as he won't always be here. His future is in Miami. His finger lingers around my ear, and dammit, my entire body is telling me to do another one-eighty and forget about the reasons we can't be together. Cripes, it was just this morning, after sleeping with him all night, that I said we were over and now here I am wanting to crawl into bed with him again. I'm giving myself whiplash.

"When will you know tomorrow, about the beach?"

"Around noon," I answer as he reaches into the pocket of his hoodie.

He pulls his hand out and stares at his empty palm. "Damn."

"What?"

"Searching for beef jerky." He chuckles. "Habit."

"I'm never getting you off those things, am I?"

He laughs and throws his arm around me. He drags me close and I breathe in the scent of him. "Listen, the protein bars were delicious. There's just something about meat sticks a guy needs." A rumble of laughter fills the air.

"What?"

"I'm glad the guys on the team don't know my love for jerky. Can you imagine the nickname they'd give me?"

"Meat stick, it might be appropriate," I tease.

"Tanner, my bud on the team, they call him Banger."

I shake my head, pretty sure I know where that comes from. "You guys have the weirdest nicknames for each other. Hey what's yours?"

He groans. "You don't want to know."

"Now I definitely want to know more."

"Fine, Hooker."

I eye him. "Is that because…"

"Because fishermen hook fish, not for any other reason you might be thinking."

"Whatever you need to tell yourself to sleep at night, Dunn," I joke. Really though, I know a lot of the puck bunnies go after the players, and I've seen firsthand how they piled on him at the pub. What I haven't seen is him playing into that, or walking around with a different girl every weekend. Most weekends, when he's not playing, he's here at home.

He chuckles and I put my hand on his thigh. I take a deep, tired breath and let it out. After an emotional morning, and a busy day of classes—no, I haven't filled the grant papers out yet—it's nice to lean on him and accept his comfort. Honestly, it's just nice to be around him.

I didn't even think I'd see him tonight, but he took up residency in the back office, and in between customers, I helped him with his calculus. I thought after we almost got caught by Danny, he wouldn't return to Boondocks. It's risky for both of us. But I just…needed to be around him tonight.

I haven't even gone inside the house yet. I'd dropped my car off at the house, because I was running a bit late, and headed straight to Boondocks. I'd texted Mom letting her know I'd opened the store this evening. She told me there were left-over in the fridge, but Liam and I had grabbed sandwiches and salads and eaten them under the old weeping willow trees at the Halifax public gardens. It was nice and peaceful there.

"Let's get you home." Liam jumps up, brushes his hands off and helps me to my feet. The wharf wobbles and I stumble against him and he groans.

"Sorry."

"Not your fault. Wharf."

"Why do you sound like you're in agony?" I'd only lightly banged against him.

He takes a fast breath and picks up his backpack. "Because I want to pick up where we left off in the kitchen at Storm House, and Abi, I just don't know what you want."

I'm not sure what's suddenly driving my actions. Maybe I'm still shaken from this morning, or maybe I feel stuck in this town. Or maybe it's Liam talking about me doing something that makes me happy. I don't know, but I go up on my toes, slide my hand through his hair and say, "Maybe this will help clarify things."

I bring his mouth down to mine and his groan of pleasure wraps around me and hugs me tight. I know what I'm about to do is wrong and risky, but goddammit, I never ask for what I need and I never just take it, but tonight I'm going to do both, because what's really driving my actions is my need to be touched and cared for by this man.

We kiss hungrily, a new kind of need gripping both of us. I feel it deep in my soul. Does he feel this strange connection too? I rub my body against his, letting him know exactly what I want tonight, and after this morning, I pray he's still willing to give it to me.

He breaks the kiss and cups my face. He glances over my head and toward the empty street. He scans the area and then, with a nod, he gestures to Boondocks. "Want to go back inside?"

"No."

There's still hope in his eyes when he jerks his finger out. "My boat."

"No."

"Oh, okay." His shoulders sag, and I like that after that heated kiss he's not pressing, but there is disappointment in his eyes.

I reach up and take a palm from my face and hold his hand. "Come with me."

"Where?"

I give a little tug. "You're walking me home."

We fall quiet as we walk along the boardwalk, our footsteps echoing in the quiet night. My car is at my house and his is back at his house, so we walk up the big hill to my place. I'm a bit breathless as it comes into view, but Liam looks like he could run a marathon.

His steps slow as we approach, and I keep tugging him. "Hart," he murmurs. "What are we doing?" He stops at the end of my driveway, and peers at me. "What about your parents?"

"They're away for the night."

He swallows, his body still tight as worry moves over his face. "This is dangerous."

I laugh. "I've always heard sneaking around is half the fun."

Liam doesn't laugh. Instead, he reaches over his shoulder and rubs the back of his neck. "I don't want you getting into trouble."

"I'm already in trouble," I tell him and don't elaborate. He might think I'm talking about this morning, but the truth is, I'm in trouble because I really like Liam Dunn. He glances at my house like he's a sheep and I'm leading him to slaughter. "If you don't want—"

Catching me by surprise, he pulls me to him, and slides his one hand around my head. "I want." He kisses me hard and deep to prove his point.

"Let's get inside before the neighbors see us."

His body is almost shaking as I lead him to my front door and I can't tell if it's from excitement or fear. I shove my key into the lock and note Liam's intake of breath. The house is dark and quiet, and I flick on the small mudroom light. We step into the kitchen, and Liam stands close behind me. The hum of the refrigerator fills the silence around us.

"No one is going to jump out at you," I tease.

A small chuckle fills the quiet of the room as he relaxes. "Where's your room?"

"Anxious much?" Truthfully, I want to get to my room as much as he does. "Don't you want the grand tour?"

"Nope, just the direct route to your bedroom." He turns me, puts his hands on my waist, and his mouth is near my ear when he whispers, "Lead the way."

I love the way his fingers bite into my hips as I cut through the kitchen and take him to the back of the house. We reach my room and he practically pushes me inside, and my heart jumps as he kicks my door shut and flicks on the light.

"Let's see what Abigail Hart keeps behind closed doors."

I turn and find him grinning as he walks around my small room, running his fingers over my desk, my dresser, and taking in the artwork on my walls. "You like watercolors, I see." He stops to examine art done by a local artist.

"I do." I examine the painting through his eyes. Seagulls flying over the water.

"You like seagulls."

"Yes, just not at five in the morning." He laughs at that. "They're pretty smart birds and they're important for our ecosystem." He arches a brow, and I continue. "They eat food waste, which reduces the amount of methane and ammonia going into the air, which makes it cleaner." He nods, and I say, "They also work as a team and alert their friends that there's a school of fish in the water by flashing their wings in a certain pattern."

"Here I thought they only stole our French fries."

I laugh, but I love the way he listens to my every word, even though I probably sound nerdy right about now. "Nope, they're smart."

"Like you." He steps toward me, my artwork no longer holding his attention. "Did I ever tell you how sexy it is when you talk so smart and teach me things?"

"You like that, do you?" I ask as he tugs me close and puts one leg between mine. It brushes up against my sex, making it harder and harder for me to think.

"Yeah, I like it."

He grips my hoodie and peels it over my head, and as his eyes darken with lust, I say, "Did you know the ocean covers seventy percent of the surface of our planet?"

"No, tell me more."

He cups my breasts through my T-shirt and I moan as he gently kneads them like two of the biggest stress balls ever. My nipples tighten and my breathing becomes a little rougher. My head rolls back as he slips his warm hands under my shirt, lightly trailing his fingers up my sides. Goosebumps break out on my body and his warm breath falls over me as he groans.

"The ocean is home to ninety-four percent of all life on Earth. We need new regulations to protect the ecosystem."

"That's a lot. I can see why you'd want to protect it. I like that."

The fishing industry is important to both our families, and my goal is to help set regulations, which could hurt the bottom line of the Dunn conglomerate, yet Liam sounds like he supports my life's ambition. He peels my shirt off and with a quick flick of his wrist, my bra falls to the floor.

"The ocean provides more than...oh..." My words fall off as his hot mouth closes over my nipple. His tongue swirls around my peak and I put my hands on his shoulders.

"Go on," he murmurs around my nipple.

What was I saying? Oh right. "Provides more than half the oxygen we breathe." He puts his mouth near my throat and breathes me in.

"Fuck, you smell good."

He slides a hand between our bodies, dipping his thumbs into my yoga pants. He tugs my pants down a bit, while his knee continues to rub between my legs, causing me to shamelessly ride him.

He pulls my pants down, just enough to expose my pubic bone. Need grips my entire body and I can't hold back a quake. "Jesus," he growls, and I suspect that shudder went right through his body too. His head lifts, and dark eyes meet mine. He holds my gaze as he slides a finger into my panties, brushing my clit as he glides lower and lower. The tortured look that comes over his face when he finds me wet and needy—for him—does crazy things to me. He loves knowing what he does to me. I move against his finger, trying to force him inside, but he simply plays with me. Fine, I can play this game. I put my hand over his steely-hard cock and give it a light massage. I'm rewarded with a growl. I grin, because I too, love knowing what I do to him too.

"Do you need me in here?" I nod enthusiastically. "Have you...been thinking about it, Abi?" God, his broken words, his hunger arouses me even more, and my mouth dries as I pant. "Have you been thinking about riding my cock and doing something just for yourself?"

The way this man can read me is a bit insane. "Yes."

"Tonight, you can take my cock any way you want. Anything you need."

Noise erupts from the kitchen, the old ice maker in the freezer clanging as it drops cubes into the tray and Liam goes still. His finger stills inside my panties. "Is that—"

"No one is coming," I quickly tell him.

A grin comes over his face as he slides a finger into my sex. "Want to bet?"

16

LIAM

As I slide my finger into her wet heat, my brain begins to shut down, but not before the realization that I'm in Abi's room, about to have sex with her hits. After this morning, I thought it was over for good, and I'm so fucking glad it's not. Yeah, I really should run outside to see if the sky is falling. If it is, there's no other way I'd want to go.

"That is so good," she cries out, as I inch into her. Truthfully, I don't know what tomorrow will bring. Maybe it will be me who decides we can't do this anymore. Doubtful. Tonight, however, I'm just going to enjoy putting my hands and mouth all over her, and with any luck, we'll get to spend more time together at the beach tomorrow evening. A few of my teammates, who are complete assholes, including Sebastian, will be there. Do I really think he'll run and tell daddy who I've been fucking? Not sure. If he does, my dad will no doubt think I'm gathering information. Will he tell Sebastian that? Will Sebastian tell him there might be more going on between Abi and me? Fuck, that could be disastrous.

But I'll deal with that tomorrow. Tonight, I have the most beautiful woman I know in my arms, with my finger inside her half naked body. The other clothed have needs to be rectified. I slowly inch my finger out and a hard quiver goes through her. "I need you naked."

"You...naked too."

I pull my hoodie off and she drops to her knees, taking my dick out before I can fully undress and there's something extremely sexy in how much she wants my cock. She licks my crown, and her moan vibrates through me. "Babe..."

She glances up at me as her tongue snakes out, trailing down the rigid length of me. It takes effort to remain erect. I mean standing. Fuck, my dick is always erect around her, and let's be honest, even when I'm not. Because when I'm not with her, I'm still thinking of her, and fuck, I'm in really deep here. Is that what makes the sex so damn good?

I reach down and shove my pants to my thighs to give her better access. I mean, tonight is all about her, and if she wants to suck my cock, I want to make it easier on her. Who knew I was so altruistic? That thought nearly makes me laugh.

She takes me deep and nearly sucks the sperm from my balls. I can't come, not yet. I want my cock inside her. I glance around the room, looking at her desk, her bed, her windowsill, all the places I want to take her.

I inch out and she wipes her mouth as she glances up at me. "What's in your backyard?" I ask.

Her brow furrows and she angles her head. "Do you mean..." She pauses her words and puts her hand over her shoulder, using her thumb to point downward, to her backside.

For a moment, I'm confused—clearly I have little to no blood left in my brain, and then I laugh. I take my cock into my hand, rubbing it, and her cheeks turn a pretty shade of pink. "No, Hart." Although now that she brought it up, is that something she'd like to try? "I was talking about your actual backyard." I point to her window.

She grins. "Well, I wasn't sure. I know you hockey players have your own lingo." She glances past my body. "Just our garden and trees, a bench and a wooden fence. Why? Do you want to have sex in my backyard?"

I step up to her, take her hand and lead her to her window. I turn her and put both her hands on the cool windowpane. I give her a nudge until her breasts are against the cold glass and an excited gasp catches in her throat.

"Oh...my nipples."

"Feel good?" She moves her body, rubbing herself against the cold window, and that answers my question. "Careful, you don't want to cut through the glass."

As she moans, I drop to my knees and tug on her pants. I tap her legs, one at a time, and she lifts each one. "What if someone walks into the yard?" she asks, her voice a harsh whisper.

"Then they'd see me fucking you up against your window."

An excited little wheezing sound escapes her throat and a fog forms on the window. "Yeah, we'd get caught," she agrees.

"Yeah, but do you not agree that sneaking around is half the fun."

"It's kind of exciting...freeing."

I had a feeling she might see it that way, and in this sleepy small town, no one is going to be walking through her fenced in yard at this time of night. It's safe, because there's no way in hell I'd do anything to expose her or put her in jeopardy.

I run my fingers up her inner thighs and the scent of her arousal reaches out to me. I breathe her in, and her aroma is like rocket fuel in veins. Her breathing is rough as I slide a finger into her hot core, and curse under my breath as she lightly squeezes around me. I fucking love how she's always so ready for me.

She moans and rocks, and I hold my finger still to let her ride it. She doesn't disappoint, me or herself. No, she's moving and grinding and taking what she needs. I slip a second finger in, and my cock aches to take its place.

Her hot juices sear my skin, and I slide a hand to the front so she can press her clit against my palm. "Oh, yes," she murmurs. I move closer, so I can kiss her plump backside as she gyrates. Her rhythm changes and she becomes more desperate. That's when I decide to give her a hand, so to speak. I move with her, sliding my fingers in and out of her hot core, aiding her as she chases her orgasm.

"Yeah, babe," I whisper, and slide my teeth over her sweet ass.

"Liam," she cries out, her fingers clawing at the window as her body convulses, teasing my cock.

"Sweet Jesus." Her hot cum spills from her body and drips down my arm, and my mouth waters, craving the delicious taste of her. I stay between her legs, helping her ride out each hard clench until her body is a hot, weak mess. Her whimpers die off and I pick her up and carry her to her bed.

I set her on the bed, stepping back to rid myself of my clothes. I love how she watches me, sated but still with longing and pleasure. Christ, I want to give this woman everything she needs and then some.

I pick my pants back up and pull out a condom and I catch her grin. "What?"

"Seems like you came prepared."

"I like to be prepared. Sue me." She laughs, but it falls off fast. I slide onto the bed next to her and brush her hair from her face. "Hey, what is it?"

She plasters on a smile. "Nothing."

Okay, I get it. I always have a condom in my pocket, and she clearly thinks I fuck anything with two legs. "I carry condoms. It's no big deal, Abi. It's just about being prepared." Prepared, yeah, right dude. You weren't prepared for this thing with Abi when you got involved.

"It's just that it's Friday night. You're missing the party at Storm House."

I groan. "I'm only living at Storm House because that's where my father wants me. I'd love to move out, but can't. He thinks it's better if I'm with the team, and he's paying for it right now, so…"

"So you have to do what he says."

"Sometimes I'd just like to run away from it all," I tell her, and wow if that doesn't make me sound like a spoiled prick, I don't know what does.

"I would too," she agrees. "Sometimes I'd like to be anywhere but here, and I know that makes me sound awful."

"No, it doesn't and once again, we're not so different, Hart." She touches my cheek and I lean into it. "But right now, believe me, there's nowhere else I'd rather be, and no one else I'd rather be with."

She smiles, reaches a hand between our bodies and strokes my cock. "Do you always talk this much during sex? I thought you said you were good at it, yet all this chatter."

I shake my head, loving her playfulness as I slide my hand down her stomach, until I reach her drenched sex. "I'd say you'd agree."

"I don't know about that."

I rip open the condom, sheathe myself, and roll over her. My fingers thread through hers and I put them over her head as my cock finds her opening. In one fast thrust, I push into her and her body tightens around me.

I groan, sinking into her heat. Why can't I get enough of her?

I think you know the reason, dude.

She wraps her legs around me and, since we have all night, I take it slowly. Each thrust hits differently than the last, and I have to admit, there's something very intimate and profound in each unhurried stroke. We move together, like we're both seeking more than just release, and it frightens me just a little.

I push my pelvis against her clit to give her what she needs, and her hands tighten in mine as our gazes meet and hold. There's something happening here, something deep and profound, something that could easily drown me. Her mouth opens and the second her muscles clench around my cock, I let go and come with her.

My lips find hers as we bring each other pleasure, and our kiss is soft, and tender, and we revel in our release. After a moment, I fall over her and she gives my hands a squeeze before she untangles hers and places them on my back.

Her heart pounds against my chest, her breath warm on my neck. As my cock deflates, I inch out of her, quickly discard the condom and crawl back, pulling her close. I close my eyes, but open them again quickly.

"Should I go?"

"Do you want to go?"

"No," I answer quickly and truthfully.

"My parents won't be back until around noon tomorrow. Can you stay the night?"

I nod, happiness enveloping me. "Yes." I close my eyes and the silence of the night falls over us. "My God, this town is quiet."

"Until five am when the boats start." She's not wrong, and I'd really like to be on one. As if reading my thoughts, she asks, "If you could do anything you wanted, what would it be?"

I slide my hand down and tap her ass. "You, again," I tease.

She whacks me. "I'm being serious." I lay still and stare at her ceiling. "You don't have to tell me if you don't want to."

"No, it's not that." She rolls toward me and lightly runs her fingers along my stomach. I flinch, take her hand and bring it to my mouth for a kiss. I don't want to come off sounding like an asshole, so I say, "I'm living the dream, Hart. Drafted by Miami. Do you know how many guys would give their left nut for that?"

"Just the left, not the right. Is the left more important?" she teases as her eyes light up playfully. "Do you call it like Boss Ball or something? Oh, maybe it's like when twins are born, the one who comes first is considered the older one, the one in charge. Is that what goes on down there?"

"Let's not talk about which one comes first, and now who's the crazy one."

She laughs at that and I take her finger between my teeth and lightly bite down. "Ow." She pulls it back. "It's okay, you don't have to tell me."

I turn to her, and my gaze moves over her face. How the hell can she read me so well? "You didn't buy that, huh?"

"Do you know you get this little line in your forehead when you're not being completely honest?"

I touch my forehead. "I do not."

"Do not play poker, my friend. Actually, let's have a game."

I laugh at that. "You want to clean me out?"

"Maybe I meant strip poker."

"Now why would I bother to play strip poker when you're already naked."

She bites her bottom lip and nods. "Good point." We lay on our sides, our hands touching each other's bodies. "It's the boats, isn't it?"

I flop onto my back, put the crook of my elbow on my forehead and stare at her ceiling. "I play for him," I admit softly, surprising even myself that I voiced the words that have been in my head for a very long time.

I turn my head and find Abi watching me carefully. "I thought that might be the case."

"I've always done it for him. I'm good at it, and who doesn't want to be a millionaire NHL star?"

"You," she says quietly.

"Fuck, I sound like a bastard. So many other guys would kill to have what I have." I turn to my side and pull Abi to me, needing her comfort. Shit, tonight was about her, and here I am making it all about me. Yeah, what an asshole. "Did you fill out your grants?"

She shakes her head and I'm about to push. "What is it you love about being on the boats?" she asks, turning the conversation back to me.

"Christ, Abi."

She lightly touches my face, pure concern in her big blue eyes. "What?"

Fuck, I don't talk about this with anyone. "I can't give up a career in the NHL."

"I understand that."

We both go quiet for a very long time as we continue to hold each other.

"When I'm on the ice," I begin. "I feel like I'm doing it for everyone else. On the boats, I'm doing it for me. Does that make me selfish?"

"No."

"It's hard work, don't get me wrong, and at times dangerous, but it's the only time I feel like I'm alive." Do I dare tell her it's the same feeling I get when I'm with her? "I have a comradery with the guys on the boats that I don't have with my team."

"My lone wolf."

I grin. "It's just that on the boats we all have the same passion. I play hockey well, yes, it's true, but the passion isn't there." I trace my finger along her arm. "I work hard on the ice because I don't want to let anyone down, you know."

"It wasn't easy telling me that, was it?"

"No." I exhale, and even though it wasn't easy, in fact I'm surprised I even said anything at all, it felt good to get it off my chest.

"Okay," she says, drawing out that one word, to make it serious. "I need to tell you something personal."

My gut tightens, but I don't get the sense she's confessing something bad. "Of course. Anything."

"I agree."

Okay, now I'm a bit confused. "Agree with what?"

Her grin is playful, and I sense the shift in the room. "That you're good at sex."

"Please," I snort, tension ebbing away. "What we just did. That wasn't sex."

"Oh, what was it then?"

I roll over her, warmth and happiness invading my soul. "That was me just getting started."

ABIGAIL

A bang in the house pulls me awake, and I rub my eyes and glance around my very bright room. Unlike last night, the town is alive, and off in the distance I hear cars, and chatter and dogs barking. That could only mean the tourists have arrived, and since they don't usually show up until around noon, when Lunenburg comes awake...Ohmigod.

I jackknife up, and turn to spot Liam spread out on my bed. The clock on the nightstand indicates it's almost noon and we slept our morning away. Not a surprise considering we were up half the night having sex, eating, listening to music, talking and having more sex.

The noise in the kitchen sounds again, and I go perfectly still, waiting for my mother to call out to me, or worse, come into my room. But why would she? She likely thinks I'm at Boondocks. I'm pretty reliable like that. At least I used to be reliable until...Liam.

"Liam," I whisper. "You need to leave."

I nudge him and he peels his eyes open. The second they land on me, he smiles, until he sees the panic on my face. Footsteps sound in the hall and his eyes go wide. "Shit."

"Yeah, shit."

I'm a grown woman who happens to live at home to help take care of things. I'm pretty sure my parents wouldn't care if I had a man over, except that man can never, ever be Liam Dunn.

Liam jumps up, and quickly tugs on his clothes. I point to my window. "That way."

"Jesus," he whispers and opens my window. He throws his legs over and slides out. "Are you okay?" I nod. "Will I see you later?"

My stomach churns. "I...don't know."

He stares at me with those dark eyes for a moment, and I spot the worry, and maybe the hint of disappointment. God, what am I doing with him? "I'll text you later," I promise. He gives a curt nod and disappears, and I quickly tug on clothes and tie my hair back. I have three minutes to brush my teeth, and get to the dock.

My bedroom door creaks as I open it and I wince as I step into the hall and see Mom coming down the stairs. So much for getting out the front door without being noticed.

"Abigail?" Mom says.

"Hey, just about to go open Boondocks."

Her brow furrows as she checks her watch. "You should have been there already."

"I slept in. Sorry. I was up late."

"What is going on with you, Abi?" She pushes past me to head into the kitchen. "You haven't been yourself lately."

I follow her into the kitchen and walk to the porch to grab my shoes. I sit at the kitchen table to tug them on. "Yeah, I've been busy with school," I say, but even as that small lie leaves my mouth, I can't help but think she's wrong. I *have* been myself lately. I have been who I really am, who I really want to be inside, all because of Liam. I'm doing more of what I want, discovering who I am, where I belong in this world. "Where's Granddad?"

"He's staying with Aunt Edna for a few days, and don't bother heading to Boondocks. I'm home now and can open."

"I'm sorry."

"I've been hearing that a lot lately."

"Where's Dad?"

"Outside, talking to Lester." Lester is our neighbor and for the briefest of seconds, panic grips me. Did he see me bringing Liam home last night...see what we did in my bedroom window?

Before I can stop myself, I blurt out, "Why does Mr. Dunn hate our family so much?"

She goes still, so still, it's almost frightening. "Why are you bringing up James Dunn?"

I try to keep my tone casual. "Oh, no reason, really. I guess I'm just curious."

"Curiosity killed the cat," is all she says as she gathers her insulated mug, and walks to the door. Her face is stern, maybe a bit pale when she turns to me, and it's clear there's more to the story than she wants me to know. "Stay away from the Dunns. They're not good people."

"Okay," I push out. "I...I probably won't be back for dinner tonight. I have some things to do...in the city."

"Will you be staying with Ocean again?"

"Probably." We don't open on Sunday. I don't have to hurry home if I stay out tonight, which is nice.

"Have you applied for the grants?"

"Not yet."

"You're going to, though?" she asks, "You're going to leave?"

I take a breath, a storm brewing inside my gut. "Mom, you can't expect me to stay forever."

"I did. Your father did. Your grandparents did, and your grandparents before them did."

Once again, guilt rushes over me like a rogue wave. If only I'd been born male. I open my mouth. I just don't know what it is I want to say. "Mom," I begin...and end.

"We'll manage," she says, and steps out the door, and I fold my hands over my stomach, and glance at the four walls that have surrounded me my entire life. My parents have always provided for me, and maybe it's wrong of me to want more.

I push myself to my feet, and walk into my bedroom. My phone pings and I tug it from my pocket.

Liam: Everything okay?

. . .

Me: I'm coming to the beach blowout.

Liam: Glad to hear it. Where can we meet? I'll pick you up.

Me: I'm actually headed to campus now. I have some work to do.

Liam: Go to my dorm. Let yourself in. I'll meet you there.

The knot in my stomach unravels a bit, stirrings of excitement careening through me. I love the idea of meeting up with Liam, of hanging out and studying in his dorm room. I wish I didn't. I really and truly wish I didn't, but I can't help myself.

I head to the bathroom, shower and change my clothes, putting on my tight jeans, a nice shirt and a pretty knit sweater. I comb out my hair, and I'm about to put it into a ponytail, when a very delicious idea hits, and I put it into pig tails. I grab my bathing suit, some heavier clothes for the beach in case it's cold, and tug a blanket from the closet. I have no idea what these beach blowouts are like but I want to be prepared. I shoot Ocean a text.

Me: Hey, you going to the beach blowout this afternoon with Easton?

Ocean: Yes, are you coming!!!

. . .

It's no wonder she's so surprised. Hanging out with the team is not my thing, and Ocean and I have been drifting apart lately. She's in a sorority house, meeting so many people and I'm swamped with school and work...and Liam. I'd recently told her a tiny bit about Liam and me, and she's still a little shocked by that, and hey, so am I.

Me: Yes, see you there.

Ocean: You have some serious explaining to do.

I laugh out loud at that, and quickly text back that I'll give her all the details when we have some quiet time. With that, I tuck my phone into my belt bag, strap it on, and grab my duffle bag, which I hadn't even emptied since I stayed with Liam. I start digging the clothes out, and go still when I see what's hidden in the bottom, beneath my clothes.

My heart jumps into my throat and a little *aww* comes out. I reach in, and pull out a chocolate coconut snowball, and I stare at it, a big stupid grin on my face. I laugh. Where did he find this? I don't know, but I do know it's the sweetest gift I've ever received, and I'm not referring to the sugar in it.

I debate on opening it, and then decide to wait and have it with Liam. I quickly pack my duffle bag, and head out to my car. I'm still grinning as I approach the city, and I glance in my rearview mirror. How far behind is Liam? I decide to make a quick trip to the store before heading to the dorm.

Once I get what I need at the store, I drive to his dorm and park in the visitor section. I sit there for a second. It's Saturday, and the guys are probably all home. My body tightens. I don't want to run into Sebastian or any of the assholes who showed up outside Boondocks that night.

I tug my phone from my bag and shoot Liam a text, asking when he'll be arriving. A few moments pass, and then he texts back and tells me to look to my left. I do and grin as I spot him coming my way. I relax in my seat and simply admire his long lean legs, his big shoulders that fill out his hoodie and the happy smile on his face as he approaches.

I open my door. "Were you here long?"

"Just pulled in." His gaze moves to my pigtails. "Jesus, Abi."

I take one in my hand. "What?"

"Are you trying to kill me?" He adjusts his pants, and the playfulness falls from his face. "You get away, okay?"

What he's really asking is if my parents gave me a hard time. "I did."

"What time do you have to be back?"

"Monday evening."

His grin widens. "Are you telling me you're mine for the entire weekend."

It's insane how much I love the idea of being his—even if only for the weekend. "I'm saying I have the entire weekend free, except for studying."

"Right." He opens my back door, snatches my backpack and duffle bag. As he eyes my duffle bag, I watch him. Is he going to bring up the snowball? When he doesn't, I lock my car and follow him inside the dorm, which is filled with guys and girls, all getting ready for the beach party.

I spot Sebastian watching us, and I turn my head and follow Liam to his room. While avoiding eye contact with Sebastian, I notice the way a few of the girls are watching me with curiosity. I get it. I'm an outsider, not someone they regularly see around here. Will they be mad that Liam is giving me attention, and not them? Will they think of me as competition, or will they want to be friends? We all know how kind college women are to one another, right?

Something niggles in the back of my brain as I step into Liam's room. He drops my bags on his small table, and when he looks at me, he asks, "What?"

"Does your father know about us?"

He swallows and reaches over his back to rub a knot in his neck. His eyes shift, and I watch him. Why is he being so cagey? Did he lie to Sebastian about that?

"That night I drove you home. I told him."

I give a slow whistle. "He couldn't have been too happy about that." He shrugs, and opens his small fridge and pulls out two water bottles. I spot the small carton of milk for my coffee and my heart thumps. He takes the lid off one bottle and hands one to me.

"Is something wrong?" I ask as he almost avoids my gaze.

"I guess he wasn't too happy about it. Parents, right?"

Okay, I don't think Liam has lied to me, and he might not be lying now. I do, however, get the sense he's not telling me something. "Are you worried about Sebastian saying something?"

"I'll deal with it if he does." He steps up to me, and rubs his finger along my arm, and a quiver goes through me. "All I know is, right now, I like being with you, Abi." There's worry in his eyes. Something is bothering him, something he doesn't want to tell me. I'll leave it for now. I have a free day, and I want to enjoy this weekend with Liam. We'll deal with real life when the weekend is over.

I glance around his room and consider where to study. "I should get some work done."

"If you want to get some work done, these have to go." He steps up to me, and pulls the elastics from my hair.

"You don't like them?" I tease.

"You know I do, and I know you have grants to fill out and I'm not going to be the guy standing in the way of your future. It's important to you, so it's important to me." A warm quiver goes through me as his big fingers unthread my hair. "Later, though." He pauses and winks. "After we get back from the beach. I want them back."

I chuckle at that, loving the way I get to him—not to mention the way he supports me—and pull my laptop from my backpack. I reach into my duffle bag to curl my hand around my snowball. I hold it out to show Liam. "I have no idea where this came from."

"Your favorite treat. Hmm, maybe it came from a secret admirer."

"Maybe, or maybe it came from someone who hates me and it's poisonous."

"I thought our story was the Capulets and the Montagues, not Snow White."

I laugh at that. "You thought that too?" He nods and I continue with, "Oh Romeo, Romeo, wherefore art thou Romeo?" He laughs as I plop down on the bed, and rip into the plastic. "Tis but thy name that is my enemy?"

"Love and hate," he says. "There's a fine line, huh?"

I eye him. "I believe the line you're thinking of is: my only love sprung from my only hate. Which means, Juliet has fallen in love with the son of her only enemy, the Montague family."

"Or in this case, the Dunn family."

A shaky laugh rumbles in my throat. "Right, if we were in love, which of course we're not."

"Right," he agrees and scrubs his chin.

I take a big gooey bite of the snowball, needing a reprieve from this strange conversation, and the intense way Liam is watching me. I mean, I don't love Liam, and he doesn't love me. We're not enemies anymore, and I like him—enough to sleep with him. There's nothing more going on here, and I'm not going to fool myself into believing there is.

Ohmigod, I'm falling for Liam.

18

LIAM

I check the time and turn to look at Abi, who's seated beside me on my bed. She's been concentrating hard, working on her grants, and while I don't want to disturb her, we should probably get going. As if sensing me looking, she lifts her head.

"How's it going?" I ask, noting her eyes are glazed like she's a million miles away.

She blinks. "Good. Just a few more essays and then I have to get recommendations from my professors." She shakes her head, clearly exasperated by the whole process. "Who knew there was so much work for a grant?"

"They should just give it to you. No one else deserves it more than you, anyway, so why put you through it?" Unable to help myself, I lean into her and press my lips to hers. Her lips are thin at first, the kiss a surprise, but she softens beneath my mouth and I moan as I savor the sweet taste of her.

She touches my cheek and I lean into her warmth as she inches back and says, "There are lots of deserving candidates, Liam."

"Nope, I'm not listening to that." I put my fingers in my ears and start humming. She grins, and pulls at my arms. I let her take my hands away, and I close my laptop.

She rubs her eyes, and glances out the window, to take in the late afternoon sun. "Is it time to go?"

There's an excitement, as well as a nervousness about her as she turns back to me, and it gives me pause. "You want to go, don't you?"

"Yeah, sure. It's just not my usual crowd." She crinkles her nose. "But Ocean will be there, so that will be nice."

"If you'd rather stay—"

"No," she answers quickly, closing her laptop and sliding off the bed. "This is a team bonding night, and I think it will be kind of fun."

"Are you going to race in a pumpkin with me?"

"Not if I don't have to," she shoots back with a laugh.

"It's fun."

"Until you drown."

I stand and laugh. "I won't let you drown. Have a little faith in me. I know my way around a boat. So do you."

"Key word being *boat*, Liam. Not pumpkin." She throws her hands up in the air. "What kind of crazy people are we here in Nova Scotia that we have pumpkin races in the ocean?"

"We're the best kind of crazy, but don't knock it until you try it." I walk around the bed and pull her to me. I slide my hands down her back and press my lips to hers. I can't seem to stop kissing her. My cock instantly thickens as she puts her hands on my chest. I have to say, it was kind of nice spending the last few hours together, working on my bed. I just like being around her and I didn't mean to spook her when I said something about love and hate. Yes, I saw the flash of panic in her eyes. She doesn't want to hear that, so I make a mental note never to mention that again.

The truth is, we are like a Shakespearean tragedy, and look how that ended. We're not, of course, star-crossed lovers, and we're not about to do anything drastic, but any kind of relationship between us is doomed to fail.

"What are you wearing to the beach?" she asks after I break the kiss.

"I'll wear jeans, and bring my swim shorts, in case the water is warm enough." She frowns, like she's considering her clothes. "Whatever you wear, make sure you don't mind getting it wet. You won't stay dry in the pumpkin."

"You say that like I've agreed to go in one." She plants a hand on her hip and looks so adorable that my heart does a little flip. "Don't put words in my mouth."

"It's not words I want to put in your mouth, babe."

Her eyes go wide, and I run my thumb over her bottom lip. "Are you talking about…"

"Food," I say. "At the beachside blowout, there's a barbecue." I grin at her as she eyes me, like she's trying to figure out if I was messing with her or not. I was. "Oh, did you think I meant…" I step up to her and press my cock against her stomach.

"Yes, I thought you meant…"

I laugh, and take her hand before I throw her on the bed and show her what I really want to put in her mouth. Later, though, I definitely plan to do that. "Come on. Let's get changed and get out of here."

Once we're dressed in jeans and sweaters, with our bathing suits and blanket packed, I grab my jean jacket in case it gets cold. "Here wear this. It could be windy."

I put my jacket around her shoulders and it's big and bulky and so damn sexy on her. It reminds me of the night I came back to my room and found her in my T-shirt. "Hmm."

She puts her arms through the sleeves. "What?"

"Maybe I'll make you wear that later and nothing else."

She grins and looks down. "Like me in your clothes huh, Dunn?"

"In and out of them. Either will do."

"Come on," she says and tugs me. My stomach grumbles as we head to the car and not entirely for food. "Hungry?" she asks.

"Always." I wag my brows at her and she rolls her eyes at my antics.

"I have something to hold you over."

"Oh?"

She reaches into her duffle bag and pulls out two meat sticks. My jaw drops. "No way. I thought you said they were nitrates holding hands."

"The ones you were eating were. These are different."

"Really." Could she be any sweeter? "You got these for me?"

"You got me a snowball. Just returning the favor."

She shrugs like it's nothing, but it doesn't feel like nothing. Was the snowball nothing, just something I saw and grabbed for her, no meaning behind it? No, it wasn't nothing. I did it because I like her and wanted to do something to make her happy.

She peels the plastic down and hands the first stick to me. I take a big bite and moan. "That's delicious. Where did you get it?"

"There's this organic pet food store just down the road. They're quite popular. I got you beef. They had chicken, but you seem like a beef guy."

"Pet food store?" I cast a glance her way and take in her grin. Then I shrug and take another bite. "Oh well, if they're organic."

"I got them at the health food store," she corrects. "I wouldn't feed you dog food, Liam."

"Try it." I hold it out to her and she reluctantly takes a bite. "Not bad, eh?"

She chews and bobs her head. "Not bad. Like pepperoni, which isn't really good for you either."

"We should get pizza later."

She laughs. "You really are hungry." She turns and takes in the streets as we drive out of town and along the shore. "Do you think the water will be warm enough to get in?"

"It's the Atlantic Ocean. Even with the hot weather we've been having, the water is never warm enough. But we're tough Canadians, so we go in anyway."

"I'm not so tough," she mumbles.

Is she kidding me? "You're tougher than you think."

She rolls one shoulder in disbelief. "I don't know about that."

"Hey, would I lie to you, Hart?"

"I don't know, would you, Dunn?" I arch my brow in disapproval as she questions my honor.

I take my eyes off the road for a second as she fiddles with her hair. She is so damn beautiful and I don't think she knows it. I know it. Heck, I've always known it. "I'm really glad you decided to come," I admit honestly.

"You know me, I'm never one to miss a good time," she jokes, and we both laugh. "How well do you know Easton?"

I glance her way and my stomach jumps. She's not interested in Easton, is she? Yes, I'm jealous. "Why?"

"I just wanted to know if he was a good guy. Watching out for Ocean. Not that she can't watch out for herself, but you know, he has a bit of a reputation. They always say he..." She stops to do air quotes. "'plays hard and fast' and I'm not sure they're talking about his on-ice plays." She crinkles up her nose. "It's not my business. She's a grown woman. I just don't want to see her hurt."

"If she knows his reputation, Abi, I think she knows what she's getting herself into."

"Yeah, you're probably right."

"You know, we've known each other forever, but she's probably still asking Easton about me."

"I think she nearly swallowed her tongue when I told her you gave me a ride and that I was staying in your dorm room. She's probably going to corner me and interrogate me."

"And what will you tell her?" I ask, as I take the winding roads leading to Queensland Beach. It's a favorite spot for the college crowd.

"Well," she begins and taps her chin as she puckers her lips. "I'll tell her you're a great hockey player and were drafted by Miami."

"What else?"

"Hmm, I'll tell her you keep your dorm room pretty tidy."

"True. And...?"

"What did I tell you about keeping your fishing to the boats?"

I laugh at that but I'm still curious. "You're basically telling her things she likely already knows."

"Oh, she knows you keep a clean room, does she? She's been in your room?"

"Yes, when we were five and she came to my house in Lunenburg. My dorm room, no."

She grins. "Okay, well, I'll tell her you're a good driver and you know about mufflers and things like that."

"More generic stuff. You're not going to tell her anything else? Like our sunrises and sunsets?"

"Nope."

"Why not?"

Her hand lands on my thigh, and as she rests it there, she says, "Those are our things, Liam. Maybe I just don't want to share them with anyone." My throat tightens. When she says things like that, I can't help but think she might want more.

"Yeah, I like that," I say quietly, a new, profound kind of intimacy blossoming between us.

"What are you going to tell your friends?"

"Nothing personal. Like you said that stuff is for us, but I will tell them you're off limits." Her brow arches. "Let's be clear here, Abi. You're here..." I stop to jab my thumb into my chest. "With me, tonight. If anyone else tries to pick you up... well, that won't happen, because you won't be leaving my side."

"Wow, so caveman and possessive."

I grin, because she's not saying it like it's a bad thing. She's always taken care of herself, never trusted anyone to do it, and I like the trust she has in me. It's not something I take lightly, and I plan to come through for her.

"Just up ahead," she points. "There's a spot between the two cars right there. Can you parallel park?"

I roll my eyes at her. "Really, Abi?"

"You're the one who said the only thing you were good at was hockey and cars."

"And sex," I say, feigning exasperation. "Why do you always forget that?"

Her light laugh fills the car, and my chest with happiness as she unbuckles, leans across the console and kisses me like she just can't help herself. My dick twitches as I put the car into reverse, and nearly swerve off the road. "Are you trying to get us killed?"

"Sorry," she chuckles and sits back. But I'm not sorry. I liked it. I ease my vehicle into the spot and kill the ignition.

"Impressive." She glances at the bonfire on the beach and her smile fades. She's nervous and trying to hide it, but she has nothing to worry about. I'm not planning to leave her side, and my buddies, the good ones on the team, are going to love her. Just not like that, or I'll have to introduce them to my fist. Her mouth drops open.

"What?"

She points to the shore. "Those are the race pumpkins?"

I follow her gaze, and take in the colorful pumpkins, painted by players and their girlfriends. "Yeah, why?"

"They're huge."

I unhook my seatbelt. "They have to be for us to fit in them."

"You mean for *you* to fit in them. That looks dangerous."

I check the side mirror before I step from the car. "We have life jackets."

"You mean *you* have a life jacket." She kicks her shoes off, and reaches into the back for her flip flops. I don't own flip flops, so I leave my sneakers on.

I reach into the back and grab our bags, meeting Abi at the front of the car. Delicious barbecue smells reach our nostrils as we cross the street and make our way along the sandy beach to where the team is setting up. There are a couple of bonfires going, and tents set up with tables, and other tents for getting changed.

As the late afternoon sun warms the sand, I see Tanner at the grill, and I drop our bags next to a pile of other bags and take Abi's hand. I lead her to Tanner and slap his back. "Two extra spicy, please," I ask when I see the sausages, and I cast Abi a playful pleading look. I'm pretty sure sausages aren't a part of her diet, but hey, when in Rome, or rather, when at Queensland Beach.

"You bet."

"Tanner, this is Abi. We grew up together in Lunenburg."

"Hey Abi." He gives her a big smile. I wasn't worried about Tanner liking her. He likes everyone and Abi is likeable. I glance around and spot Sebastian downing a beer. Great, a drunk Sebastian is not what the day calls for. Not that I think he'll do or say anything, especially while Coach Jameson is still here, but Coach won't be here all night.

I spot Coach talking with his daughter Sawyer and her fiancé Chase. Chase used to be on our team a couple of years ago and is now on the Boston Bucks NHL team. I heard he had a three-game suspension for fighting, and is still pissed about it. Sawyer is an actress and runs a small theater just outside of Halifax and she and Chase somehow make the whole long distance thing work. I never liked the idea of it, and I can only hope Abi goes to Miami, but hey, look at me getting ahead of myself. Tonight could very well be our last night together.

Tanner puts the sausages into the buns and hands them to us. "Best sausages on the planet," he assures Abi.

"Because you made it?"

"Yes."

She laughs and nudges me. "You guys don't have modesty problems, do you?"

"Hey, I heard that," Tanner jokes. "And just for that, I'm going to beat you guys in the pumpkin race."

"It's also because they're Scandinavian sausages. Tanner's family is originally from Norway. He gets them from a local Scandinavian market here, and naturally thinks they're the best." I bite into mine. "He's not wrong."

Her eyes go wide. "Oh, that's why they call you Banger. Like bangers and mash. Bangers are sausages."

His mouth drops open. "What are you talking about? People call me Banger?"

She blushes. "Oh, I'm sorry. I thought..." Her gaze goes from Tanner to me, and there's a pleading look on her face. I'm about to come to her rescue, and let her know Tanner is messing with her when Tanner nudges her.

"I'm kidding. I know they call me that. Bangers and mash are British. Bang is my last name."

"Oh, I didn't know."

Just then Isla appears, and she snuggles up to Tanner. "I'll be your partner if you don't already have one," she says to Tanner. She turns and points to one of the pumpkins. "I painted the one with the words PUCK written above a painted black hockey puck."

We all turn to see it, and I gulp, because the paint in the P dripped, and now looks like an F.

Tanner smiles at her and says nothing about the pumpkin. "Sure," he says, seeming rather indifferent to Isla. She's pretty and nice, but she doesn't strike me as Tanner's type. Who is Tanner's type, and if he's not into Isla, why did he say he was going home with her the other night? What is going on with him?

Now is not the time to ask, so I slap his back again. "Fucked," I say quietly, "That's what you're going to be when we beat you."

"Not a chance."

Isla beams and her attention turns to Abi. She lets her gaze race down the length of her and I stiffen. She'd better play nice. Last week I saw her hanging out with Conner, Sebastian's best friend. He was one of the guys responsible for Abi's ripped bag, and fuck knows what he's been saying about her.

"I'm Isla," she says, sounding friendly enough.

"I'm Abi. Nice to meet you, Isla. I love your shirt."

I glance at the loose white shirt covering a bathing suit top. I'm not sure it's anything special, not that I would know, but it's in Abi's nature to be kind.

"Thanks, I like your coat."

"It's Liam's." She waves a hand my way. "I wasn't sure if it was going to be cold or not. It's pretty warm here. I don't think I'll need it, after all," she mentions but makes no attempt to take it off.

Isla leans into Abi. "You must be very special."

"What's up, Isla?" I ask, worried about what she's going to say next.

"Why do you say that?" Abi asks before Isla can answer me.

"Because our boy Liam here never brings a girl to anything."

Abi turns and smiles at me, and I sense she likes that I'm not a man-whore like most of the other guys. But hey, I'm not going to judge them. They're single and can do whatever they want.

Abi weaves her hand around my arm, and steps closer. "My lone wolf," she whispers, and my cock thickens as the heat of her breath washes over me. I'm surprised she's being playful, or even displaying affection in public. Maybe she's tired of giving a fuck too. She puts her mouth near my ear. "Later, I plan to make you howl."

Holy shit.

19

ABIGAIL

After spending the afternoon chatting with some of Liam's teammates, eating a delicious sausage, and roasting marshmallows around the campfire, it's now time for the pumpkin races. While I'm actually having a really nice time here, I would have preferred to watch the sunset alone with Liam on the dock or on his boat. I think we're both a little introverted. But we always have tomorrow night...I think.

"Are you really doing it?" I ask Ocean as she stands beside one of the pumpkins and looks it over. I don't remember her being so adventurous, except for maybe that one time she talked me into going to the party, and look how that turned out—Sebastian starting rumors about me. But it's nice to see her trying new things, and she's not the only one.

She knocks on the side of the big pumpkin. "It seems sturdy and seaworthy."

"Says the architectural student," Easton pipes in laughing, as he throws his arm over her shoulder. She beams up at him, and it's easy to see how much she likes him. I have to admit, I am as curious to hear their story probably as much as she is to hear ours. We just haven't found the time to talk one on one. All my spare time is spent with Liam, and I want to take advantage of that because I don't know how long it will last. I just hope she knows what she's getting into with a guy who's known to *play hard and fast*.

Maybe you should ask yourself that question, Abi. Do you know what you're getting into?

Yes, I absolutely do. Okay, maybe not absolutely. But I kind of know. Sort of. Okay, I don't know what I'm doing at all, other than falling for a guy I should never be falling for. I stiffen and try to fill my lungs as they tighten.

"You okay?" Liam asks, moving closer, always attuned to my body language.

I shake myself from my reverie and smile, not wanting to admit my inner thoughts. They'd terrify him, I'm sure. "Yes, just considering how one is supposed to climb inside that thing without tipping over." I slip off my flip flop, and put my foot in the water to test it. Damn, that's cold. Let's just hope we don't end up taking a dip.

"That means you're doing it?"

I eye him suspiciously. "Was there something in that sausage? I've heard of liquid courage before, just never—"

"Sausage courage," Liam teases.

I shoot a glance toward the barbecue. "Where's Tanner? I'm sure he did something to my sausage."

He laughs and grabs two lifejackets from the pile. "Sailing a pumpkin is all kinds of fun."

"Said no marine biology student ever."

His brow arches, hope in his eyes. "Ah, but maybe said by the daughter of a fisherman, one who loves and wants to protect the ocean."

"No," I state soberly as I reluctantly take the lifejacket. I glance along the shore, and note the players laughing and pushing one another. Everyone is having fun, and I like that. "I want to protect the ocean of course. It's just, if I catapult out of that thing and land a mile from shore, the ocean isn't going to protect me."

"No, but I am, and for the record..." A cute grin plays on his lips. "...There's no ejection seat, so you won't catapult anywhere." My heart swells in my chest as I take in his sweet face, sincere eyes, and the way he just put his arm around my waist in a protective manner. If I hadn't already fallen for him, this might have been the moment. "I'll be right back. I need to grab oars."

"I'll help," Easton chimes in, leaving Ocean and me alone. Her eyes go big and I brace myself.

"Abs, what the hell?"

A small squeal catches in my throat. Honestly, Liam makes me so happy and I can't quite contain it. I feel like a silly schoolgirl with a crush, all tingly from head to toe. "I know, I know," is all I can tell her.

She shades the late day sun from her eyes and glances down the shore. "Are you two an actual couple?"

I follow her gaze, and spot Liam talking to Sebastian. My body tightens. That can't be good. I try to focus on Ocean. "No, like I said, he gave me a lift and offered me a place to sleep."

"Oh, come on. I wasn't born yesterday, and I have eyes." She holds two fingers out and points to her face. "It's easy to see there is more going on." Her big brown eyes get even bigger, like she just had a lightbulb moment. "You're sleeping with him." It's a statement, not a question and I consider my response. I don't want to keep anything from her, but I really don't want to hear that I'm making a mistake.

I kick my foot around in the sand. "I wouldn't exactly say we've been getting any sleep." Last night we stayed up until the wee hours of the morning having sex, and I was late waking up, which is why Mom and Dad are angry with me. That thought fills me with angst and guilt.

She grabs my arm. "Ohmigod."

"Wait, no, that's not true. We spent a night on his boat, and actually did sleep." I put my arms around myself, my body warming. It was so cozy with him on that boat, his big arms holding me all night. Heat begins in my core and spreads.

She stares, almost aghast. "We don't hate him anymore?"

That makes me laugh. I love how she's sides with me no matter what. "I don't think so. I actually think he's really sweet."

"My God, is the sky falling?"

"I figured you'd think something like that."

She goes quiet for a second, and her eyes narrow. My stomach tightens, because I know what she's going to ask. "Your parents?"

I spot Liam and Easton coming our way. "Look, I don't really know what is going on. We're getting along and having some fun. It can't go anywhere. So, I don't see the sense in mentioning anything to my parents."

"Right," she agrees, and frowns.

"But for now, we're just...I don't know. Getting along. What about you and Easton?" I ask quickly before they reach us. "I didn't see that coming."

"Neither did I."

The guys reach us and she doesn't say more. Liam's hand lands on my waist, and my thoughts evaporate as his warmth seeps under my skin. I catch the frown line on his forehead before he bends to set the oars in the boat.

"Have you been telling lies?" I tease when he straightens and his head rears back, his body tightening.

"What?" he asks, the line in his forehead deepening.

My throat squeezes at his strange reaction as little warning bells go off in my brain. What the hell is going on? I quickly turn and find Sebastian watching me. I can't tell from the distance, but is he smirking? My gaze jerks back to Liam and something tells me their conversation was about me. What was said?

"What's going on with Sebastian?" I ask.

He turns toward the pumpkin, and moves it around when he explains, "He asked about us. Again."

"What did you tell him?"

"I told him we were hanging out, and he needed to back the fuck off." He looks back at me, his gaze holding mine, almost like he's waiting for me to challenge that, or come up with a better explanation of what we're doing, but I don't have one. He rubs his forehead. What, is he not telling the truth about us and trying to hide evidence of it?

God, what is going on with me? Why am I being so paranoid? Liam has been nothing but sweet and honest, and he's not done anything to make me distrust him. This is on me and my own issues.

"Why is he smirking?"

"Because he's an asshole."

"Yeah, okay," I say and step up to the pumpkin. "Are we doing this or what?"

He runs his hand through his hair, momentarily agitated, before giving me a nod. "I'll hold it and you get in." He grips the pumpkin and I put my hand on his shoulder to put one foot in. Beside me, Ocean squeals as Easton jumps in and her pumpkin rocks. But she's smiling and having fun, so I'm not worried. I get one leg in and then another and sink down onto my knees.

"You good?"

"As good as I can be in a pumpkin on the water," I joke.

Liam carefully gets in and uses the oars to push us from shore. We're unstable at first, and we both hold the sides until we get our balance.

"You know we got this, Abi. No one knows their way around a boat like we do."

"You want to win, huh?" I ask. "I guess I should have realized you were competitive." When his brows pull together, I add, "A hockey player and all."

"I want to at least beat Sebastian."

"Me too."

He mumbles under his breath and hands me an oar. "Let's get to the starting line." We instinctively row in sync, because yes, we both know our way around a boat, and how to navigate one. "What we do is go from the starting line to that buoy out there. We sail around it, and come back to where we started and the first one to cross wins."

Tanner flicks water at us as we pull up beside him, and we laugh and splash him back. "That's damn cold," Liam yells.

Once everyone is lined up, a whistle blows and we all start paddling and I have to say, it is kind of fun. We bump pumpkins with Ocean and Easton, and we all holler and hold on as we become tippy. As Ocean and Easton start going around and around in a circle, we get ours under control again, and I take stock of our position.

"There's only one pumpkin ahead of us." Sebastian and some girl I don't know. "Let's get them," I say and Liam grins.

"I'm not the only one with a competitive nature."

We work together, and soon enough we're flying across the water and circling the buoy. "Just a bit harder," I yell to Liam.

We both dig in harder as we race toward Sebastian and the girl I don't know. Before we can pass them, Ocean and Easton come out of nowhere and bang into us, sending us straight into Sebastian. We tip and the next thing I know, Liam and I are in the freezing cold water, and those watching from the shore, begin to clap and laugh and I know all of this is going to be online at any moment. Thank God, my parents don't do social media. That doesn't mean someone won't show them, though.

We're close enough to shore that I can touch the bottom, but swimming is faster than walking so that's what I do. Liam swims beside me as our teeth chatter. "I'm sorry," he yells.

"Not your fault. It's Ocean and Easton who are going to pay," I tell him, but it's all rather funny, and horribly cold.

We reach the shore and we're dripping wet, and people run to us with towels and blankets. We shrug out of our lifejackets, and we're led to a big bonfire to warm up for a second.

"Ohmigod, Abi, I'm so sorry," Ocean says as she comes running up to me.

"Where'd you get your license?" Liam jokes after Easton slaps him on the back.

"Sorry, man, lost control. Don't have a license like you do. Hey, you think with your experience you could have gotten out of my way?"

As the guys joke with one another, Ocean rubs my arms. "Are you hurt?" she asks, as she looks me over and from somewhere behind me, I'm pretty sure I hear someone whisper fish bait.

My mind goes back to the night Sebastian threatened to dunk me before he would fuck me. The blood in my veins turns cold, but it's not because I'm soaking wet. I don't want to look around to see Sebastian or any of his friends making fun of me.

"Hey," Liam says, and pulls me to him, clearly thinking my sudden change in demeanor is because I'm cold.

"Let's get changed." I want to get away from those assholes. If Liam overhears them, it will only lead to trouble, and with their coach here, I don't want that. I don't want to be the reason Liam gets benched or kicked off the team.

"You guys can get changed in the tent," Jesse, Liam's teammates tells us, and Liam runs and gets our bags from the pile. He puts his arm around me, and we duck into one of the tents for privacy.

With his arm that's around me, he pulls me close. "I didn't quite see things going down that way."

I realize he's upset with himself. He told me he wouldn't let anything happen to me, and then we tipped. I go up on my toes and kiss him. "At least Ocean and Easton won, and hey, it was kind of refreshing."

A tiny, sincere smile tugs at his perfect mouth as he makes a fist and nudges my chin. "Thanks for being a good sport."

Any other time, I might have hated a cold dunk. If I were with Liam, I might even skydive, and I don't like heights. Okay, maybe that's pushing it. I inch back and struggle to get his coat off me.

"Let me help." I turn around and he peels the coat from my shoulders and uses a towel to wipe my neck and chest before helping me with the rest of my clothes. It's so odd, getting naked with him in a tent like this, while his team is just outside.

I pull on my dry clothes quickly, and then help Liam out of his wet clothing. "I like getting naked with you," he grumbles, as I tug on his jeans, struggling to get them down.

"I don't hate it," I tease. "Do you have to hang out here longer or do you want to head back to the dorm?"

He grins and grips his pants, helping me lower them. "Actually, before we go back there's something I want to show you."

I laugh as he shimmies his pants down. "I bet there is."

20

LIAM

"**W**hat do you think?" I ask. "As good as a sunrise, or sunset?"

Abi's eyes dim with happiness as she takes in the view before her, and I brush her hair back, as her lips part. "It's so big. I never really took time to admire it like this before. I could stay here and just appreciate it all night." I turn and follow her gaze, taking in the big, full moon high overhead. "You knew it was a full moon tonight?" she asks.

"Yeah, I thought you'd enjoy it."

"You're right. I did."

Off in the distance, the party is still going hard, and I'm glad I found a quiet spot on the rocks away from the others to enjoy the full moon with Abi. Sebastian and his goons have been drinking all night, and even after I explained—okay, lied to him about my relationship with Abi—I don't want her near him. He might open his big mouth and say something I don't want Abi to hear.

She takes a big breath and her body relaxes as she puts her hand on my knee. "Thanks for this."

"So, out of the three, sunrise, sunset, and full moon, which is the best view?" I ask.

"Out of those three, I'd have to say sunrise is still my favorite." She puts her hand over mine. "There's another view, though. One that might trump them all."

"Oh, yeah?"

Her grin is playful. "Yeah."

"Are you going to tell me," I ask and laugh as she lays her head on my shoulder.

"I don't know."

"You don't know?" Her soft chuckles curl around me. "Why not?"

"I think maybe I'd rather show you."

"Okay, show me then."

She stands, and reaches for my hand. I give it to her. "We have to go back to your place for that view."

I pick up our bag, and my cock twitches. "I like the sound of that." We walk along the shore, and up to the road where I parked along the side of the secondary highway. Back at my car I toss our bags in as Abi climbs into the passenger seat. I slide in beside her and she leans into me and gives me a kiss on the cheek.

"What was that for?"

"The full moon."

"I'm not really in charge of the full moon, Abi," I tease. "I wish I was, though." She sinks back into her seat, lethargic, but happy. "If I get a kiss for a full moon, what would I get for a shooting star?"

"You'd have to show me one first."

"Hmm," I say. "I might have to get you back on the boat. I seem to see many in the night sky over the water." I start the car and turn the heat on as the cooler night air wraps around us. Abi might still be chilled from our dunk, and I don't want her to get sick. I can't imagine what her parents would do if she was sick and unable to work every evening. I guess they'd have to figure it out, just like they'll have to figure out what they're going to do if she goes to Miami. I hate that she feels guilt about wanting a future.

It's funny, and she was right when she said something about our guilt, her wanting to go and me wanting to stay. I pull onto the road and head back to the city.

"Are you and Ember close?" Abi asks.

"Yeah, we are," I answer, not sure why she's bringing up my sister. "She thinks I'm too overprotective, though."

"I can see that."

"Hey," I shoot back.

"What? I'm not saying there's anything wrong with that. You protect those you care about, Liam. That's nice."

I steal a sideways glance and find her watching me. Does she know that's why I want to protect her, because I care about her?

"She's going to be at the academy next year," I grumble.

"You don't like that idea?"

"I just don't want her around any of the hockey players. You know what they're like."

She stares at me like intelligence has spent a lifetime chasing me and I've always been faster. "You know *you're* a hockey player, right?"

I snort. "You know what I mean."

"I'm sure she'll make good choices. I don't think all hockey players are players. Tanner Bang," she says, adding emphasis to his last name. "He seems really nice."

"Stay away from him," I warn.

Her head jerks back at my sudden outburst. "What, why?"

Oh, because I'd be jealous. "His nickname is Banger, Hart. Need I say more?" I'm joking of course. He's a good guy. A bit brooding at times, but a good guy, nonetheless.

"He's called Banger because of his last name," she shoots back. "Although it was funnier when I thought it stemmed from his love of sausage." She immediately cringes. "Wait, that came out wrong."

I groan. "Can we not talk about Tanner's sausage?"

She laughs and it fills my chest with happiness. "What will you do if Ember falls for one of the guys on the team?"

Right now, Ember seems more interested in my best friend Josh than any other guy. I grip the steering wheel harder. She's too young for him, and the idea of my best friend and my sister...no...just no. "She's too smart for that."

She whacks me. "Hey."

"What?"

"Are you saying I'm not smart?"

"Wait, what…" My heart hammers as I cast her a glance. Is she saying what I think she's saying? Should I ask? Before I can stop myself, I blurt out, "Are you saying you've fallen for me?"

Her smile instantly flatlines, and her entire body tenses. "No, no. that's not what I'm saying," she corrects quickly. "I just mean she's a smart girl and not all guys on the team are players, and it could happen."

"Can we go back to talking about Tanner's sausage?" She laughs out loud, and puts her hand on my thigh. "Or we could talk about what might trump the sunrise, sunset and full moon."

"We will, when we get home."

Home.

Funny, I kind of like the sound of that.

"I'd rather talk about it now," I tell her.

"Wow, I didn't realize you had zero patience, Liam."

She's wrong about that. I have lots of patience. Hell, I waited far too many years wanting her. I honestly still can't believe she's been in my bed, and I've been in hers. It's all too good to be true and you know what they say about that. My gut tightens and I swallow.

"Are you sulking?" she asks, mistaking my reaction.

"Maybe," I joke.

"We're almost there," she announces as we approach our Halifax exit. I ease off the highway and take her hand in mine. I drive through the city streets and park in my spot at Storm House. The place is quiet, with most of the guys still at the beach. I spot Easton's car. I guess he and Ocean had other plans for tonight as well. Abi seemed a little less worried about her friend after she met Easton. I hope the guy doesn't hurt Ocean.

I gather up our things and take her hand, leading her into the building and straight to my room. Once inside, I drop our bags and pull her into my arms, running my hand up her back to hold her to me.

"Finally, I've got you alone."

"My lone wolf," she teases.

"What was that about making me howl?" She reaches down and places her hand over my dick, and I give a little howl, which makes her laugh, as my gaze zeroes in on her mouth. "I've been dying to ravage this mouth like a hungry wolf all fucking night."

She takes a fast breath, heat turning her cheeks pink, and my dick thickens. I tug on her sweater. Her hand falls from my dick as she lifts her arms and lets me peel her clothes over her head. I release her bra and it falls to the floor. I stand back for a moment, just wanting to admire her perfection.

"This is better than any of those views," I murmur as my body throbs for more and my mouth goes dry.

A little laugh catches in her throat as I reach over my shoulder, grip the back of my hoodie, and peel it off. My T-shirt follows, and she leisurely lets her eyes roam down my body.

Once she's finished admiring me, she steps up to me, drops to her knees and unbuttons my pants.

She pulls them and my boxers down, much easier now that I'm dry, and I kick them away. As I stand before her, naked, she takes my swollen dick into her small palm. She gives me a little squeeze and moans, the heat from her breath arousing me even more. After a long slow lick around my crown, she goes back on her heels.

"This is the view I like best," she says, her voice so full of need, my dick throbs, aching for her mouth. I take my cock into my hand as she sits back on her knees and opens her mouth. I inch closer and tap her bottom lip with the tip of my dick before I feed it to her. As she devours my dick, her moans of pleasure vibrate all the way to my aching balls. Pleasure wraps around me and teases my nerve endings. She sucks me deep and I grip the back of her head as my body shakes.

I clench my teeth as her head bobs, taking me to her throat, then retreating repeatedly. When I'm close to blowing, I pull her free and lift her to her feet. I turn her so her back is pressed to my chest and walk her across my small room until I reach the long mirror on my wall. She moans as I stand her in front of it, my hands all over her body.

"How about this view?" I ask, as I run my palms over her breasts, stopping to play with her nipples. She watches me with lust-imbued eyes and wets her lips as I tease her pretty pink buds. I slide one hand lower, and she whimpers as I prod her feet wider apart.

She wiggles against my throbbing cock, and I use two fingers to spread her wet lips, exposing her needy little pussy in the mirror. "Liam," she murmurs, her body moving against mine as I look at the gorgeous view before me.

I slide a finger inside her and she whimpers, her sex muscles tightening around my finger as I go deep and hold still. "Fuck my finger, babe."

She begins to rock her hips back and forth and it's pure fucking torture watching my finger disappear into her body and come out soaking wet. My dick throbs and leaks against her back, wanting in on the action.

"You are so beautiful, Abi."

Her eyes lift and find mine in the mirror and my heart pounds as she fucks my finger. I add a second for a snug fit and her juices soak me as she grinds against my palm and takes what she needs. My God, she is amazing. I can't even believe the years we lost together because of our feuding parents. But I don't want to think about that right now or how that could come between what is blossoming between us.

"Liam," she cries out as her muscles clench in the most carnal way, and I stop breathing as she lets go, so I can etch the gorgeous sight before me in my brain. I keep my fingers inside her and let her ride out the waves and when her body stops spasming, I pull my fingers out. I turn her and back us both up until I reach the bed, and sit on the edge.

As she stands before me, press warm kisses to her body and breathe in the scent of her skin as I kiss her stomach. She holds my shoulders and puts her knees on the bed, and I glance up at her, knowing exactly what she wants. I reach around her, grab a condom and quickly sheathe myself.

"Babe," I whisper as I take my dick into my hand and hold it as she moans and lowers her body until my cock is sliding into her tight opening. "Fuck yeah."

"Oh God, Liam," she moans as she slowly sinks down, burying my dick inside her. She puts her arms around me and I hold her hips. Fuck, I love taking her like this. I move her up and down on my dick, and her tight pussy massages the long length of me until I'm panting and doing a shitty job of keeping my orgasm at bay.

"I'm close babe."

"Let me feel you," she murmurs.

I move her body, working it harder and faster over my cock, and she whimpers, throwing her head back. She moves with me, lifting and lowering herself, and as she milks my raging hard-on, I reach up her back, grip her hair and tug it.

Her pussy clenches around me, and a new kind of intimacy grows between us. Does she feel it too? Christ, it's all-consuming, all-encompassing, making nothing else in the world matter but this woman on top of me. I can't think, I can't breathe, all I can do is feel and what I'm feeling is so damn intense and beautiful I don't ever want this to end.

"Fuck, Abi."

"Liam," she cries out and a gush of heat spills from her body, searing my cock into submission. I let go, and come into the condom high inside her tight channel. I press my mouth to her throat and kiss her as we both succumb to the pleasure.

"Babe," I murmur, no blood left in my brain as she continues to take deep gulping breaths. "Love this...love you."

21

ABIGAIL

The morning light shines in Liam's room, and I blink against the bright rays as last night's memories pull me wide awake. Did Liam say he loved me? I slowly turn my head and my heart beats a little faster when I find him asleep beside me, one arm on his forehead. His blanket hovers around his hips, giving me the perfect opportunity to admire his gorgeous, hard body.

God, I still can't believe I'm having sex with the guy I've hated for years—that my family still hates. But holy God, the sex is so good—addictive, really—and I'd be lying if I said I didn't want more. The problem is, I'm not sure I'm talking about sex when I think...more.

But he couldn't have said he loved me, right? I was gasping from my orgasm, and my heart was pounding in my ears, so I probably heard him wrong. If I didn't, it likely spilled out because the blood had left his brain and he wasn't thinking straight.

As if sensing me watching him, his eyes open. He smiles when he sees me, and rolls to his side to face me. I'm about to snuggle in when his smile turns shaky, and his chest begins to rise and fall rapidly. I tense as his dark eyes narrow, like he's recalling details from last night, and that he might have said some things he shouldn't have said.

Not wanting to have that conversation with him and ruin a beautiful night of sex, and not wanting to hear an apology—heck, I want him to think I never heard it—I say, "For the record, I saw shooting stars last night."

He angles his head, the hard, worried lines of his face smoothing out, as one hand goes to my arm. He lightly runs his fingers over my skin. "Oh yeah?"

"Yeah, and you were responsible."

He grins, clearly understanding where I'm going with this. "I was, huh?" He glances past my shoulders to the window. "I guess I forgot to close the curtains."

"Nothing to do with that."

"No?" he asks.

"No, I saw shooting stars each time you brought me to orgasm." I moan as my body warms, and he laughs and pulls me to him, kissing me on the top of my head as I snuggle into the crook of his arm.

"So what do I get for that?" he asks.

"Tell me what you want."

"Head outside and spend the day with you." he answers quickly, like he'd already been giving that a thought.

I lift my head to see him, loving the idea of spending the day with him too. Here I thought he'd be asking for something sexual, but no, he wants to spend the day with me, and my heart does a little happy dance, but then I remember, I should probably get home.

"What do you want to do outside?"

"Head up to Citadel Hill for a picnic." I glance at the clock. "But if you have to go?"

I think about the cleaning that is done at Boondocks on Sunday. I always help get the place scrubbed before we open on Monday. Would it hurt if I was a little bit late? "I think that sounds like a fun idea."

A smile lights up his face. "Why don't you shower, and I'll run out and get some things at the market."

I nod, a bubble of excitement welling up inside me. He pulls last night's clothes on, grabs his keys, and tosses me a fast glance before he heads out. I step into the bathroom, and turn on the shower, my body gloriously sore from all the sex. I adjust the spray, climb in, and use his body wash. I kind of like the idea of smelling like Liam all day.

I take my time washing up, lingering longer in the shower than I normally would. I don't expect Liam back right away. When I finally turn the water off, I grab a towel from the hook and wrap it around myself. When I hear the door opening and footsteps on the floor, I hurry out, only to stop dead when I find Sebastian standing there, staring at me.

I tighten the towel and walk toward the bed, putting it between us. His gaze moves down the length of me and the hairs on the back of my neck stand up. "Liam will be right back," I tell him. "I thought you were him, actually."

"Oh yeah," he says with a smirk that sends shivers down my spine. I glance around for my clothes and notice the way his gaze is following mine.

"Did you need something?"

His head jerks back to me. "Just looking for my buddy."

Buddy?

Since when have Liam and Sebastian been buddies?

"Is there something I can help you with?" God, I shouldn't have worded it that way. Now he's wetting his bottom lip in a disgusting, sexual way. "Like I said, Liam will be back in a second. I think I hear him now."

He smirks, like he knows I'm lying and that I'm frightened to be here with him, half dressed—and that he has the upper hand.

"I was going to see if he wanted to hit the gym, but I can see he's busy *hitting* something else." The way he says hitting, his gaze dropping to the bottom of my towel, turns my stomach. I snatch up my clothes, ready to bolt to the bathroom and lock the door, when I spot movement behind Sebastian. My entire body tenses, fight or flight kicking in. If it's one of his asshole friends, I could be in trouble, again. Although Liam warned them, and I'm in his room, so maybe I'm okay. Wow, look at me giving Sebastian the benefit of the doubt.

"What the fuck?" Liam pushes past Sebastian, drops a brown paper bag onto his table, and stands between the two of us. I nearly cry with relief. "How did you get in here?" he challenges Sebastian, as he widens his legs and fists his hands at his sides.

Sebastian's demeanor completely changes, and he stands up a little straighter. "Door was unlocked. I just opened it. Thought you were in here. Didn't know you had company." Oh, I'm company now, am I? Not someone Liam was *hitting*. Bully that he is, he's not so brave when someone bigger and stronger is around.

"I was sure I locked it." Liam glances at me, worry on his face. I try to remember if he locked it and can't. I was in a hurry to get to the shower and he was in a hurry to get to the market. "I'm sorry, Abi."

"I'm going to change." I practically run to the bathroom and shut the door. Their voices are muffled as they talk and then I relax a bit when the dorm room door closes with a loud thunk. A moment later, knuckles rap on my door.

"Abi."

I open the door and Liam looks me over. "I'm sorry. I must not have locked the door."

"You didn't know Sebastian was going to burst in."

"He's never done that before."

"He somehow thinks you two are buddies now."

"Yeah," is all he mutters, his eyes narrowed as they lock on me. "Did he say anything to you?"

"Just that he wanted to see if you wanted to hit the gym."

"Anything else?"

"No." I take in his stiff jaw, and the way he's grinding his teeth. "Are you worried that he called me names again?"

"Did he?"

"No." What he said wasn't nice, but he didn't call me fish bait.

"He didn't say anything else?"

What is going on here? My mind races back to the pumpkin races when they were having what seemed like a very private chat. "What do you think he said to me?" I ask, my heart picking up pace as my brain runs through different scenarios. God, here I go again, letting my mom and dad get into my head, so I automatically think the worst of Liam.

"I don't know. He needs to mind his own fucking business."

"About us?"

"About everything," he responds, his voice angry, his hand practically shaking as he scrubs his face. A second later, he lets out a breath and puts his hands on my arms, leans in and gives me a kiss. "I'm sorry. I'm just...he just...pisses me off. I didn't mean to sound angry with you." His warm gaze moves over my face. "Are you sure you're okay?

I'm a little shaken, but otherwise I'm fine. "I'm okay. Why don't you have your shower, and let's get outside. We don't need to let Sebastian ruin our day."

He nods, walks around me, and starts stripping off his clothes. I drop my towel and tug on a T-shirt, hoodie and my yoga pants as he climbs into the shower. As the room begins to steam up, I head into the other room, and glance into the brown paper bag sitting on his small table. I've never been on a picnic before, except with my grade three class. This seems rather romantic. Is Liam trying to be romantic? Is what's going on between us about more than sex? God, I want that, I truly do, but how can we make it happen? Then again, I might be reading more into this, and maybe he does this with all his girlfriends. Not that I think he's had a lot of girlfriends.

I grab my comb and run it through my hair, and when I get a knot and it pulls, my body comes alive. My God, am I going to spend the rest of my life getting turned on while combing my hair?

I check my phone for messages, and don't find any from my folks. I'll have a quick picnic with Liam and then head back. The shower turns off and I sit on Liam's bed and go through some school emails. He comes from the bathroom, completely naked, and I laugh—even though there's nothing funny about a naked Liam. I just love how comfortable he is in his own skin, and around me.

"Something funny, Hart?"

"Nothing funny at all," I respond, trying to wipe the grin off my face as my body heats up.

"What, you've never seen a naked man before?" he jokes.

Grinning, I gesture with my hands, waving them up and down at his body. "Not that kind of naked," I admit as I admire all six feet of hardness.

"Wow, I need to keep you around." He bends down and kisses me. "You're good for my ego."

"Your ego needs no stroking," I inform him and he groans loudly in response. I angle my head, take in his tight jaw. "Was it something I said?"

"You can't talk about stroking when I'm standing before you naked, half fucking hard."

I glance at his thickening dick and tap my chin. "Well, I could talk about it, or I could put my money where my mouth is."

I'm about to slip off the bed, and put my mouth where his cock is when he stops me.

"As much as I want that, and believe me I do, I promised you a picnic, and we need to get out of this dorm and into the sun." I blink up at him, a little surprised. "But I'd like a rain check."

I laugh at that. "Of course, you do."

"Jesus, Abi, I'm a red-blooded male, so yeah." He shakes his head and starts pulling on clothes. "What the hell is wrong with me?" he jokes. "Maybe I should get checked for a concussion." Under his breath, he adds, "Who the hell turns down a blow job?" More grumbling and then, "I really hope it fucking rains soon."

I can't help but grin, and while I wanted to drop to my knees —I love bringing him pleasure—I am looking forward to spending time with him outside the bedroom. He's fun to be with, and I love getting to know him.

Love.

There's that word again.

Heck, maybe for him this isn't all about sex, Abi. Maybe he did say he loved you.

Maybe he's not the only one with a concussion.

22

LIAM

I take the last piece of cheese and hold it out to Abi. She takes a bite and moans around it. "Delicious."

"Got it at the market. You know, this cheese is made by Dane's family in Bass River."

"Dane is on the team?"

I laugh. "Was. I should have explained that. You've heard of The Gouda guy."

She nods. "Wow, that's amazing."

"From what I understand, Dane is opening his own artisanal cheese shop, and a biking trail."

"Weird combination," she says as she washes the cheese down with a big drink of water.

"Apparently, both of those things are his passion."

She nods. "I love it. Wait, what do you mean was? He's no longer on it? He doesn't want to make the NHL?"

"Right."

"Oh wow. I thought all you guys wanted that."

"Nope."

"Well, I'm happy for him. Everyone should follow their passion. Which reminds me, I need to get my grant paperwork in order. I already emailed my professors for recommendations."

I brush a crumb off her face as she recaps the water and begins to clean up, putting the garbage back into the brown paper bag. "Now, if we could only incorporate commercial fishing into your NHL career."

"Ah, can't see that happening, Abi. But that doesn't mean I can't have a boat someday." It might not be the same, but it'll be enough.

"Miami is the perfect place to have a boat." She drops back onto the grassy hill and stares up at the sky and I mimic her position. Off in the distance, dogs bark at the park, and a few people are flying kites. Up above, the clouds form shapes, and I study them. The historic Citadel Hill often fills up with families on the weekends, along with the expected tourists, and oddly enough, fills me with a sense of loss, and longing.

"Want to come on my boat in Miami?"

"If you drive a boat anything like you drive a pumpkin, that's a big fat no."

"Hey, that's not fair." I nudge her. "We were killing it until Ocean and Easton hit us."

"Yes, well as a good captain, you should have been able to avoid that."

"Come out with me tonight, I'll show you how good of a captain I am."

She sits back up and checks the time. "I'm not sure I can." She glances around the hill and smiles when she sees a young boy playing with his dad. "I should probably get back. I have work at Boondocks."

"Okay." I push to my feet, and hold one hand out to her. She takes it and gathers up the garbage after I pull her up. We head down the hill and back to Storm House. Our steps are unhurried, like neither of us want the day to be done, but reality calls and I should get back home too. I have one thing to do before I go, though, so I won't be able to follow behind her.

We reach Storm House and after we gather her bags from inside, I put them in her trunk and stand by her door. "Sunset?" I ask.

"We'll always have sunset," she tells me and I lean into the car and give her a kiss. "When do you head back?"

"I have a thing," I say and randomly point over my shoulder. "It's a team thing we do."

"Oh, okay, don't let me keep you. I'll talk to you later." I tap the roof of her car and back up, standing in the parking lot until she drives out of sight. Once she rounds the corner, I start walking to the children's hospital, where the guys and I often go on the weekend.

I walk by the commons and a wayward soccer ball comes my way. I kick it back to the kids playing and stand there for a moment to watch them as they go through drills. Twenty minutes later, I get to the children's hospital and start visiting with the patients. They're always happy to see me, and they love all my hockey stories. They're very excited that I've been drafted by Miami. Today I'll be visiting with Trent.

I walk into his room, and his mom is sitting beside him on the bed, and they're reading a book. Trent glances up at the sound of my boots and my heart hitches as a smile lights up his face.

"Liam," he calls out, and runs his hand over his hairless head. Childhood leukemia fucking sucks and I'm happy I can put a smile on his face, and the faces of a few of the other kids here, whenever I get the chance.

"Hey buddy," I say, and cross the room. His mom stands and gives me a grateful smile. She knows our visits are something Trent looks forward to during this difficult time in his young life.

"I'm going to grab a coffee," his mom Belinda announces and gives me a wink. "Trent has something for you."

She leaves and I grab the big bulky chair in the corner and pull it up to his bed. Beside him, machines beep and he moves carefully, not wanting to disturb the IV in his arm and it fucking breaks my heart.

"How have you been, bud?" I ask. He shifts on the bed, and it showcases his weak body. "Let me help you."

"Nope, got it." I grin. He's an independent little guy and I pray to God he beats this and is able to grow up and play hockey like he wants. He hands me a picture, and my throat tightens as tears prick my eyes.

"Hey, is that me?" I ask, trying to keep my voice normal as I point to the hockey player with Miami written on his jersey.

"Yup, and that's me." He taps the paper, jabbing at the boy in the picture that's not that much smaller than me, and he too has Miami on his jersey. I love that he sees himself bigger than he is.

"I can see the resemblance," I tell him. "Look at those muscles." He gives me a big toothy grin, and I reach into my hoodie pocket. "I have something for you too."

"What?" he asks, and sits up a little straighter.

I pull a puck from my pocket and hand it over. A wide smile fills his face, and I tell him, "That's a winning puck from our last game."

He turns it over and over in his small little hand. "It's signed."

"Yeah, a lot of the guys signed it for you."

He blinks, as his eyes pool with tears. "Thank you, Liam. When I play, I want to score, a lot."

"You will, buddy."

As he continues to admire the puck, my entire body tightens. This little guy really looks up to me. Many here at the hospital do and dammit, I don't ever want to disappoint them. I don't want to disappoint anyone, actually, my father included. Right now, he doesn't really know much, but if he found out how much time we were spending together, and I wasn't with her to get dirt on her family, he'd likely lose his shit. Patience isn't one of his virtues and the man can hold a grudge. I'm still not sure what really went on with him and the Hart family, but it was from a long time ago, and he's not over it.

I swallow as my throat goes dry. I have to play hockey for kids like Trent. I want to give them hope, and a future to look forward to. I'm not here on any type of scholarship, though I'm not sure my father would really cut my funding. He wants me in the NHL. That's his dream. Still, I shouldn't take a chance, and that means I should probably end things with Abi.

I take a fast breath, my heart pounding a little faster. Did I really tell her I loved her last night? I push back in the chair as my blood runs cold. Jesus, how could I have been so stupid. I'm not sure if she heard me, but if she did, she clearly didn't want to talk about it. *And why is that, Liam?* Oh, because this relationship doesn't have a future. Which means I shouldn't drag it out.

I'm so lost in thought, I miss what Trent just said to me. "What's that, buddy?" I ask, and give him my full focus.

He pats the side of the bed. "Do you want to read with me?"

I stand just as his student nurse comes in. "Hey Trent," she says, as she does something to one of the machines. I hear a few beeps and then she turns her attention to me and offers a big smile. "Nice to see you again, Liam."

I perch on the edge of the bed. "You too, Gabby."

She hugs a clipboard to her chest with one hand and twirls her ponytail in her other. It reminds me of the way I pulled Abi's hair and how much she liked it. Jesus, I can't think about that right now.

"Great game last week," she tells me, lingering close to me.

"Thanks." Honestly, I don't know her well, only from my visits and I spotted her outside the rink a few times after a home game. Like I said, I usually grab a fast beer with the guys and disappear.

"Look what he brought me," Trent pipes up and her eyes go big.

She focuses on the puck. "That is so nice."

Trent hugs it. "I'm going to take really good care of it."

"I know you will," she says, and turns back to me. "I'm looking forward to your game on Friday."

"Thanks for coming out and supporting us."

"Tanner was in for a visit the other day." She leans in. "I think my friend has a crush on him."

I chuckle. "Who doesn't?"

She shrugs, writes something in a clipboard, and casually mentions, "I was thinking, maybe the four of us could do something after the game."

The first word to pop into my brain is, no. The only girl I want to be with is Abi, but I'd just come to the conclusion that I need to break things off with her.

"I...uh..."

"Here." She scribbles something on a piece of paper and hands it to me. I glance at the sticky note, and see her name and number. "Text me after the game. We'll figure the details out then."

"Yeah, okay," I say, my stomach in knots as I tuck the paper into the pocket of my hoodie. I should text her, should double date with Tanner and her friend, but it feels horribly wrong. But maybe it will help me move past Abi. Fuck knows, we can't keep doing what we're doing.

She leaves the room and Trent giggles.

"What's up, little man?"

"I think she likes you," he tells me as I shift to sit beside him. "Is she going to be your girlfriend?"

"Nah, we're just friends."

He sets the puck on his lap and opens the book he'd been reading with his mom. "I don't have a girlfriend."

"Lots of time for that."

"I bet when I play hockey, I'll have a lot of girlfriends."

"I bet you will." I point to the book, not wanting to talk about girlfriends, or what a mess my life is in, because that's exactly what I want Abi to be, and it can never happen. "Why don't you read to me?"

I sit back and listen to the story, as he puts his finger on the page and moves it as he reads along. His mother comes back with a coffee for both of us and I graciously accept it. I'm tired from last night and I still have the drive back home to Lunenburg. I could stay the night here at the dorm. If I did, I wouldn't be able to see the sunset with Abi. That's a good thing, though, considering I need to end this with her—not just for my sake, but for hers too. She doesn't need the shit her parents would give her if they ever found out. Jesus, they're hard enough on her as it is.

I flip the plastic tab back on the coffee cup and take a much-needed sip. Belinda knows how I like my coffee. She always gets me one when I visit. She pushes the big clunky chair back and takes a seat. Worry lines frame her eyes as she smiles at her son, and I can't even imagine what this family is going through. It makes all my problems trivial and makes me want to be a star player in the NHL all the more. Not for me, but for all those counting on me.

Soon little Trent grows tired, and his eyes begin to slip shut. Belinda stands and takes the book from his hand. I slide off the bed and fix the blankets around Trent as he sinks into his pillow.

"Thanks for coming, Liam," she says quietly. "Your visits make all the difference in the world. He talks about you non-stop and is determined to grow up and play for Miami."

"Good, I can't wait to play with him. But I'll be an old man by then," I joke.

She puts her hands on my cheeks. "You're a good man. Your parents must be so proud of you."

"They are," I tell her, matching her low tone. Am I proud of them? Honestly, I'm not sure I am. I'm not sure wanting to destroy the Harts, to secure their land, or for whatever reason my father wants a vengeance, makes me proud of them. "I'll see you in a week."

"Take care," she whispers. "Oh wait, don't forget this."

She hands me the drawing, and I smile as I walk to the door. I fold the picture and put it in my hoodie pocket, my fingers connecting with the sticky note. I turn back. "Is he doing okay?" I ask, always a little afraid to do so.

"He's doing good, Liam."

"He's a great kid."

"Thank you."

I head outside and walk back to the dorm, my mood a little low as I grab my books from my room and jump in my car, even though everything inside me urges me to stay in the city tonight.

With the plan to end things with Abi on my mind, I drive through the city and hit the highway. I turn on the music to drown out my thoughts, and when I make it about halfway home, I spot a car on the side of the road—a car that looks suspiciously like Abi's.

Fuck.

I slow and pull in behind it, and Abi jumps from the car. "Abi, are you okay?"

She nods, but looks a bit frazzled. "I don't know what happened. It started making a funny noise again. I thought I should pull over."

"How long have you been here?"

"Not that long," she answers, but I do the math and even though I'm not good with numbers, I realize she's been here a while.

"Did you call anyone to come get you?"

She shrugs. "I don't have CAA or anything, and my parents are busy on Sundays."

Jesus fucking Christ, I hate that she has no one to count on, and didn't I say I wanted to be the guy who was there for her?

"What were you going to do?"

She shrugs, almost sheepishly. "I guess I knew you'd be by, eventually."

I tug my phone from my pocket. "Did you text?"

"No."

"Abi, Jesus." A flash of anger grips my gut to know she was out here, all alone, not knowing who to turn to. "I want you to know you can count on me, okay?"

"I know you had things to do, and I didn't want to interfere." The trust and warmth in her gaze sucks the air from my lungs and fills me with a need I've never quite felt before. She steps closer and takes my hand. "That's why I waited. I knew you'd come along."

I stare at her and my heart hammers. How the fuck did I think I could walk away from her and end this? I fucking love her. I've always loved her. That first day on the playground in elementary school, when I saw her in pig tails, I knew I was a goner. But how and where do we go from here? I really don't fucking know, but I have to fight for her...for us.

23

ABIGAIL

I steal a glance at Liam as we watch the tow truck pull onto the highway, towing my car behind it. I'm so happy Liam came along before dark. I wasn't really worried I'd be stranded. I knew he'd recognize my car and could probably diagnose the problem, maybe even fix it. I just wasn't sure how long he'd be, and he could have decided to stay in the city overnight.

If it came to that, I would have called a tow truck myself, but Liam jumped all over it when he realized there was a suspension problem, whatever that means, and it was too dangerous to drive. He was right, though. He does know a lot about cars. Just because he's not a great student doesn't mean he's stupid. I hate that word, hate that he even uses it, or thinks that way about himself.

"I'll pay you back," I say again, and he nods. He wouldn't let me use my credit card, and insisted on putting the charge on his. I'm a little short on cash after getting my muffler fixed. He didn't seem to mind covering for me. That's what friends do, right?

Friends...ah, but is that what we still are?

"I'll drive you for the next couple days, until your car gets fixed. What nights do you have to work?"

"Things are getting slower with the season coming to an end, so we're only going to be open Monday to Wednesday evenings for October. It'll pick up again in November with lobster season."

"I have a game Monday and Friday night. I'm going to be late. How about Monday you take my car home, and I'll crash at the dorm. You can drive it back in the morning."

I glance around his car, not sure if that's a good idea or not. It's an expensive vehicle, and I'd be terrified of dinging it. I ding mine all the time, but it doesn't much matter.

"Thanks, but that's okay. You need your car. I'll find another way home."

"What I need is for you to be safe and to have a way back and forth between home and school." I don't miss the hint of anger in his voice as I glance straight ahead. "Hey," he murmurs, his voice softer. "I'm not upset with you. You just finished saying you knew you could count on me."

"I can." My stomach twists. I don't mean to upset him. It's just not easy for me to lean on others. "I just don't like to ask for things."

"I know that, and you didn't ask. I offered. You're taking my car, and if I have to duct tape your hands to this steering wheel, I will."

I shake my head and laugh. "Extreme."

I stare at his handsome face in the dim dashboard light as he turns my way. "You'll take it, then?"

"Did you not just say I had no choice?"

He rolls one broad shoulder. "I mean you have a choice, I just—"

"I'll take it, Liam." Warmth rolls through me, and I lean back in my seat. "Thank you." I close my eyes. Quietly, I inquire, "Did you get done what you needed to get done?" I refrain from asking about the specific task. If he wanted me to know he would have told me, and I can't help but feel a tinge of sadness and dejection. He's always assuring me of his trustworthiness. Does he not think the same of me.

"Yeah," is all he answers, and I turn my head in time to see the muscles in his jaw tighten.

"Good."

I stare out the window, leaving it at that, until he begins, "I was at the Children's Hospital."

My chest tightens. "Is everything okay?"

"The guys from the team visit the kids often." A small, but pained smile tugs at his lips. "I usually visit Trent." A beat of silence and then he reaches into his hoodie pocket. "He made me this." I don't comment on the hitch in his voice as I take the paper from him and unfold it. "That's me and that's Trent," he explains pointing at the two figures on the paper.

"He wants to play for Miami too huh?"

"Yeah."

"You're his role model. That's nice, Liam." He nods in response, but it's clear that something is bothering him. "You don't want to be his role model?" I ask cautiously, not wanting to tug at whatever it is causing him pain, but wanting him to open up to me.

"I do. I don't want to let anyone down." A long moment of silence and then, "Life just isn't fucking fair sometimes."

"No, it's not," I agree. I take his hand and put it on my lap, knowing he's talking about his family as well. He wants to live up to everyone's expectations of him. But what about what he wants? "Tell me about Trent."

"He's a tough little bugger," he says and smiles, and it lightens the mood in the car. "Positive, independent. Wants nothing more than to play professional hockey." He casts me a fast glance. "I don't ever want to take my future for granted."

"I know." The guilt on his face hurts my heart. "He's going to be okay?"

"Yeah. His mom said my visits really help, and I like that, you know. When he gets better, I'm going to take him to the rink and teach him some tricks."

"Maybe one day you'll both be playing in Miami."

A small chuckle catches in his throat. "Wouldn't that be something."

"You like kids?"

"I like Trent." He goes quiet for a long time, and then asks, "You want to come watch when I take him to the rink?"

My heart does a little happy dance at the inclusion. "I'd love to."

He gives my thigh a squeeze, and I briefly close my eyes, my brain running through a happy scenario. Liam and me both living in Miami. I'm doing my master's degree while he kicks ass in the NHL. It's a happy dream, and there's a small part of me that revels in it, revels in the small chance that we could have a life together outside this small town, and maybe children of our own. Then another thought hits. Liam loves the game, and plays for all his fans—especially the sick children—but is a life in Miami, away from the boats, what he really wants? Would it make him happy?

With exhaustion taking over me, I drift off. The next thing I know, his voice is pulling me awake. I open my eyes as he eases off the highway, taking the exit to Lunenburg.

"I'm so sorry," I murmur and rub my eyes. "I didn't mean to fall asleep."

"It's okay, you needed sleep. I didn't mind." I sit up a bit straighter. "Do you want me to drop you at Boondocks or home?"

I consider it a second. "Home will be better. I have my bags." That, and my parents are likely at Boondocks, and they're angry enough with me as it is. I don't need to add fuel to the fire by having them see me with Liam. He nods, and I'm pretty sure he knows the real reason I want to go home.

A couple of minutes later, he drives down one of our many one-way streets and pulls up in front of our house. I glance up and find the porch light on. "Thanks. See you in the morning."

"No sunset?"

"Probably not tonight." I crinkle my nose, and check the time before opening my door, and light floods the car. "I'm late getting home and will have lots to do at Boondocks. Don't forget your picture." I fold it, and that's when I see a sticky note, stuck to the back of it. I glance at it, and see a woman's name and a phone number.

"It's not what you think," he says quickly, his voice filled with concern.

"It's okay," I respond, trying to hide my sadness. Did he ask a woman for her number?

"She's a nurse at the hospital," he explains. "Her friend has a thing for Tanner. Wants to double date."

"Oh, that sounds like fun," I manage to push out, forcing a smile. Deep down, though, a pang of sadness grips my heart. Liam and I are not an official couple, and yet, with each passing moment, I find myself falling harder and harder for him.

"Abi," he whispers softly, his voice laced with hope and desperation. "It's you I want. It's you I want to be with."

I blink back tears my voice trembling as I state, "Yet you took her number."

He reaches for my hand, holding it tightly. "I took it. Jesus..." He swallows, his expression laced with regret. "I thought...I don't know what is going on with us."

"I don't either," I admit, unable to hide the sadness and confusion welling up inside of me.

"I want to be with you, Abi, it's just..." His words tail off, a mixture of longing and frustration evident in his eyes.

"Our families," I begin, my voice tingled with resignation. "I know."

He pounds the steering wheel. "Christ, my father would disown me."

"I know. It wouldn't be any better for me." I shift in my seat, the weight of our situation bearing down on me. "So you thought you'd go out with someone else."

"I thought maybe it would help me get over you." I stare at him, never having seen such vulnerability before. He pounds the steering wheel. "But I don't want to." He takes a couple of deep fueling breaths, like he's gathering his courage. "I...I'm in love with you, Abi."

My heart thunders in my ears, happiness, and worry mingling within me. I meet his gaze, my eyes welling with tears. His hand gently touches my cheek, his fingers tender and cautious. We stare at each other, the silence pregnant with uncertainty.

"Abi," he finally whispers, desperation lacing in his voice, and etching lines on his face. "I can't be in this alone. Tell me I'm not."

"You're not," I respond, my own voice barely above a whisper. He cups my neck with his hand, drawing my mouth to his. The kiss that follows is bittersweet, a delicate blend of longing, need and the weight of what's ahead of us. It wraps around my heart, a mixture of happiness and sadness as we connect on a deeper level.

A bang in the distance cuts through the silence, and I slowly inch back. "I...need to go."

"I know." He takes my hand and gives it a squeeze, neither of us wanting to leave. "Does eight tomorrow work for you?"

I have no idea how I'll make it through until eight tomorrow as I nod and jump out, grabbing my bags from the back. I give a little wave and stare at him as he drives off and the second I turn around I nearly jump out of my shoes. How long has my mother been standing there?

"Mom," I blurt out quickly, as my gaze flies to the road, to where Liam just disappeared. Did she see us sharing the most important moment of my life? "What's going on?"

"I could ask you the same question," she answers, her tone laced with worry, and warning.

"Oh, my car broke down, and I had to get it towed, and I got a lift home."

Her gaze goes to where his car just rounded the corner. "With that Dunn boy?"

"He was driving by and helped me out."

She looks back at me, and I try not to fidget under her scrutinizing gaze. What I just said wasn't a lie. Not exactly. "You stay away from that family, Abigail. James Dunn is trouble, and you know it."

"How would I know it? No one has ever told me why you hate Mr. Dunn, and I know it was long before the incident with the traps. Why do we hate them, Mom? Why? That's all I want to know."

"We just do."

Feeling somewhat defeated, my shoulders sag and I try a different tactic. "And anyway, Liam is not his dad. He gave me a ride—" I struggle to explain, my heart still wobbly from what transpired between us in the car.

"That family is no good. They tried to destroy our business and stole from our traps," she shoots back, her eyes blazing.

My stomach is so tight, it begins to hurt. "It was a drive. It was either that or walk, and I was a long way from home." Her back straightens, because yes, I was basically just saying I couldn't call them because I couldn't count on them. "I should get to Boondocks," I say, working to keep my voice and body from trembling as I step around her frozen body.

I hike my backpack up higher, and Mom notices it. "Is that a new bag?"

"Yes," I croak out. "I wasn't able to use the last one, after all."

"Abigail."

I turn back around, and nearly shrink under Mom's stern gaze. "Stay away from that boy."

As soon as the words leave her mouth, something snaps in me, and I lift myself up taller. "I can't. I'm going to catch a ride with him back and forth to school until my car gets fixed, and he's actually lending me his car tomorrow night because he has an away game. I can't just hang around and wait for him to get back because I have to work at Boondocks," I inform her, my voice filled with determination as I stand my ground, something I've never done before. Anger floods her face. "I need to get to my classes. I have a scholarship to maintain. College might not be important to you but it's important to me." They want me to take over the family business, but I want other things, and I'm starting to feel a little less guilty about that.

"I don't like this, Abigail."

"I have to do what I have to do, Mom."

As I walk away, she talks to my back. "Most of the work is done at Boondocks. All that is left is the floors."

"Okay." I step inside and head straight to my room. From the sound of water running upstairs, Dad is in the shower, and the brief break from the guilt I had earlier is short-lived. My stomach cramps again, and I drop to my bed to take a couple deep breaths as the four walls around me close in.

Liam and I have no future because I'm never getting out of this place, and the weight of that realization fills every ounce of me with shock and despair.

24

LIAM

It's Friday night and game time, and my parents, sister and girlfriend are in the stands, ready to watch the Storms kick some Cape Breton ass. *Girlfriend.* Did I really just think of her as my girlfriend? Yes, I did but I'm not sure I'll ever get used to it. I'm also not sure if I'll ever get to call her that in public. She told me all about her conversation with her mother, and how her mom warned her to stay away from me. How do we possibly go public after that, and I have my own dad's warnings to think about.

There's so much tension and I detest what our folks have done to us. They all might have a past full of hate, but does that mean Abi and I need to have a future full of it, too?

But right now, as I stretch out on the ice, I need to get my head in the game. I don't want to let Coach, my teammates, Miami, or any of the children watching the games, down—especially Trent. As pressure bears down on me, Tanner comes skating over, distracting me, and that's when a cheer erupts in the stands. We both glance up and I spot Gabby and her friend making noise and waving a big foam finger.

"Fans?" Tanner asks.

"Yeah," I reply, dropping and stretching out my legs. "Do you recognize Gabby from the hospital?"

He takes another quick look. "Oh, right."

"She wants to double date tonight." Tanner goes quiet and frowns. "We're not. I didn't call, but I have the number if you want to."

"I might," he says and skates off. My gaze goes back to Abi and Ocean, and from her stillness, I guess she saw the exchange. She knows she has nothing to worry about. I've been honest with her about my feelings, and she feels the same way. It's incredible knowing she loves me.

Abi loves me.

That's something else I'll never get used to. My heart races a little faster as I finish stretching. I really hope I can spend the night with her, in her bed. Since her car is now fixed, this is the last time I'll be driving her home. Her parents are going to pick up her grandfather at her aunt's house. They'll be staying the night which means Abi will be opening Boon-docks tomorrow afternoon. That happens to be the last day for her to submit her grant application. Yeah, I didn't forget and hopefully I'll be with her to cheer her on as she sends it off.

The whistle blows and I get my head into the game, and for the next two and a half hours, I focus only on hockey. I play my best, always putting my heart and soul into every game, and when I intercept a critical tying shot just before the final buzzer, and the crowd goes wild. My buddies and I all hug, and after we shake hands with the Cape Breton Bears, we make our way to the change room.

"Hey," I say to Tanner. "Here's Gabby's number."

"Thanks." He takes it from me. "You don't want to call?"

I shrug as Sebastian sidles up to us. "Who don't you want to call?" he asks, and I resist the urge to tell him to mind his own business.

"Couple women in the stands," Tanner explains and shows him the number before dropping it into his bag.

Sebastian grins like we share a secret, and I guess we do. "He's got his hands full right now." He nudges me. "Isn't that right, buddy?"

He's so not my fucking buddy. "Yeah, that's right," I agree between gritted teeth.

Tanner peels his jersey off. "What's going on?" He asks as his gaze goes back and forth between the two of us, like something bad is about to go down, and I'm really fucking worried it is.

"Our resident fisherman Hooked here, got some bait on the line."

He snorts and I clench my fist, wanting to punch that smirk off his face. It honestly takes every ounce of control I have to stop myself from smashing his face in. Coach wouldn't be too happy about a fight right now and I can't risk trouble. Tanner's questioning eyes narrow and I shake my head.

"It's nothing," I say.

Sensing I want it left alone—at least one of the guys in front of me has a clue—Tanner goes back to undressing and walks toward the showers, and I turn from Sebastian, wanting the conversation to end, but he has different plans.

He puts one arm on the locker and leans toward me. "Saw your family out there."

I toss my jersey into my bag, unease gripping me. "Yeah."

"Mine are here too. Dad has some big political thing tomorrow, so I'll be skipping the party and heading back to Lunenburg with them."

"Okay." Why the fuck is he telling me all this? I don't give a shit, and we are not friends.

"Your sister is all grown up," he hints slyly.

"Don't even fucking think about it," I growl.

He smirks, clearly enjoying this comradery he thinks we have. "Yeah, no I get it, but you had us all fooled, Hooker."

"What are you talking about?"

"You and Abigail. Didn't know other things—"

I glance around, aware others are within hearing distance. "Shut the fuck up, Sebastian."

He follows my gaze, and leans in all conspiratorial like. "Right."

If my father sees me with Abi, he's going to think I'm doing what he asked of me. He'll likely cut me from his life when I don't do what he expects. Doesn't he know I play hockey for him, giving him the future he wanted? I do everything for him, because family is important, and I want my family in my life. They've honestly given me so much, including the opportunities to be the player I am today. I wouldn't have succeeded without them. I can't lose them. But I can't lose Abi, either.

Overwhelmed with conflicting emotions, I walk away and head to the showers. The hot water washes over me, but it does nothing to wash away the turmoil burning inside. Once I've cleaned up, I grab my gear, and step out into the cool night. My heart races as I find my family waiting for me. Mom and Ember give me big hugs and Dad claps me on the back.

"Great game, son," he compliments me, but the pride in his eyes is mixed with something else, something that looks a lot like anticipation...hope.

Fuck.

"Thanks." I search the noisy street, wanting to catch a glimpse of Abi. But she's nowhere to be found. She knew my parents were going to be here and isn't about to come anywhere near us. But later...I'll definitely see her later. "Are you guys staying long?" Shit, does it sound like I'm rushing them off.

"No, no you go join your friends at the pub," Dad booms. "Ember has gymnastics tomorrow morning and we have a long drive ahead of us."

"See you later, big brother," Ember says, and I run my knuckles through her hair, living up to the annoying big brother status she bestowed upon me years ago. She leans in and asks, "Hey, have you heard from Josh lately?"

My phone pings, and I snatch it from my pocket. "This is him now. Congratulating me on the game."

Her smile grows big. "Tell him I said hi."

I tuck my phone away, with no intention of doing that. "Yeah."

"Go, have fun, but not too much fun," Dad says with a laugh. I hike my bag over my shoulder, trying to mask the unease creeping through my veins.

"Thanks for coming."

"Will you be home later?" Mom asks, clutching her big, over-stuffed designer purse tighter. She doesn't much like coming into the city, and her worry seeps into her words.

"Tomorrow," I answer, and Dad leans in.

"We'll talk then, son."

My heart leaps as I turn to my father, take in his firm jaw, and the tight way his eyes are examining me. He's a big man, larger than life, but I'm a grown-ass man too, and should be able to see who I want. What was that I said to Abi, not that long ago: What if we didn't give a fuck what others think?

Maybe I should start actioning that statement. I open my mouth, take a fueling breath and say, "Yeah, I'll see you tomorrow sometime."

Goddamn chicken shit. Fuck, why can't I tell him?

Oh, because the worst thing for you would be for him to cut you out of his life. *Is it though, Liam?* Is that the worst possible thing? How about having Abi cut out of your life?

Just as she races through my brain, I spot her with Ocean and Easton. I can't help but stare as her gaze quickly, nervously sweeps over me. That's when I realize my father is watching me, closely, and he's a very astute man.

Just when Abi is about to dash off, Dad turns her way. "Abigail Hart, is that you?"

Her sudden halt mid stride sends my heart into my throat. I try to speak up again, but Mom's voice interjects, reminding me this might not be the right time or place—or maybe it's really reminding me I truly am a chicken shit.

"What are you doing?" Mom asks as she tugs on his coat. "We don't talk to that family."

"This isn't going to be good," Ember mumbles and inches back.

"Yes, it's me," Abi says, maintaining a cautious distance. "How are you, Mr. Dunn?" Her shaky gaze slides to my mother and sister. "Mrs. Dunn, Ember?"

My dad rocks forward and backward. "Lovely to see you here at the game, supporting the Storms."

My stomach knots. It makes me uneasy how friendly he's being. Although it's clear there's something between Abi and me. Anyone near us can pick up on that and a moment ago, maybe our gazes lingered just a few moments too long.

I put my hand on Mom's arm. "I'll walk you to your car."

"We're not far. You go do what you need to do," Dad says, and I don't like the smirk on his face. It reminds me of Sebastian's.

"Drive safe," I tell him, as they turn and disappear into the night. I scan the crowd and search for Abi, but she's gone. No doubt they're headed to the pub, so I pick up my pace and race along the sidewalk. I spot her, Ocean and Easton up ahead and I call out to her. She stops, says something to her friend and comes my way.

"Hey," I say after we close the distance, and all I want to do is kiss her.

She blinks nervously. "I'm sorry...I didn't mean..."

"You didn't do anything wrong, Abi."

"Your father, he was being so strange. I can't remember the last time he spoke to me when I'd run into him."

"I don't know what that's all about," I fib and her gaze moves to my forehead. Shit, do I have that telltale line she was talking about? "Want to get out of here?"

She glances over her shoulder. "I thought you had to all meet."

"I really don't give a shit about that right now. I just want you...alone."

Her smile wraps around me. "I'd like that too, Liam."

I take her hand in mine, and we head back to my car parked outside the dorm. I drop my bag into the back, and we climb inside.

"Great game, by the way."

I laugh. "Thanks."

"Did Tanner take that girl's number?" I eye her. "I saw them cheering and saw you talking to Tanner."

"Jealous?"

"No."

"Good, because it's you I love, Abi." The smile that comes over her warms my heart but when it quickly falls, I know exactly where her thoughts went. "Tonight," I begin. "Let's have tonight. Just the two of us, alone." Tonight, we can pretend we have no worries, no families rooting against us.

She nods. "Tonight."

I reach for her hand and squeeze it. "Is your application all ready to go tomorrow?"

A nervous little sound catches in her throat. "Just have to read it over once more, and then...submit."

"Good."

We both go quiet on the drive home, lost in our own thoughts. The soft hum of the engine provides a backdrop to the unspoken tension and roadblocks we decided to shelve for tonight. I take our Lunenburg exit, and break the quiet. "Do you want to go home first and we can walk to Boondocks?"

"Actually, let's go there first." She crinkles her cute nose playfully as she rubs her stomach. "I was hoping for nachos at the pub—"

A fast wave of regret overcomes me. I'd been so selfish, wanting to be alone with her, I hadn't thought she might have been hungry. "Oh, I'm sorry. We should have gone."

"No, I'd rather be with you and we can make some home fries at Boondocks, smothered in cheese and gravy."

"Poutine. Mmmm." I turn toward Boondocks. "Hey, wait, that's not healthy."

A quiet sigh escapes her. "Maybe tonight, I just want to live a little, Dunn. Do something that brings me happiness."

"Poutine brings you happiness, huh?" Her laugh is light, as it fills the car and helps lift the rest of the weight from my shoulders. Tonight is for us, and us alone.

"Yes." Her response is swift and playful, but the want, love and need in her eyes wraps around my heart.

I swallow hard as everything I feel for this incredible woman rises to the surface and makes me want her impossibly more. "Would doing *me* bring you happiness?"

Her gaze softens. "More than you'd ever know."

"How about this, then? I make the fries while you relax and go over your grant proposal."

A flicker of surprise flashes in her eyes. "You know how to work a fryer?"

I frown, as her surprise reminds me I lack talent in a lot of areas. "Yeah, you're right." I shrug. "I just wanted to do something for you."

"You're a smart guy, Liam, and I know you can do anything you put your mind to."

I shrug, hiding my sense of inadequacy. "Thanks for the vote of confidence."

She takes my hand, having none of that. "I know you're capable of a lot of things," she says firmly, forcibly and honestly, making warmth spread across my chest. "I know how smart you are."

Honestly, I love the worth she sees in me, and as I stare at her, it ignites a spark deep in my soul and forces me to contemplate my worth beyond being a hockey player—not to mention my dad's unspoken threats. How much am I sacrificing for my family's approval, to make them happy, because being cut out of their lives would be catastrophic? I once told Abi she needed to do what made her happy. Maybe it's time I prioritized my own happiness and future to really fight for the love I share with Abi.

25

ABIGAIL

With my belly completely full from all the poutine, and my heart stuffed with all the love I have for Liam, I lock the door to Boondocks. Warmth races through my body as Liam stands close behind me, his mere presence messing with my mind and body.

I breathe in his scent as he lightly runs tender fingers through my hair. Feeling somewhat dazed I turn the key and double check the door, amazed—considering the way my brain is shutting down—that I remembered to even lock up.

I turn to Liam, and the light from the moon falls over his towering body as he smiles down at me. My heart misses a beat as his eyes fill with loving warmth. It was so sweet of him to cook for me, to serve me, and to clean up afterward as I re-read my grant essays. I can't believe I spent years hating this man, when now all I want to do is love him.

His knuckles brush my cheek and my insides quiver. Ever since we confessed our feelings, there's a new kind of intimacy between us. I've never felt anything like it, and from his gentle touch, it's clear he feels it every bit as much as I do. Either that or he's an incredible actor, which he's anything but. He leans in and lightly presses his lips to mine, and I sigh.

"Let's get home," he whispers.

Home is my place tonight and I love having him in my bed. Will there ever be a future where we don't have to sneak around? Maybe when we're in Miami. But even then, he'll be photographed so much, we'd never be able to go out in public.

Nope, not going to think about that. Tonight is about us and us alone, which means, I'm going to forget all my worries for the next few hours. We walk to his car and he drives up the winding hill to my place. We don't speak, but we continue to sneak glances at one another as excitement builds up inside me.

He parks on the street and I pull out my key as we walk into the house, going straight to my room. I flick the light on, and the next thing I know I'm in his arms, his mouth devouring me with a deep hunger that screams of something more.

I step back and he growls as I break the contact, but it turns to a moan as I begin to undress. He does the same and a minute later, we stand before each other with our bodies bare and our hearts wide open.

"Liam," is all I can say as my heart thunders.

He takes my hand and leads me to my bed. I pull back the covers and we both slide in, enjoying the warmth of each other's bodies as the cool bedroom air swirls around us. Shifting, he goes onto his side while I stay on my back, and he lightly runs his fingers over my arms, and belly, heading lower. I quiver.

"I love the way you touch me," I admit.

"Probably not as much as I like touching you."

"What a team, we..." My words fall off as he spreads my thighs and lightly pets my damp sex. "God, that feels good."

"That's what I want, Abi. I want to make you feel good." His voice is so thick with emotion it wraps around my heart and tugs.

My chest quivers as I breathe. "I want to make you feel good too."

"This makes me feel good," he tells me and slides a thick finger into my core. My hips come off the bed, the world around me spinning as this man touches me. He slides his finger in and out of me, and I put my hands on his body to explore his hard and soft angles. Who knew there'd be such a soft side to Liam Dunn? My enemy turned lover.

He repositions and moves between my legs, pressing his hot mouth to my core, and once again I see shooting stars. He knows my body so well now he can take me to the moon in seconds. But maybe it's more than that, maybe it's love that makes this so much better.

I run my hands through his hair, and he angles his head until his eyes meet mine. I smile down at him, and I can't tell, since his mouth is on my sex, but I think he just smiled back.

He turns his attention to my clit and I gasp, my hips coming off the bed. He slides a second finger inside me and my body shuts down, spilling all around him.

"Babe," he murmurs and laps at me, and before I even stop spasming, he's rolling on a condom and sliding his hard cock inside me.

"Jesus, you're still coming." He grunts and gasps and grabs a fistful of my hair as my muscles clench around him. "Babe," he murmurs again.

I run my hands down his back, my heart full and happy as he starts riding me, searching for his own release. I move with him and realize what we're doing… this isn't sex. No, this is lovemaking, each of us wanting to give pleasure, more than we want to take. If that isn't love, I don't know what is.

He groans. "I'm so close."

It's crazy, because we're getting good at this sex thing, which means we should last longer, but tonight it's different. It's the first time we've been together since we told each other how we feel, and we just can't fight to hang on.

"Come for me," I say, and he pushes deep inside and buries his face in my neck as he let's go. I hug him tight and concentrate on the pulses. "I'm going to go on the pill," I tell him. "I want to feel everything."

His head lifts, the love, surprise, and utter joy in his eyes sucks the air from my lungs.

"Really?"

"Would you like that?" I ask and run my hands through his hair.

His grin is big and silly as he nods emphatically. "Yeah."

I kiss him and guide his head back to my chest. We stay wrapped up in each other for a long time, neither wanting to move. He eventually rolls off me, discards the condom, and sets an alarm on his watch before snuggling back in. Yeah, neither of us want to accidently sleep in again.

I close my eyes and the next thing I know, sirens and alarms —very close by—pull me awake. I jackknife up and check the time to see it's only six, before my gaze goes to my window. The smell of smoke seeps into the house, and panic erupts inside me.

"Liam," I yell, and he stirs awake.

"What?" The sirens speak for me, and he too sits up quickly, and rubs his eyes. "What's going on."

"There's a fire somewhere."

"Shit." He slips from the bed, and goes to my window, glancing into the back garden. "It's really smoky out there."

A horrible, sickening knot tightens in my stomach. "Liam..." I begin, barely able to speak, to push his name past my lips. He spins as I'm jumping from my bed and pulling on last night's clothes. "Did you...last night...the fries...the fryers."

He goes completely still, his eyes locked on mine. "I shut everything down." He blinks and glances down. "I'm sure I did."

"Oh, God, Liam." I don't wait for him. I'm out the front door in seconds, and when I see the fire is coming from the waterfront, I take off running. Within seconds, Liam is beside me, grabbing at me.

"Abi, you can't go down there."

"I have to. What if it's Boondocks?"

"You still can't go."

"I have to know." I shrug away and start running down the hill and as soon as I pass the bank, which has been blocking my view, and I take in the sight unfolding before me, the world around me collapses and I sink to the ground. "Oh my God. Oh my God. Oh my God."

Liam drops next to me, and puts his arms around my body as fire trucks screech down the street below us. "You need to move back."

"I need to call someone. I need to do something." I reach into my pants, and my phone is still in my pocket from last night. I call up my contacts and a second later, my mother answers.

"Mom," I cry out.

"Abigail, what is going on? It's six in the morning."

"Boondocks. It's on fire." Tears fall down my face as guilt strangles me. This is my fault. I was in charge of securing the place last night, and ensuring everything was properly shut down.

"How bad?" she asks her tone edging on panic.

"Bad, Mom. It's bad. The firetrucks and police are here," I wail, hysterical now. "I can't get close."

I hear muffled sounds as she says something to Dad. "We're on our way. We'll be there in about an hour."

"Okay," I say, and breathe heavily as I watch plumes of smoke spread into the air. Noise erupts around me as residents all rush from their homes to see what's going on. Liam remains quiet beside me as panic forces me to my feet, desperate to do something, anything.

"You should go back home."

"No, you should go home," I shoot back, and he tenses. I pace the street, unable to think.

He reaches for me, and I pull back, the blood in my veins ice cold. "Abi—"

"Liam, you should go. My parents are on their way back." Oh God, when they ask what happen, I'm going to have to tell them the truth. Will they think Liam did this on purpose? I lift my head slowly and meet Liam's dark eyes. As old insecurities and fears pierce my brain—and, as years of warnings from my mother and father come back in a whoosh—I can't help but wonder if he did do it on purpose. My gut clenches as I remember how nice his father was, like he knew something I didn't, and how Sebastian was always smirking at me. I instinctively wrap my arms around myself and moan as bile punches into my throat.

He stares at me, his face pale as he somberly states, "It's my fault."

I try to swallow as my body trembles, and I drop down onto one of the stairs of a local pottery shop. "Liam..." I begin and shake my head as memories of last night, and how sweet he's always been to me curl around my heart. Of course, he didn't do this on purpose. I shouldn't even be thinking like that. But wait, what did he just say? "What?" I ask and blink up at him.

"It's my fault."

Those three words blast like fireworks in my brain. He's admitting that he did this? What the hell is going on? I'm not thinking clearly, and neither is he. "Liam," I try again.

"No, I can see it all over your face, Abi." An invisible sword pierces my heart as he turns toward the fire, and inches back and as he moves further and further away, it feels like he's slowly dragging the blade from my body, leaving me to bleed to death on the stairs. "Do you want me to go?"

"I don't know, my parents..."

Just then, Sebastian comes rushing around the corner. His father's house isn't too far from where we're standing. I don't miss the way Liam stiffens and reaches for Sebastian before he can get to me. But Sebastian is laughing and patting Liam on the back.

What the hell?

"Baited and hooked," he blurts out, and before he can say another word, Liam punches him in the face. The entire world wobbles around me.

"Jesus Christ, Liam." Sebastian covers his face and licks at the blood on his lip. "What did you do that for?"

"I need you to shut up."

Sebastian swipes at the corner of his mouth. "Yeah, okay, man. Sorry. I just thought—"

"Sebastian," Liam growls, his hands fisted. "Shut the fuck up."

"Thought what?" I ask and stand, everything inside me unsteady and panicked. I grip the rail on the stairs to hang on.

Sebastian, who has never been the brightest bulb in the pack, looks from me, to a growling Liam, back to me. "Nothing, man," he says, and my body goes weak.

"Are you saying Liam baited me?" I try to keep my words even and steady. "That I was bait?" He shifts, looking suddenly nervous. If he thinks he spilled secrets that could get Liam into trouble, he'd be right.

"It's not what you think," Liam blurts out quickly, and that's when I see the deep line in the middle of his forehead.

I glare at him. "Are you saying it wasn't your fault?" my mind rewinds back to the night I helped him with his calculus and I found him with invoices in his hand. Was he snooping?

"No...just...Jesus..."

"You were with me the night my grandfather said we didn't have insurance. You remember that, right?"

His eyes go big, like he's remembering something he forgot. Damn, he is a great actor. "Yeah, but...it's not—"

"It's not you luring me in, baiting me. Making me think you love me, so you could destroy my family, our livelihood, and my future." A groan crawls out of my throat and tears fall as my future plays out before my eyes. "I can forget about submitting my application today."

"Abi, don't."

"You think I can leave here now, Dunn?" My God, my parents need me more than ever, after this mess. It's over, everything is over. A hallow laugh rumbles in my chest and I catch the gleam in Sebastian's eyes. He's enjoying this. I did nothing to the guy other than turn down his advances and he's been out to ruin me ever since. I guess he and Liam have more in common than I realized. "Sebastian knew, didn't he? You said something to him, about me being bait?"

"I..."

"It's a simple yes or no, Dunn?"

"Yes, but it's not at all what you think." He reaches behind his neck, a desperation about him as he rubs his shoulders. Sure, he's desperate; he doesn't want to go to jail for arson. "I told him you were bait, but only to shut him up."

"And that makes a lot of sense." He shakes his head and I continue, "With no insurance, your dad can finally buy up our land. Congratulations," I pause to clap my hands. "You all got what you wanted."

Sebastian laughs, and covers his mouth with his hand, and I get it, I've nailed it. That's exactly what's been going on. I stare at Liam, a part of me refusing to believe this is really happening. The weak, wounded part I never should have trusted. My brain, however, is telling me another story, and Sebastian here is backing that up with his smirk and remarks.

Liam goes deathly still, his dark eyes piercing mine. "Is that what you think?" he asks through clenched teeth.

I shake my head and try not to collapse as hurt and pain rains down on me. "What I think is this. I knew you were capable of a lot of things. I told you that last night." I glance toward the plume of smoke, and add, "I just didn't think you were capable of this."

My tongue is thick, my throat tight, like it's being squeezed by a noose as I stumble backward, away from Abi, not wanting to go, but knowing I can't stay and help her either. She thinks I'm a monster, that I burned her family's place to the ground on purpose, that much is clear. Did nothing we did over the last month matter? Did she not see that I wasn't a chip off the old block? I choke back a fucking sob as she stands there shaking, refusing to even listen to me. It's obvious nothing I do or say is going to change her view.

"Hey man, where are you going?" Sebastian asks and puts his arm over my shoulder, and because my legs are fucking shaky, he nearly knocks me to my damn knees.

I shrug him off, needing to escape before I punch him in the face again. Sure, he's not helping my situation, and he might be the world's biggest douche-bag, but what's really going on here is Abi doesn't believe in me, in us.

"Back the fuck off, Sebastian," I growl.

He removes his arm and holds his hands up. "Whoa man, what did I do?"

I have no energy to get into this with him, so I pick up my pace and practically run up the hill to get my car, which is still parked outside Abi's home. Once I'm inside, I stare at Abi's house and take deep gulping breaths. If I left the fryer on, I really did ruin everything for her and her family. As that truth bounces around my brain like a runaway pinball, my guilt turns my stomach against me, and I nearly vomit as I pound my steering wheel.

Abigail Hart thinks I burned her business to the ground—on purpose.

Wow, just fucking wow. Doesn't she know how much I love her, that I'd do anything in the world for her? It hurts to swallow as I start my car and drive on autopilot as I sift through the fog in my brain, and finally find my way home. Dad is on the front steps, staring at the smoke in the sky, when I get there. He has a cup of coffee in his hand, and he's dressed in a T-shirt and pajama pants. I guess now the whole town is aware of the fire. Soon enough they'll be aware that I'm behind it.

My blood runs cold as I slam my car into park. My father's attention turns to me as I climb from the driver's seat and close the door with much more force than necessary. His eyes are narrowed in concern as they move over me, and the clothes I was in last night outside the rink, but I think the worry I spot there is for me, not the Harts' place of business. Jesus, he can't be happy about this. He can't be, otherwise I have to admit that I'm the son of a monster and the Hart family had every right to hate him all these years.

"What's going on?" he asks, his tone a mixture of worry and...happiness.

Jesus fucking Christ.

"Why do you hate them so much?" I blurt out, and square my shoulders, ready to have this out here and now. I've spent my entire life not knowing, not challenging my father and I'm fucking over it. If he can feel happiness about someone else's disaster, then he's not a man I want to please, a man I'd do anything for, even play hockey. As he stares at me, his dark eyes hardening in the way they do when he's not getting his way, I no longer care about making him proud.

He pushes himself up to his full height and sets his coffee cup on the deck rail. "What's going on with you?"

"Answer my question." He stares at me long and hard, and I don't shatter under his scrutiny like I have in the past. As I stare back, he turns his focus and studies something past my shoulders. "I want the truth. What did the Hart family ever do to make you hate them so much?"

Every muscle in his body tenses, like whatever happened between them is still as fresh today as it was all those years ago. "Let's not—"

"Tell me right fucking now, or I'm walking out of here, and I won't be back."

His head rears back. "You can't talk to me like that."

I widen my stance, a power move, and shock registers on his face. I get it. I never stand up to my old man, but things have gone too far.

"I just did."

His face turns red, his eyes blazing. "If you walk away—"

"What, Dad? What?" I shake my head, and push my pent-up anger into pacing back and forth in front of him. "Are you going to pull my college funding? Fine. There are other things I can do."

He shakes his head like I've lost my damn mind. I get it. I'm not a great student, but there are other jobs, ones that don't require me to wear a suit, or a jersey. Jobs that are for me and me alone. Don't get me wrong. The NHL is no hardship, and I do play for a lot of reasons. But I'm always playing for others. Never for myself.

"Liam. You need sleep." He reaches for me, and I flinch back.

"What I need are answers," I say, clenching my teeth together. "What happened between you and the Hart family? And if you're wondering where this is coming from, it's because I'm in love with Abi, and I think I just accidently burned down her business."

He takes a fast breath, and I can almost hear his brain racing. "You didn't do it on purpose?"

For one brief second, I'm shocked that he just asked me that. Then I find my voice. "No, for fuck's sake. How..." I rake my hand through my hair, and turn toward the fire, my eyes burning but not from the smoke. If my own father doesn't believe me, and thinks I'm capable, it's no wonder Abi turned on me. "I'd never do anything to hurt them."

"You were hanging with her and not getting dirt?"

My gaze jerks back to him, the accusation in his tone infuriating me. "That's right. Did you miss the part about me loving her?" I wave my hand toward the fire. "I can't believe you think I'd do something like that."

"I never asked you to burn her place down, son."

"No, but what you asked was ruthless, a means to an end to ruin them. Just like a fire. Why the hell do you want to ruin them?" I fold my arms and stand there, refusing to budge until the truth comes out.

He finally exhales and that's when I notice his tired eyes, and the fine lines surrounding them. "Miriam Hart and I...we go way back."

"Everyone in this town goes way back."

He nods. "We were...a couple."

I stare at him, a little surprised by this. "And?"

He snorts but it holds no humor. "I offered her the world, Liam." He waves his arms. "Look around, look at what we built here."

"Your father built it, you inherited," I point out, which earns me a scowl. I don't much care if he's angry with me or not right now. I'm fucking angry with him.

"Nevertheless, this could have been all hers, but..."

His voice falls off, and that's when understanding hits like a hard body check to the board. My head spins for a second as I stand there, the pieces of the puzzle falling into place. "Are you kidding me?"

"About what?" His shoulders sag, making him look less like a giant to me.

"All of this," I begin and wave my hand around. "The hate, the destruction, the wanting to hurt the Hart family is because you were in love with Miriam and she didn't love you back."

He frowns, and rubs the center of his forehead, and I notice the line there, the same line I have. Apparently, it's a lie line. At least, it is according to Abi.

"Of course not, son."

"I want the truth," I demand, even though I'm pretty sure I know the truth.

Just then Mom pokes her head out of the door, and when she sees the look on my face, a deep sadness comes over her. My chest practically caves in when I see the hurt on her face. All these years, all these years and hateful acts was because Miriam was the one who got away. How must that make Mom feel? I pinch the bridge of my nose to fight the tears. I refuse to let my father see me cry.

"She went with that..." He waves his hand. "That Hart boy. He had nothing. Came from nothing, really. What was she thinking?"

Oh, my fucking God.

"This...all this mess, and years of hate was because Miriam chose a boy from the wrong side of the tracks? Are you kidding me? You dragged this on for years, because you couldn't accept defeat and move on. Mom loves you, Dad. You have a family that loves you."

He slumps, and in a low voice says, "He was not good, Liam. He wasn't right for her."

"Who are you to say that, or judge? We can't help who we fall in love with," I state, my voice much lower. "Her life was hers, not yours."

"It was just as easy for her to fall in love with someone who could give her the world, versus someone who couldn't."

Jesus, is he still trying to convince me—or maybe himself—that he's right? Still trying to justify his actions? "Look at them. Living hand to mouth, season to season. They have prime oceanfront land and haven't even done anything big or important with it. They could have an empire."

"Maybe that's not what they want. Maybe running a small business is what makes them happy. Whatever they do, it's not your business." I just wish they'd cut Abi some slack and let her live her own life. I get it, they want her to take over the family business, most people in this town do, but it's not for her and they need to accept that and move on, just like Dad needs to accept that Miriam was never, and never will be, his.

"Son."

I hold my hand up, having heard enough. "There's going to be an investigation. They might even call it arson, and I might be charged. If I left the fryer on, I want you to know it was an accident—"

"You won't be charged," he says quickly, and straightens again.

"If I'm responsible, I have to pay the consequences."

His head lifts. "I'll hire the best lawyers and see to it that you walk away."

Yeah, I get it. He's a powerful man, with powerful political connections, and I plan to put those connections to use—for the good of Abi's family. "They have no insurance and you're going to make this right. Not because I made a mistake, but because you need to make up for all the hurt you brought them over the years and all the hate that Abi and I have had to endure." He goes quiet for a long time, like he's considering his options, but he doesn't have any. "If you don't do this, you won't see me again, and you can forget about me ever playing for Miami."

Shock registers on his face, and his jaw drops. "You...love hockey."

"I love the game, but you and I both know it's not where my heart is."

"Liam, the boats aren't for people like us."

"People like us," I practically scream. I take a breath to keep my anger in check. The entire village does not need to be privy to this conversation. "I am not better than any anyone else. None of us are. You were born into privilege, just like I was. That does not make us any better."

His head drops. "I loved her."

"Yeah, well, I'm sorry you were hurt, but she loved someone else, and life isn't fair. Get over it." I'm being cruel, I know, but I'm angry, with him, with the situation, with Abi for thinking I could do something like this to her. I'm also angry with myself for leaving the fryers on.

"I've lost Abi, Dad. I don't want to lose you too, but I will leave here and not look back if you don't make this right."

"Son."

"I've spent my life wanting to make you proud, because family is the most important thing to me. I thought I'd be nothing, no one without you. I thought I wasn't smart enough to do anything other than hockey. I was wrong."

"Hockey is your life."

"Because you made it my life. I could go back on the boats, but you obviously won't allow me on yours. Did you know I'm good with my hands, Dad? Maybe I'll be a mechanic. I enjoy that kind of work."

He looks almost aghast. "No son of mine—"

"Have you not heard anything I just said?" I glare at him. "I play hockey for everyone else, Dad." Heavy silence falls, only to be broken by the sound of another fire engine approaching the scene. "Do something. Rally your workers, the neighbors, whatever you have to do, to help them rebuild."

"Liam."

I shake my head and continue to stand my ground. "Do it or I'm gone."

He goes quiet like he's once again weighting his options, but he only has one. "You'll continue to play hockey?"

"Yeah, but this time it's not for you." This time it's for the woman I love.

My heart pinches tight in my chest as a fire truck flies by. Abi might never speak to me again, and she might have just accused me of horrible things, but that doesn't mean I'm not going to ensure she doesn't get the future she deserves. "Also, I'm going to need you to call in some favors."

It's Monday afternoon, and I need to get myself together, and get myself to campus. I've already missed my morning classes, and I can't miss my afternoon ones too, not without risking my scholarship, but I can't seem to drag myself out of bed. Probably because I don't quite see the point. Everything I've been working for...gone. And at the end of the day, does it matter if I get my degree? It's not like I can do anything with it living here in Lunenburg, becoming what my parents always wanted.

After my parents returned Saturday morning with my grandfather, I told them everything. I told them how long I've been seeing Liam, how I've been staying with him in the city, and how he cooked for me the night of the fire. They, of course, had a lot to say about that, including *I told you so.* They're right, they did tell me so. They were livid, of course —their world just burned down around them—and I vowed to stay home and help rebuild it, doing whatever was necessary, even getting a job in town.

Did your world not just burn down too, Abi? Who is helping you?

I roll over in my bed, which is still wet from all my crying overnight. I touch my face, which is dry now. I don't think I have any tears left in me. I put my hand over my head, and listen to the silence of the house. There was a knock on the door early this morning. Mom and Dad left without a word to me. I guess they don't feel like they owe me anything. I heard Granddad shuffling around, then his bedroom door closed. At least I know he's home and safe. I have no idea where my parents have gone, only that for two people with nowhere to go, they've been gone a long time.

My phone rings and my heart jumps into my throat. Who could be calling? I usually only ever text and it's with Liam and Ocean, sometimes my mother. No way is Liam calling me. I roll over and snatch my phone off the nightstand. I stare at Ocean's number as my phone rings, and my heart is so heavy I'm not even sure I'll be able to speak. The call ends, and starts up again. I slide my finger across the screen because maybe she needs my help with something.

"Abi," she says quickly, and I hear muffled voices in the background. She's obviously walking along the campus. "I just heard." I groan. "Are you okay?"

I'm about to say yes, I'm fine, but am I fine? No. Am I tired of not reaching out or letting anyone help me when I need it? "No, I don't think I am," I answer, my voice low, defeated... exhausted. "How did you find out?"

"Easton told me. I don't know how he knew. I think maybe Sebastian." My stomach knots, and a cry catches in my throat. "I'm coming home."

"No," I say and sit up. "You have classes."

"Liam didn't do this, right?" A beat of silence, and then, "There are rumors."

My world tilts on its axis and once again the embarrassment and shame I felt when Sebastian spread rumors about me, completely drains the blood in my veins. Fresh tears fall, and I sniff.

"He's not here today. Easton said he didn't show up for practice."

I hold my phone, having no idea what to say. A creaking noise sounds outside my door, and I listen for a second. When everything goes silent again, I chalk it up to Granddad wandering around.

"There's an investigation going on into what started the fire," I tell her.

"I'm so sorry. Is there anything I can do?"

"No," I tell her, and start crying harder. "Everything is a mess, Ocean. I didn't submit my grant application. What's the point? I have to stay here and help my family. I...I...loved him, and he was so sweet, and he told me he loved me too, and how could this have happened?"

As I speak the words out loud, a part of me warns that I have this all wrong. That Liam wasn't behind the fire or out to hurt my family. But the things Sebastian said, the way he backed up everything that happened...

"Hey, Abi," she says softly.

"I don't know what will happen. All I know is I won't be going anywhere now. I don't know how we can rebuild, but no matter what I'm here for good." I snort. "Mom and Dad always wanted a son who'd stay home and follow in their footsteps. I guess they're getting what they want." A hysterical laugh catches in my throat. "The Dunn family will likely buy our land, and they're getting what they want. The only one not getting what they want is me." I'm rambling like a spoiled brat, I know, but dammit. "My world is falling apart around me, and I'm powerless to do anything about it."

"Maybe Liam's world is falling apart around him too."

My racing thoughts come to a resounding halt. "What?" Holy crap, is she taking Liam's side on this?

"I think you need to talk to him, Abi. I've seen the way he looks at you. He loves you. Easton said the same thing. Maybe it really was an accident."

I cry harder. "Even if it was," I say, blubbering like a toddler now. "Even if he didn't do it on purpose, we're over." My throat is so tight it's screaming in pain. "I accused him of sabotage." I stare at my window with blurry eyes. "He's never going to talk to me again."

Knuckles rap softly on my door, and I jump. "Abi, can I come in?"

"It's my mother, can I call you back?"

"I'm here if you need me."

I end the call, swipe at my eyes and prepare myself for another scowl from my mother, or another lecture. "Come in."

I sit up straighter as both Mom and Dad come in, not with scowls on their face, but with something that looks like regret, and gentle understanding. What is going on?

"Can we talk?" Mom asks, her voice low and sad. I want to ask if everything is okay but that would be a stupid question.

"Sure."

I move to the center of my bed and they both sit. "I'm sorry," Mom says first, and it's followed by Dad agreeing.

"For what?" I ask.

"For not being who you needed us to be." I stare wide eyed, sure I'm dreaming. Mom takes my hand. "We were making you into what we wanted you to be, but we never stopped to think about what you needed."

"In our generation, it was natural for children to take over the family business," Dad explains. "I guess we thought you'd get married, stay here, take over and realize this was your dream after all."

"It's not," I say quietly. I think Liam's father is the only one who doesn't want his son taking over. He wants him to live his own life and as much as I hate the man, I guess that's something.

Mom pats my hand. "We know and we're sorry."

"We're sorry for not supporting you," Dad adds. "For you thinking we wanted a son." I stare at him. I guess he must have overhead me on the phone. "It's just that handing things down is tradition in this town."

I take a big shuddering breath. "There's nothing to even hand down now." They exchange a fast glance and my heart jumps. "What?"

"We spoke to the fire marshal."

"And?" My gaze jerks back and forth between the two of them.

"The fire started in the back office. Faulty wiring."

I cover my face and start sobbing. Mom shifts closer and pulls me into her arms. "I'm sorry, Abi."

"Things are going to change around here," Dad says. "We're looking at a retirement home for Granddad and taking a lot of the responsibility off you."

"Responsibility. What responsibility now? Boondocks is gone." They exchange another look. What are they keeping from me?

"We want you to concentrate on your studies, and go to Miami and make changes in the world."

A sobbing laugh catches in my throat. "I didn't submit the grant papers. It's too late for that." They exchange a third look which has the hairs on the back of my neck tingling. "What is going on?"

"We're rebuilding. The community has come together under the guidance of the Dunn family."

"Are you kidding me?" The sky must be falling.

"No. We had a long talk with James Dunn this morning."

I stare at them. Honestly, I'd be less shocked to hear that they got me an elephant, the pet I wanted for my sixth birthday. "What...what?" Is all I can say.

Mom's shaky hands pluck at an imaginary piece of lint on my blanket. "You need to talk to Liam."

Panicked, I start kicking the covers off and try not to hyperventilate. "Does he want to talk to me?"

Mom hesitates, her blue eyes darting between Dad and me. "Not that we know of. It's just...I think you two have some things to figure out."

I get up and pull on my hoodie and tie my hair back, even though I have no idea what I'm planning on doing or if I plan to do anything at all. I just can't sit still any longer. I grab my keys off my dresser, and before I head out the door, I turn back.

"I love you both very much."

They both give me soft, appreciative smiles. "We love you," they tell me.

I run out the front door, jump in my car and start driving. I find myself at Liam's big house, but his car is nowhere to be found. I turn around and drive through town. When my search still comes up empty, I pull over and reach for my phone.

My fingers hesitate, worried if I send him a message he won't answer, or worse, say something hurtful, something I deserve. I debate on what to say, and then finally shoot off a text.

Abi: We'll always have sunset.

I wait forever for a response, and when none comes, my heart sinks into my stomach. I drop my phone and stare out my blurry window. I don't go home, instead, I drive the winding streets aimlessly, searching for Liam's car until it's almost sunset. I eventually park, gather all my courage and head to our dock, which fortunately was spared the fire.

I make my way down the wobbly wharf, and nearly cry when I find the two Adirondack chairs empty. I drop into one of them, put my elbows on my knees and cry into my hands. I stay like that for a long time, until I hear footsteps behind me. I gasp, and jump up and a garbled noise catches in my throat as Liam angles his head to take me in and the love I feel for him bursts in my heart.

"It was you," I whisper.

"What?"

"I don't like to ask for much. I don't like to ask for anything, but this morning, I couldn't help but think I was staying home to help my parents after their world burnt down. It occurred to me, my world burnt down too, and I was wondering who was helping me. It was you, Liam. You were helping me. Why?"

His face is full of warmth and vulnerability when he says, "Because I love you."

I sniff, hating myself for the things I said to him. "I love you too. I'm sorry for accusing you...Sebastian."

"I did tell Sebastian I was working with my dad to take over the Hart family land."

"Why?" I ask quietly.

"It was stupid. Dad asked me to get dirt on your family. I never wanted that, Abi. I wouldn't do it. I refused. Then Dad realized we were together, and assumed I was doing what he wanted. Sebastian started asking questions, and I foolishly thought the only way for us to be together without him saying there might be more going on between us, was for him to think I was in on something with my dad. I was wrong to do that."

"I understand," I say as I glance at Boondocks and all the destruction. "I'm so sorry for everything."

"It's okay. I understand, Abi. I know where that distrust comes from." He grins. "When I was little, my mom gave me a cookie. The raisins were made to look like chocolate chips. That's when my trust issues started."

I can't help but laugh at that. "Thank you, Liam." A hiccupping sob rises in my throat. "Thank you for... everything. I'm so sorry."

He steps up to me and pulls me into his arms. "Actually, I'm the one who's sorry." I blink up at him in confusion. "I'm sorry it took so long to get here. I was in the city with my dad. He had a meeting."

I nod, not really understanding why he would be at his father's meeting. My heart lurches. "Wait, does your father want you to take over the business? Are you going to be back on the boats?" In his heart, I know this is what he wants.

"No, I'm going to Miami."

My heart thumps. "Liam, is that—"

"You're going to Miami too."

I gasp. "What?"

"That's why Dad and I were in the city. He has connections." I open my mouth and he cuts me off. "Please, let him use them for good, Abi." He takes my hand. "You are smart and deserving, and this scholarship is yours. You know that."

"I didn't submit it," I explain as sweat breaks out on my body.

"I figured as much. Go ahead and submit it. Dad told the board there were extenuating circumstances. It's not too late. I promise."

"Oh my God, Liam."

"We're going to Miami, babe," he says, and it takes me a moment to wrap my brain around that. "Wait, Liam, how did you get your father to do all this?"

"By telling him I'd still go play for Miami."

I shake my head, my heart hurting. "You made a deal. You put hockey on the line."

"Yes."

"But...you play for everyone else. I know that, Liam." I lightly pound his chest. "What do you want?"

"Don't you see, Abi? For the first time in my life, I'm playing for me."

"No, you're playing for me," I correct. I shake my head, my body trembling. "I don't want you to ever regret it, or come to resent me for it."

"How could I ever regret it? I'm actually being selfish, Abi, and I'm not just playing for you, I'm playing for myself, because playing for you is giving me exactly what I want—everything I want."

Happy tears begin to fall, and he pulls me to him, lightly brushing away the tears with the rough pads of his thumbs. "Say yes. Say you'll submit the grant and come to Miami with me."

I stare up at him, as the world around me begins to take shape and form and right itself. "Yes," I say, and throw my arms around him. His lips find mine for a deep kiss, and when we inch apart, he lightly holds onto my shoulders, his eyes very serious as his gaze holds mine.

"Do you remember a long time ago, when I asked you to promise me that you'd apply for the grant?"

I nod. "I'm keeping that promise. Late, but I'm keeping it.

"Remember you told me I had to promise something in return."

"You told me you had to think on it, and you said I should probably be afraid," I say.

"I've thought about it. A lot. Here's what I promise. I'm going to love playing in the NHL, because I get to come home to you every night. I promise to go back to fishing, after my career, when you've changed the world and created a sustainable ecosystem." I smile up at him. "I promise to always love you, do right by you, and be the man you need me to be."

I nod as my heart overflows with love. "That's not scary at all."

"Not scary at all," he agrees as he picks me up, presses his lips to mine and spins me around. After a hug that squeezes the air from my lungs, he sets me down and turns me toward the sunset. I sigh and lean against his chest, encircled by his arms. I remember what he said he loves about sunsets.

"Time for dreams…"

"Nah, our dreams are becoming a reality," he whispers in my ear. I smile liking that. "So, do you agree, sunsets are just as amazing as sunrises?"

"I agree."

"A honeymoon in Santorini, then?"

I spin to face him and take in his smile as he begins to drop to one knee. "Liam?"

"Oh, I forgot to mention when I was in the city with Dad, I made a pit stop." He pulls out a gorgeous diamond and I gasp. "Will you marry me, Abi? If you say yes, I promise to make you the happiest woman in the world."

I nod as I sink down with him. "How many promises does a girl need?"

He puts the ring on my finger, kisses me and whispers, "All the promises, Abi. All the promises."

EPILOGUE

Liam

"I'm here, I'm here," I shout out as I come through the front door of our gorgeous new home in Miami, overlooking the Atlantic Ocean, an ocean Abi and I are both very familiar with having lived on the East coast of Nova Scotia all our lives.

"We're in here," Abi calls out.

I follow the sound of her voice. "Sorry, traffic was awful." I've been living in Miami for two years now, and I'll still never get used to the sheer amount of traffic at all hours of the day. It baffles me, which is no surprise, considering we didn't even have one traffic light in Lunenburg, the small town we both grew up in, but I wouldn't trade my life for the world.

Happy voices boom from the living room and trickle down the hall to my ears as I hurry to the kitchen. I drop the brown paper bag on the island next to Abi, leaning in to give my smiling fiancée a kiss on the lips, despite the fact that both sets of parents are watching us from the living room.

I hear a masculine groan, or maybe it was two, from our audience of four. "What?" I ask, laughing and shrugging as Abi glances into the bag. I take in her hair, tied in pigtails. Is she trying to kill me? Seriously though, she looks so gorgeous and sun kissed, dressed in a light blue, loose-fitting dress that matches her eyes, and makes me want to tell our parents to go to a hotel so I can have her all to myself. I simply can't get enough of her and I wouldn't want it any other way.

But sending my parents to a hotel when we have a big house with four spare bedrooms would be ludicrous, right? Of course, it would. They're only here for a week and we want to enjoy every minute with them—except for the nighttime minutes, all those are reserved for Abi, alone in our king-sized bed.

"Did you get the limes?" she asks as she fills a reusable bag with snacks for our afternoon boat ride. God, she looks so happy and relaxed, it fills my heart with all the love I have for her.

I wink at her. "Can't have margaritas without the limes," I say, my damn shorts suddenly feeling like they've been shrunk in the dryer, not good considering the company in the other room. A contented sigh escapes my throat as I glance at the four parents, all chatting happily.

Life is crazy, isn't it? Abi and I spent so many years hating each other, only to fall in love in college. Although I'm pretty sure I've been in love with her since I first saw her in pigtails on the playground. We plan to get married in Santorini, to see all the beautiful sunsets, as soon as the time is right. She's currently swamped with her master's degree at the University of Miami and I'm so damn proud of her. She's been working with the Department of Natural Resources to support environmentally friendly practices and influence environmental policy creation. It's everything she's ever dreamed of and she's going to make this a better world for the next generation.

Me? Well, I'm still working my butt off to prove myself to my team. They're a great bunch of guys, and I know a few of them from the Academy. I'm honestly loving every minute of playing in the NHL, because at the end of every night, and after every away game, I get to come home to the most amazing woman in the world.

I've kept my promise to Abi, to enjoy every moment in the NHL, and it's an easy promise to keep. While I can't wait to call her my wife, we're in no hurry because we're in love, we're together and we ended a lifelong feud between our families and for now, that's enough for both of us.

Besides, getting married in Santorini… Well, I always wanted my best friend Josh to be my best man, and sadly enough, we had a falling out. I now think of that dark night as…the incident. My heart is still fucking broken over that. I swallow down the pain, and try to push the memories of our fight to the back of my brain.

I listen to my parents and Abi's parents chat in the next room, and my stomach cramps. Wait, am I being stubborn and stupid like my father, holding a grudge when I should have let painful shit go a long time ago? Jesus, maybe I am. Didn't I lecture my father on the same thing? Maybe I should pick up the phone and call Josh right now. Christ knows I miss him in my life. The truth is, I want him by my side when I get married. Maybe that's why I've been holding off.

I reach for my phone, my hands a bit shaky, and Dad's voice booms from the other room. "Are those margaritas ready? A man could die of thirst around here."

Abi laughs. "No, I'm going to make them on the boat. I have everything we need now." She snatches up the brown paper bag, checking inside one more time. "Babe, can you run to the bedroom and grab the bag with our spare clothes?"

Everyone stands and picks up their bags, and my dad slaps Abi's dad on the back like they're lifelong friends and I hope from here on out they can be. After the fire, Dad rallied the town, and everyone worked to rebuild Boondocks into something so spectacular it drew in way more customers. Abi's folks hired some locals to help, and that helped with Abi's guilt. She was able to enjoy her summers in Miami without the worry, and with the extra money Boondocks is bringing in, her grandfather is now getting the best care possible at a nursing home.

Abi naturally received the grant money, and spent her summers here in Miami. I flew back and forth as much as I could, and now, here we are making a life together. The only thing that could make it better is if Josh and I were still friends.

I dart to the bedroom. That's when I see the picture Trent gave me years ago. Abi framed it. She's so sweet like that. I was never happier than when Trent fully recovered, and Abi and I took him to the rink for one-on-one ice time. He's playing league hockey now, and Dad and I sponsor him and other kids. It has really brought us closer together. As for Trent, I still keep in touch with him, and really hope to play with him someday in Miami. I turn my head and see a picture of Ember and me during Ember's high school graduation. She's still at the Scotia Academy, doing a literature degree. My heart thumps. I miss her. She doesn't talk to me much, not since...the incident.

Josh is the best guy you know, Liam. What is your fucking problem?

I snatch up the bag and walk back into the living room. While I have everything I've ever dreamed of, and I'm so happy that our families are getting along—I never in a million years thought I'd see it happen—I miss being close to my sister, and I miss having Josh in my life. I want it all back.

"Need some help?" I ask Abi as she juggles a couple of bags.

"I think I got this."

I laugh. Isn't that just like her. So damn independent, but she knows she can count on me. "No, you don't." I take the bag from her and follow her out the front door. I lock up behind us, and we all head to the dock, our parents chatting happily.

I note the way Abi is watching me, and I turn to her. "Are you okay?" Abi asks quiet when our folks are out of ear shot.

I bend and kiss her again, amazed at how well she can read me. "I am."

She smiles at me. "Maybe you should call him."

"I think I will."

"Come on, son," Dad bellows as he steps onto the boat. It's one of the first things I bought after moving here. Abi and I spend most of our free time on the boat, watching sunrises and sunsets.

"You can head back to the house for privacy, if you like," she suggests gently.

"I'll call tonight," I tell her and she takes my hand and gives it a little squeeze. The gorgeous sun warms my body as we walk down the dock and climb onto the boat. Abi, her mom and mine start making margaritas while our dads go over the details of the boat. It brings a smile to my face, watching everyone get along.

I sit for a moment, just to take it all in, when my phone rings. I'm not expecting anyone to call, so for a second, I think about ignoring it. But as it continues to ring, and I catch Abi's eyes, I pull it from my pocket and my heart jumps into my throat when I see it's from Josh.

———

Thank you so much for reading Abi and Liam's story. I hope you loved it as much as I do. To find out what happened between Liam and Josh—the incident—check out HARD BURN. Stay turned for Scoring Fast, the next book in my Scotia Storm Series.

ALSO BY CATHRYN FOX

Scotia Storms

Away Game (Rebels)

Warm Up (Rebels)

Crash Course (Rebels)

Home Advantage (Rebels)

Shut Out (Rebels)

Moving Target (Rivals)

Face Off (Rivals)

Scoring Fast (Rivals)

Opposing Teams (Rivals)

Deal Breaker (Rebels)

Hard Burn (Rivals)

Fake Out (Rivals)

End Zone

Fair Play

Enemy Down

Keeping Score

Trading Up

All In

Blue Bay Crew

Demolished

Leveled

Hammered

Single Dad
Single Dad Next Door
Single Dad on Tap
Single Dad Burning Up

Players on Ice
The Playmaker
The Stick Handler
The Body Checker
The Hard Hitter
The Risk Taker
The Wing Man
The Puck Charmer
The Troublemaker
The Rule Breaker
The Rookie
The Sweet Talker
The Heart Breaker

In the Line of Duty
His Obsession Next Door
His Strings to Pull
His Trouble in Talulah
His Taste of Temptation
His Moment to Steal
His Best Friend's Girl
His Reason to Stay

Confessions

Confessions of a Bad Boy Professor

Confessions of a Bad Boy Officer

Confessions of a Bad Boy Fighter

Confessions of a Bad Boy Doctor

Confessions of a Bad Boy Gamer

Confessions of a Bad Boy Millionaire

Confessions of a Bad Boy Santa

Confessions of a Bad Boy CEO

Hands On

Hands On

Body Contact

Full Exposure

Dossier

Private Reserve

House Rules

Under Pressure

Big Catch

Brazilian Fantasy

Improper Proposal

Boys of Beachville

Good at Being Bad

Igniting the Bad Boy

Bad Girl Therapy

Stone Cliff Series:

Crashing Down

Wasted Summer

Love Lessons

Wrapped Up

Eternal Pleasure Series

Instinctive

Impulsive

Indulgent

Sun Stroked Series

Seaside Seduction

Deep Desire

Private Pleasure

Captured and Claimed Series:

Yours to Take

Yours to Teach

Yours to Keep

Firefighter Heat Series

Fever

Siren

Flash Fire

Playing For Keeps Series

Slow Ride

Wild Ride

Sweet Ride

Breaking the Rules:

Hold Me Down Hard

Pin Me Up Proper

Tie Me Down Tight

Stand Alone Title:

Hands on with the CEO

Torn Between Two Brothers

Holiday Spirit

Unleashed

Knocking on Demon's Door

Web of Desire

Pinterest http://www.pinterest.com/catkalen/